How the Vortex Changed my Life

Pamela K. Kinney

Acknowledgements

I like to thank my beta readers, Penny Arrighi, Carol Smith, and Judith Howell, for their invaluable first read of the full manuscript. And I also like to thank the critique group led by Joe Erhardt in Richmond, as they were the first to critique the beginning chapters of this urban fantasy novel. Without everyone's help, this book might never have gotten off the ground. I also like to thank my husband, Bill, for his patience while I worked on this book. He's a hero in every way!

Most of all, I like to thank my readers, for without you, this urban fantasy might never become words upon the pages.

Couldn't we just cancel the apocalypse until next week? I have nothing new to wear for it.

~Cat Viggolone

CHAPTER 1

Some days, a girl just can't get a break. I wanted to get married, have kids, and a career that I loved. Instead, I married Jeff, who had an affair with his secretary, and divorced me so he could marry the bimbo. As for the kids, he didn't want any. Of course, last week I got the news from his snide mother that his bimbo was pregnant. Of course, she'd always blamed me for us not having kids. As for that career—working a window at the Virginia Department of Motor Vehicles wasn't quite what I'd dreamed about.

At age thirty-three my life was boring. Then the vortex opened.

***

Friday at the DMV bulged with people. I took money for license renewals and fielded the same old questions I've always gotten about why some folks' licenses were revoked. "Next!" I called out, slumped over my counter, little devils jackhammering away at my brain into a growing tension headache.

My eye on the hands of the wall clock as they drew closer to five o'clock, I swore one more person who wanted to know why her little teenaged darling hadn't passed the road test, I would scream.

When five o'clock rolled around, I escaped to my car. I didn't know why I hurried; no doubt it would be another tedious weekend for me.

The cranky old junk heap did its usual old ritual of coughing and backfiring before finally the engine gave up and turned over. I just wanted to get home, soak in a hot bath, and order a chicken mushroom pizza from my favorite pizza delivery.

But just as I was about to turn into my driveway, a gigantic quadrilateral of swirling neon colors—reds, purples, and hot pinks—appeared out of nowhere right smack in the middle of the street. It created a gale that blasted the neighborhood. Trees uprooted and flew into it, along with a couple of cars, a bicycle, and one yodeling cat. People ducked into their homes. That's when my car decided right then and there to break down. My heart pounded so hard, I thought it might break through my chest. I tried to restart the engine, but it remained dead. I leaped out and bolted for my house. Unfortunately, that path happened to be in alignment with the destructive force.

I never made it.

***

I opened my eyes. A dull pain pounded on the right side of my head. Reaching up, I found an egg-sized bump underneath my tangled hair. Dizziness assaulted me and my stomach lurched. I leaned over to my right and threw up what remained of my snack from my afternoon break. Chocolate doesn't taste good coming back up. I squeezed my eyes shut as the pain and wooziness went the next level of crazy amusement park ride vertigo. A few seconds later, I popped one eye, then the other open. I still had the dizzy spell, but it'd lowered to passable lightheadedness.

"Great," I muttered, wincing, "just really great. I must have banged my head on the steering wheel or something. Heck, maybe I had a nasty nightmare and fell out of bed and smacked my head."

I combed the matted locks out of my face, but it didn't work. That only made my sore head hurt worse. "I'd like to know how I tangled my hair from a clout on my head. I need my brush. Where's my purse?"

I looked around. "Wait a minute, this isn't my bedroom. Not my car either." To tell the truth, it didn't look like I was anywhere on Earth. Okay, maybe the *Twilight Zone*. That's what the whole scene reminded me of. I saw nothing except a place filled with gray mist. A creepy, cobwebby kind of mist. I expected Rod Serling to come out of hiding and start his spiel.

"Hello!" I called out as I crawled to my knees and from there tottered to my feet. My voice echoed back.

In the distance, I saw something. Indistinct because of the mist, it grew more and more distinguishable as it drew nearer. As it drew nearer, I saw it was two separate beings. One was a single eyeball with a dark blue iris about the size of a miniature poodle. It hovered in mid-air. The other, a gigantic black wolf with red eyes.

Wolves don't get that big, do they? And what is the other thing? I almost pissed my pants. "Stay back, whatever the hell the both of you are," I said, stepping back and holding my fingers out in the sign of the cross.

"That only works with vampires, and to tell you the truth, it doesn't work well with them either," said the wolf, its voice deeply male. "At least, so the movies claim."

Oh God, the wolf talks.

"Wolves don't talk."

"Of course, they don't," snapped the wolf, "because I'm not a wolf. I'm a shapeshifter." He cocked his head to one side. "I see you don't understand what shapeshifter means. Try werewolf. That's what you humans named us in all those stories."

Run, just run! The whole place full of thick mist made it hard to see more than a few inches in front of me. Who knew what else I might have stumbled into? Besides, I found that what they say about freezing in terror happened to be true. I stood there, staring at both the werewolf and the floating eyeball, my heart drumming at ninety miles a minute.

The eyeball drifted nearer to me until we almost touched nose to...iris?

"Jesus!" I stumbled backwards and tripped. "Owww." I landed on a harder surface than I thought.

The wolf sighed. "Larry, get away from the lady. I don't think she likes anything of a supernatural bent."

'Larry' levitated back over to the wolf and floated by his side. Its movement reminded me of a cork attached to a fishing line, bobbing in the water.

A nervous giggle escaped me. I clapped both hands over my mouth as I realized how that might be interpreted by the monsters.

When I felt more in control of not letting any more titters escape, I asked, "Why would something like that be called Larry?"

The werewolf snorted. "His parents named him, just like I'm sure your parents named you."

"What kind of parents—? No, don't answer that. I don't even want to know."

I got off the ground and dusted off the seat of my pants. Not because of dirt, but from whatever else might be on lingering on the ground. "I assume that this place is inside that big swirling mass of colors that appeared in my neighborhood. Did you have it kidnap me or something?" I stared at the werewolf. "Sorry, but I didn't catch your name, Mr. Werewolf."

"I didn't give it, but it's Connor Rojas. And no, we didn't have you kidnapped, or anything else."

"Were you and Larry sucked into here the same as me?"

Connor sat down, his tail encircling his body to tuck neatly between his forepaws. "Larry has always been here, in this dimension. He's a demon. I ended up here about six months ago, when the vortex opened above my apartment in El Cajon, California. Unfortunately, that was the first night of the full moon and I had just changed. I've been stuck as a wolf ever since. Guess it has to do with whatever counts for the laws of this place."

Larry made a strange little squeaking noise and Connor stopped, his ears twitching toward the eyeball as if listening. "Thanks, Larry." He swept his gaze back at me. "Larry wanted me to tell you about this place. We're in a dimensional entrance, kinda like a foyer or lobby. There are doorways that lead to several different places. Places like Faerie, and worlds of the Norse gods, Greek Gods, and so forth. One doorway beyond this 'stopping place'—about twenty paces to our left—takes you into what you humans call Hell, or what passes for Hell, depending on your take on religion, of course. The opposite way leads to Heaven."

Hearing the word Hell jolted me. "You mean I'm in ...Hell?"

"No, like I said, not quite, just a lobby that leads to it, along with the other places I mentioned."

The werewolf stood up on his hind paws. I stepped back, staring up at the creature towering over me. I'm tall for a woman at five feet nine inches in my stocking feet, but as I bent my head back, I figured he had to be at least six feet three inches, and this was on his bare, uh, paws. I felt small and insignificant, a frightened Red Riding Hood cowering before the big bad wolf. Thoughts of 'But Wolf, what a tall body you have! How tall are you?' flitted through my mind, with the rejoinder being 'The better to snap off your head, my dear.'

As if he knew what I was thinking, Connor spoke in a softer tone. "Don't be scared. I won't eat you."

That didn't reassure me. After all, he had fangs, claws, and an intimidating height. I stared down at the swirling mist circling my shoes, feeling that was better than up into a pair of werewolfish eyes. I heard him sigh.

My heart thumped painfully in my chest. I snuck a glance at him. "How do I get out of here and back into my world?"

"With luck, the vortex is still open in your neighborhood and maybe if we all move together and leap about ten paces to your right, we'll end up there."

"What do you mean, if we all leap together we'll all end up back at my home? You're coming with me?" I frowned at the eyeball. "Along with...that Larry? I don't think so."

"I want to go home too, and I don't want to leave Larry here. I fell through the doorway to Hell after I got sucked up. If it hadn't been for Larry, I'd still be there, a plaything for demonic entities. And he's not exactly popular with Hell right now." His eyes lit up. "Oh, I get it. You think once I leap, I'll remain as a werewolf?" A laugh—at least I thought it was a laugh—issued out from between his large, sharp fangs. "Nope. Once I'm back on Earth I change back into a man. Naked, but a man, nevertheless. I assumed the full moon just ended, right?"

"I guess. I don't look at my calendar to check if it's that time of the month. You know, is it a full moon, or is it a waxing crescent?" *That's it, Cat, smart off to the big furry with teeth almost long as your arm. Can't you keep your big mouth shut for once*? I heard sounds coming from him and with surprise, stared up at him.

Deep guffaws slipped out of his maw, his chest heaving in and out. Then he stopped and looked at me, a glint in his eyes. I hoped from interest and not with hunger. "I like you. What's your name?"

"Cat Viggolone. Cat's short for Cathleen, although my husband, Jack, always claimed it was because of the sharp claws I unsheathed whenever we had a fight."

"Husband?" Connor's voice seemed to hold a hint of disappointment to it, but I might have imagined it. "You're married?"

"Not anymore. We've been divorced for seven months now. He preferred his secretary. She's younger, something I'm not."

"He sounds like an idiot. I see a beautiful woman."

A tear slipped out of the corner of my left eye and I wiped it away. Being called beautiful was something I hadn't heard from Jack. But I couldn't afford a good cry now. I had more important things, like leaving this place. "You said we're able to get out of here?"

"Follow me."

Connor dropped down onto all four paws, and with Larry trailing like a floating balloon, we turned to my right. One moment I wandered among swirling gray mist, the next I was jerked off my feet and found myself deposited back in my front yard. I lay on browning grass and stared up at the vortex. It began to shrink and shrink until it. . .departed. But not before I heard something roar. I shivered and wondered if that might be Lucifer, or something just as bad. It sounded immense and terrifying, something I hoped never to meet face to face.

I turned my head to my right and saw Connor, no longer a wolf. Instead, a lot of nude male flesh obscured my view, which to my shame, I didn't mind. Well, okay, I'm lying. I enjoyed every bit of his nakedness. His eyes, no longer red, were a deep chocolate brown, framed by long soot-colored lashes. Maybe due to being a werewolf for six months, a thick beard covered his face. A lock of black hair fell over his forehead, and I realized he must be Latino—or had some Latino in him. The man had a nice even tan everywhere. I swept my gaze lower, down his chest to—*Oh, my.* My face grew warm as I looked away.

He said, "I'm glad that my body meets with your approval, but can we get inside your house? I mean, a naked man and a floating eyeball are sure to cause some notice in your neighborhood."

"Yes, of course, uh—" I jumped to my feet and dashed to my car, which still sat where it had broken down. I fetched my purse and the keys from inside, hurried to my house and unlocked the front door, whisking Connor and Larry inside. Thank goodness, the vortex had frightened people so much that they had stayed in their homes. With it gone, I felt sure that someone would call the police or fire department. I didn't feel like explaining about the nude man, but most especially about Larry. Floating eyeballs are not natural to this neighborhood. To be honest, I don't think Larry would be considered natural anywhere on Earth.

After I turned on the lights in the house to see if the electricity still worked, vortex or no vortex, I dug up some old clothing of Jeff's from a big bag in the laundry room that he hadn't taken with him when he'd left. I handed Connor a pair of jeans and a ragged T-shirt that Jeff had outgrown—in other words, it meant he'd grown too fat. But they fitted Connor nicely, and I saw that he filled them out in all the right places. A rip in the front of the T-shirt let me see a male nipple and black chest hair. I looked away from that and looked up into his face.

"Sorry, but Jeff didn't leave any shoes here. It wouldn't matter anyway; I think his feet are smaller than yours." Connor's bare feet peeped out from beneath the jeans, and I noticed dirt on them. "I guess Hell, or wherever that place is, must be dirty."

Connor blushed, which I assumed must be rare, right? I mean, when you need to be naked to shift into a wolf there's not much point to it, is there? Embarrassment had to be lacking.

"When I change back into a man after wolfing around, I usually take a shower. It wasn't just from being inside that vortex for six months, but from the roof of my apartment building where I made the change. It's fairly mucky up there." He added, "Sorry to soil your carpet."

I took his hands and peered at the dirt on his palms and crusted under his nails. I gestured at the hallway. "There's a bathroom at the end of the hall. It's the first door to the right. Why don't you go in and grab a shower? When you're done, dress in these clothes. While you're showering, if I can get my car to restart, I'll go and buy you some shoes. What's your size?"

"You don't have to. I mean, if I can get to a branch of my bank, I'm sure I still have a checking and savings account with them. There's plenty of money in both."

I shrugged. "Well, you can repay me later, but for now, go take that shower. Your shoe size, please?"

"Thirteen."

I watched as Connor walked down the hallway before I grabbed the TV remote to turn on the television, so Larry could watch it. Though why I thought he would want to, I couldn't imagine. But what else could an eye demon do? Besides, I didn't want him floating through my house peeping into places.

Thank God, my car's engine did turn over and I drove to a nearby Wal-Mart. When I returned home an hour later with a pair of men's black leather jogging shoes in a plastic bag, I found a showered and shaved Connor sitting on my threadbare couch. He was using the TV remote and flipping through the numerous channels. Larry hovered beside him and stared at the set. Did that eye ever blink? As for Connor, now that he'd sheared the beard off his face, his smooth cheeks were... Hold on! How did Connor shave? My moisturizing shave gel and pack of disposable shavers I kept for my legs came to mind. *Oh, yeah.* I made a mental note to see how he left the sink and shave gel. Jeff always made a mess after his morning absolutions.

Connor looked up. "So, we're still in Afghanistan? And Trump, a businessman, won the presidential election?"

"Yes, to both questions."

He sighed. "Damn, the news you miss when you've been trapped in Hell." He shut up when a special news bulletin came on.

Two news people sat behind a desk, one reporting about the vortex that had disappeared in my neighborhood. Now it had apparently materialized in another part of town—downtown Richmond. The newsman talked about creatures stampeding out of the vortex. Ghastly, terrible creatures.

Connor glanced at me. "This isn't good, not good at all."

He was right. Halloween looked to be arriving early this year, and giving tricks to everyone, not treats.

CHAPTER 2

Larry bleated like a sheep and threw himself against the TV screen. After several repeated attempts at solericide, he dropped senseless to the floor. Connor tossed the remote on the coffee table and leaped up from the couch.

"Come on," he said, grabbing my hand, "and let's go."

I narrowed my eyes, suspicious. "Go where?" An awful thought came to me. "Oh God, you want us to go to where the vortex is. Where those...those things are." I yanked my hand out of his and sat down on the couch. I plucked the shoes out of the bag and tossed them at Connor. They struck him on the shins. "There are your shoes, and you can go with Larry to that vortex. Me? I'm staying home. I'm not 'the save the world' kind of woman, thank you. One encounter with that vortex is enough for me."

I added, "I think I'll order some pizza. Mmm...a chicken with mushrooms appears good to me." I picked up the receiver of the phone by my couch, intending to call the pizza delivery.

Connor slipped on his new shoes and dropped to one knee to tie the shoelaces. Not looking at me, he rose to his feet.

"Come on, Larry, let's go see if we can do something about that vortex."

He jogged out of the house, Larry right after him. The door slammed shut behind them with a decisive bang. A picture of a mountain scene mounted on the wall fell to the floor and cracked. Sighing, I put the receiver back down and got up. I set the picture upright against the wall, figuring I could buy a new frame for it tomorrow, or donate it to a thrift shop.

I waited to see if Connor and Larry would return and, after five minutes, it looked like they wouldn't. Upset, I headed into the kitchen for the half gallon of chocolate ice cream I had in my freezer.

Nothing made me feel better than chocolate ice cream. Okay, maybe chocolate cake, candy, pizza...Whenever I become upset or frightened or in any negative mood, I always ate. The divorce itself had put ten pounds on me. Maybe tomorrow I could start a diet. Today though, the ice cream called to me. I cracked open the freezer door and something grabbed me by the waist, yanking me back against a solid form.

"I'm not leaving you. Let's go," growled Connor's voice in my ear as his hand covered my mouth. He whirled me around. A scowl on his face knitted his eyebrows together and his eyes looked almost as red as they did when he was the werewolf.

Jubilant, I grinned. "So, I can't grab anything to eat?"

"No."

I dropped the smile. "Look, except for an afternoon snack that mostly came back up, I didn't have anything to eat since lunch. Being stuck in the vortex and escaping it can make a person hungry."

"The world is in big danger and all you care about is your stomach?"

I added, slyly, "I also thought about staying alive."

"Look, I need directions to where the vortex opened up. You live in this city."

"It's good to know how important I really am to you."

He stared at me, silent.

I sighed. "All right, all right, I'm coming."

I followed him to the front door, swiping my purse and keys on the way out. Inside my car, Larry rested on the back seat. Before I could even climb in the driver's side, Connor jumped behind the wheel and flipped a hand, palm-side up.

I glared at him, jiggling my car keys. "Excuse me, but it's my car, and only I drive it."

Connor blew out an exasperated breath. "Larry and I decided we couldn't hoof it over to that part of town and not have him seen. It's why we needed a car, but without the keys, I couldn't start it and I sure as hell don't know how to hot-wire a car. Please, hand over the keys, or can you drive like a race car driver so we can get there pretty quick?"

"I work for the DMV and I have never gone over the speed limit. Never got a ticket, ever."

"Well, honey, I can and have broken the speed limit before, and with no qualms about it. Get in and give me the car key for the ignition."

Like I didn't figure that out about Connor. The keys bit into the palm of my hand as I stared at him. He just stayed in the driver's seat. Finally, I dropped them onto his palm. I knew arguing wouldn't get me anywhere. Sighing, I climbed in the passenger side. Not even allowing me any time to buckle up, Connor coerced the car into life and tore out of my driveway. The scenery became colorful blurs, merging together like splatters of wet paint. Houses melted into trees and lawns, lawns and trees into playgrounds, and playgrounds became blurs speeding along the street. Growing dizzy, everything spun out of control as I hooked my hands onto the dashboard and hung on for dear life.

I yelled, trying to be heard above the roar of the engine. "Stop! For God's sake, stop! We're going too fast." I closed my eyes. "Oh God, I feel sick!"

"Sorry, Cat. But if Hell has found a way into our world—"

A sound, small and indistinct at first, growing and growing louder...a siren! I opened my eyes and glanced in the rearview mirror. It held a reflection of flashing blue lights. A police car tailed us. I punched Connor's shoulder.

He snarled, "Cut that out. Do you want me to crash this car?"

"Pardon me for being so rude to point this out, but we have a police car pursuing us. Geesh, I thought werewolves have sensitive hearing."

Connor cut his gaze at me. "Yeah, I heard that police car way long before you."

"You knew, and didn't think to tell me? Pull over or into a parking lot."

He made a right turn and drove into a nearby shopping center's parking lot. The police car followed us in. Connor found a parking space and shut off the engine. Looking through the back window, I saw a tall figure rise out of the driver's side. Dressed in green, with a cap of the same color jammed on his head and dark sunglasses shading his eyes, the policeman had a shiny badge pinned to his shirt. His thumbs were hooked into his belt, the pinkie finger on his right hand not far from the gun in the holster. The officer walked with determined steps to the driver's side. Connor rolled down the window.

The officer bent down a tad. "Did you realize you had been driving above the speed limit?" His mouth tightened. "In fact, I'd say you went above and beyond speeding."

Connor didn't answer but stared at the steering wheel.

The officer straightened up and pulled out a pad and pen from his shirt pocket. "May I see your driver's license and car registration, please?"

I glanced into the rearview mirror and saw Larry drifting toward the policeman, obviously to get a closer look. Spying an old stadium blanket on the back seat, I grabbed it and threw it over the eye. I yanked him into the front seat with me, keeping him on my lap. I tried to make him stay still, but the officer noticed the movement.

"Lady, what do you have there?" he asked, using his pen to point at the covered Larry squirming in my arms.

Unbidden, a nervous snigger burst out of me. "Oh, this on my lap? It's just my dog, Officer. He gets nervous around strange men, and I didn't want him to bark at you. I'm keeping him covered and holding on to him until you're done with us." I prayed in my head that he believed me. Thankfully he must have, as he diverted his attention back to Connor. I shoved Larry down onto the floor at my feet.

Lowering my head, I whispered, "Larry, stay down there and don't move." I grew more threatening. "No movement, no noise, nothing. Understand?"

The blanketed form bobbed up and down as if in agreement. At least, I hope he concurred with me.

I looked at Connor and the policeman and heard the officer's voice rising in pitch, demanding that Connor hand over his license and car registration again. Wonderful. I kept the car's registration in the glove compartment because I owned the car. Connor had no license. Maybe back in California he did, but not here in Virginia, and not on him. No way would we be able to finagle our way out of this predicament.

Connor directed at me a tight grin of large white teeth. "Darling, this nice officer wants to see my license and vehicle registration." The starry glints in his eyes told me something, something I didn't care to know.

With a moan, I gripped the dashboard tight with my fingers. I knew what Connor would do, and I saw myself spending the rest of my life behind bars. In a cell where there would be hardly any room and where the toilet facilities stunk to high heaven. And where no doubt, my roommate would be a big tough-looking woman named Big Bertha wanting to share my bunk with me.

Connor turned the key in the ignition and the car roared to life. He slammed his foot on the accelerator and the car bounced forward, barely missing the policeman who leaped away. Connor sent the vehicle zooming out of the parking lot and back onto the street. He drove like a crazy person, heading toward downtown where the vortex waited. In the rearview mirror, I saw the angry cop running to his patrol car, his form shrinking as we drew farther and farther away from him.

A horde of sirens reached my ears, and I knew more police had joined our cop in the chase. Connor ignored them and kept going, our destination his only concern. My stomach churning, I glanced aside at him and saw grim determination etched in every line of his face. A single black curl fell over his forehead, flopping over an eye. Something bobbed at my feet and I glanced down. Larry had thrown off his blanket and kept making loud chirping noises—most likely an equivalent of screaming or demon cursing.

Connor slammed on the brakes. I grappled for the edges of my seat and Larry rolled around, knocking into my feet. Connor was about to turn off the engine when the car died.

That's when I saw it! The familiar swirling of colors. My stomach cramped as my heart drummed beneath my breasts. This time though, the vortex had an ash gray circle in the middle. As the circle kept growing, it blotted out the colors. And from this circle, horrible, ghastly fiends popped out. What scared me even more than the demons was seeing that grayness drifting like fog from the vortex. The nasty stuff leached all the color from the surrounding area. Like watching a color film become black and white. It slipped over one old man holding onto a stop sign to keep from being dragged into the vortex. He let go of the sign and lurched away, ashen and with eyes empty of life.

I said, "Oh no, that creepy stuff changed that man. . ."

Connor said, "We got to get out. Grab Larry and let's go."

I stuffed Larry under my arm like a football and sprang from the car. Connor leaped out from the opposite side. My car trembled and lifted into the air, spinning like a top and went right into the maelstrom. The vortex stopped drawing other things in after that, but it continued to spit out demons.

We sprinted away, trying to beat the seeping gloom as it gained ground and drained the life and color out of everything. It changed the flesh of people and animals, making them into the stumbling undead. One of the nasty beings from the vortex gave chase. Ten feet tall, the grisly creature had long, green wiry hair all over its body and a single red eye in the center of its head. It opened a maw full of dagger teeth and a long tongue, yellow as a banana peel, whipped out.

I screamed. "Oh God, something's after us!"

Connor spoke, not sounding out of breath. Unlike me. Um, right, werewolf. "Keep running and don't look back. We have to keep ahead of the demons and that hell vapor." He fell silent; the only sound, his shoes slapping the concrete of the sidewalk.

I let Larry go and the eye floated beside us, keeping pace without any effort. We ran as fast as we could, but the entity kept pace not far behind us. It made strange, crass sounds, a cross between someone throwing up in a toilet and gaseous bubbles breaking. Not anything pleasant to hear. I wondered if it had an odor to match the noise and thanked God we were not downwind of it.

Connor and I arrived at some stone steps. We clattered up and into the Richmond Public Library. After we stepped into the foyer and passed the circulation desk we looked around, unsure of where to go. I saw a room to the left of us, pointed at it, and we slipped inside. Rows and rows of books on shelves lined the area like soldiers marching behind each other. A portly man in khaki pants, white shirt, and a blue, flowered tie sat behind a desk. He looked up and smiled.

"Can I be of assistance?" His smile faltered as he stared past me.

He's seen Larry. This won't be good.

He stood, his forehead wrinkling. "That's pretty life like. What is it? A balloon? I can't see any string attached to it."

Deciding not to beat around the bush, I blurted, "He's not a balloon. He's an eyeball—actually, he's a demon."

The man said, "Are you trying to say that whatever it is, is alive?"

"Kinda. I guess demons are sort of alive."

The librarian walked over to us and poked at Larry. Larry didn't like it and started that weird bleating noise he could make and bumped against the man. He bumped him so hard, he almost knocked the librarian over. The man managed to stay on his feet and took a couple of steps back as he wiped the finger on his pants as if Larry had given him cooties.

Connor grabbed the librarian by the same finger and squeezed hard. The man cried out.

Connor let go. "Larry doesn't like people poking at him." He glared. "It's rude. Besides, how would you like it if I poked at you?" Connor proceeded to do just that.

The librarian stumbled back. "Okay, okay. But what is that thing? The lady called it a demon, but demons aren't real. Right?"

Connor snorted. "That *thing* is a demon like the lady said and if it wasn't for him, I'd been dead within hours after I got trapped in Hell." Larry bumped against Connor and made another noise I'd never heard before, like a cat's purr. "I find Larry is a lot more 'human' than you humans are."

"Well, you look as human as the rest of us," said the librarian with a snotty attitude, "and that eye beastie definitely doesn't." He narrowed his eyes. "This library is for humans only. I mean, non-human things can't get a library card issued to them." He saw Connor give him a glowering look and inched away. "Well, I'm pretty sure that's the rules."

I spoke up. "We're not here to borrow a book." I snuck a look at the front entrance. "We needed a place to hide in. You see, a monster is after us. A very big monster. And there are others outside like it and Larry here. A vortex opened not far from here and downtown Richmond is turning gray and I don't mean Confederate gray either. Richmond's new address is now a part of the Hell dimension. The whole world is doomed. And I don't think it really matters whether Larry can be issued a library card, or what species can use this library."

The librarian's mouth opened and shut in shock, his eyes bulging and looking like tennis balls. He sputtered, "You're nuts." He cut a glance at Larry who hovered closer to him. "I think you guys are pulling something on me. That thing has got to be fake."

I grabbed him by his ugly tie. "Look, Hell is taking over Richmond, and soon, Virginia, not long after, the U.S., and from there, maybe the world. So, get over it. Larry is not fake. He's a demon, plain and simple, but maybe you can't comprehend it. I know I couldn't at first. That means no more people checking out books, no more Christmas, cute fluffy kittens, no more anything good and right for humankind. Just demons, Hell, and the end of life as we know it."

The librarian ripped his tie out of my hand and looked at me like I'd sprouted horns and a pitchfork myself. I must have been tougher on him than I thought.

A growl reached my ears, along with an awful miasma slamming up my nostrils. I reeled around. With an African American lady librarian clasped in one clawed paw and a patron speared by the claws of the other, the monster that had been chasing us stood by the circulation desk. The patron kept screaming while the librarian hung unconscious and limp like a wet noodle.

I watched with horror as the monster snarled and slurped the patron's head into its mouth, effectively cutting off the screaming. The librarian with us took off, yelling something about monsters not being in his job description.

Connor grabbed my hand again and drew me toward the elevators. He kept pushing at the button for up, one eye on the monster now busy eating the rest of its meal.

It still clutched the librarian, who hadn't yet regained consciousness.

Finally, the elevator door slid open with a ping and Connor thrust me inside, with Larry and him crowding in right behind. He punched the button for the second floor and the door slid shut.

I began to cry, not dainty little tears, but big ones that redden your face. It had been a terrible Friday so far, with working a long shift at the DMV, handling irate customers; and then ending up in the corridor 0outside of Hell's dimension. Now it looked like I would become Purina monster chow for some demonic creature, and the world would be destroyed. My life sucked. I'd give anything to have my boring old existence back.

Our ride stopped and the door pinged, sliding open. We stepped out onto the second floor. People stood to the left of us, staring over the banister. Horrible sounds drifted up from the first floor and I knew what the looky-loos watched.

Connor grabbed a metal statue and swung it, slamming it hard against the buttons. A flash of smoke, a buzzing sound, and the elevator became useless. He looked at me and shrugged. "At least the monster won't be able to use it. Though being a demon, I won't promise it won't be able to magick its way up here."

He glanced at the onlookers still staring down at the first floor. "Hey, over there. If you're all smart, you better find a way out of here or someone may watch you being eaten alive." Only one person appeared to have heard him and the man turned to give us a wide-eyed look. Then he swept his gaze back to the scene down below. Stupid, stupid idiots. Connor snorted. "Come on, let's find another way out."

Larry floated away from us but came back. He bleated.

Connor arched an eyebrow. "Looks like Larry found some stairs."

"You really do understand him," I said, jogging after him and Larry as we went down a short hallway to some stairs. I hesitated. "This leads back down, and I think the only way out is right where we came in."

Connor shook his head. "I'm hoping there might be a back door or something. You know, to escape fires if the front entrance is blocked."

He started down the steps, Larry in his wake. I trotted after them. Tired and sweaty, I wondered if I was about to be on a demon's dinner menu. Even if we did escape the library, we might run smack into that terrible grayness enveloping Richmond. I thought about how I didn't fancy being eaten or that I didn't quite fit as quality undead material.

Back on the first floor I noticed that the creature finished gnawing on the patron and began to nibble on the librarian. The librarian woke up and shrieked, trying to pull her leg out of its mouth. It smacked her head against the floor, silencing her. Worse, the gray mist now hovered inside the library, bleaching the color out of everything. It encroached further inside, like some terrible thing in an old Fifties movie. I touched Connor on the arm and pointed it out.

"I see it, Cat. Let's hurry and find another way out."

He emerged into the shadows at the opposite end of the hall but came back looking dejected. I pointed back at the stairs.

"These stairs appear to keep heading downwards. Maybe there's a way out further down."

Connor agreed. "You might be right. Anyway, we don't have any other options."

We bolted down the stairs. It led to the basement. We searched a couple of rooms and found two librarians working on some projects in one. Before we could warn them, Larry wandered over to one and the women screamed and fled, showing us the way out through a small door that opened to the outside. North of us, we noticed the street draining of all color, turning gray and lifeless. The librarians who had been in the basement dashed right into it.

Connor said, "We can't go that way. We'll head south instead. If we're lucky, maybe we can hitch a ride and head back to your house, Cat." He frowned. "Maybe."

Larry whistled like a songbird.

The grayness crept closer. My heart pounded harder. "I'm guessing that what Larry said is that it's better to try and go down fighting than let the Hell take over. I don't want to become a mindless zombie."

Larry twittered like a mad thing and took off like a small jet. Connor and I tried to keep up. We ran for three blocks. Every so often, I'd glance back over my shoulder. The nasty mist appeared to be drawing closer. I wondered if it was only a matter of time before it caught up with us.

We had just hit Main Street when a yellow Nissan putt-putted down the street, the only sign of anything in the area other than us. Connor leaped in front of it, waving his arms, and the car screeched to a halt. The driver, a little old lady with white hair in tight curls and wearing pink tortoiseshell glasses, leaned out of the opened driver's side window and shook a fist.

"What do you think you're doing, young man?" she yelled. "I could have hit you and then I'd lose my license for sure. I already have one speeding ticket."

Speeding? Maybe she had gotten a ticket for obstructing the flow of traffic, but I doubted it would have been for driving over the posted limit. She couldn't have been going more than fifteen miles per mile when we ran into her.

Connor walked up to the window. He leaned over and smiled. The smile dripped of raw sex, something I hadn't seen for myself before. Yeah, and when he did it, it was to a lady old enough to be his grandmother.

"Ma'am, our ride left us stranded downtown and we need to get back to—" He flashed me a look, arching an eyebrow.

I folded my arms together and mumbled, "400 Statute Street in Chesterfield."

His grin grew wider. "400 Statute Street in Chesterfield."

Granny reached out and patted one of Connor's hands.

"Well, you all look like fine, decent young people. Mind you, I don't give rides to hitchhikers normally, but in your case, I'll be lenient this time. Hop in."

With her two myopic eyes on Connor's 'decentness' I noticed that she wasn't aware of Larry yet. If she had seen him, or even saw him floating in after me as I climbed into the back seat, I bet we wouldn't be getting this ride. It surprised me that she even meant to include me and not just Connor. Deciding to be safe, I forced Larry down to the floor. When I looked back at Granny, I saw her eyes gleaming as she gave Connor the once over. I waited for her to lick her lips in anticipation. It put me in mind about the grandmother and the wolf in "Little Red Riding Hood." Except, in this case, the little old lady had become the Big Bad Wolf.

Connor said, "Thanks, er...what's your name?"

Granny flashed him another smile. "Mrs. Mabel Porter, but you can call me Mabel."

Huh, not a word to me about calling her Mabel.

Mabel waited until Connor climbed in, before she said, "Please buckle up, it's the law," and she set the car in motion. Just in time too, as I sneaked a peak out the back window and saw the fog reaching the area we vacated a few minutes ago. I pivoted my head back around and whistled in relief. Though the way the old lady drove, it might catch up to us yet.

She took her time. If a turtle raced us, the turtle would have won. Connor motioned for her to pull into a convenience store parking lot. She did and shut the engine off.

Mabel smiled at him. "I thought you wanted to get to Chesterfield?"

Connor fumed. "At the rate that you're driving, we might get there by tomorrow morning. I'm taking over the driving."

Granny frowned. "Oh, no, you're not, young man. This is my car—"

She broke off as Larry drifted into the front seat and her view. He stared into her two eyes, which grew wide with fright. "What in tarnation kind of critter is that?" she squealed, her Southern accent thickening. She clutched her chest, her breathing heavy. "Oh, my poor heart—I can't take this." She slumped down in her seat.

I leaned forward. "Oh, dear God, did Larry kill her?"

Connor laid a hand over her chest. He looked at me. "No. Her heart's still pounding. She just fainted." He climbed out of the car and walked over to the driver's side, where he opened the door and lifted her out. He motioned for me to get out and I did, leaving the car door ajar. Gently, he placed Granny in the back seat and buckled her in. She looked like she was peacefully sleeping. I climbed back in next to her to keep an eye on her.

Connor settled into the driver's side and started the car. Before he drove off he got my address from me and added it to the GPS he found in a cup holder under the dash. He handed the GPS over to me to hold. Larry nestled into the seat on the passenger side as Connor drove down the road. Unlike Mabel, he didn't worry about the speed limit but forced the car to go faster.

"What will we do when she wakes up?" I asked.

Connor didn't answer.

"We did steal her car." I looked at her. "I know we needed to escape what is happening downtown, but for God's sake, this is a carjacking, and we just kidnapped the owner, too."

Connor gave a one-handed dismissive wave while keeping the other on the wheel. "We're borrowing it. Besides, with the vortex, and all those things escaping it, I think the police have more to worry about than one stolen car. As for Mabel, we kept her from being zombify earlier."

We rode onto the ramp for I-95 and merged with the traffic. Light, only a few cars, a couple of trucks and one semi rolled along the asphalt—not unusual on I-95 around this time of the day. With Connor zooming along at almost seventy, we made it back to my house in no time.

He parked the car on the street. Thank God it was night, for that meant my neighbors huddled inside their homes, watching the news, or eating dinner. This way we could sneak Larry and the still unconscious old lady (who had awakened, but seeing Larry again, had passed out) into the house without anyone seeing the eye or her. Connor carried Mabel to the bedroom I used as a guest room and deposited her on the bed, and locked her inside, just in case she awoke and began to make trouble for us. Before he did, he searched her purse for a cell phone, but not finding one, tossed the purse on the bed beside her. Unless she had one in her vehicle, she couldn't make a 911 call.

I snatched up the remote and clicked on the television, changing channels until I found the evening news. On the large video monitor behind two news anchors sitting at a desk, I saw what had to be a live picture of the vortex. A newscaster reported on it from a news helicopter hovering far enough away. As we watched, the grayness took over people in its path, zombifying them. Suddenly, the show switched to a meteorologist who reported that the weather was a nice 60 degrees. "Great for an evening walk," he said, pointing at the green screen with a shaky finger, "but not downtown."

Larry lowered down onto the couch and stared unblinking at the TV. I tossed the remote and it landed beside him. Connor followed me into the kitchen and sat down at the kitchen table. I made a salad, scrambled some eggs, and poured water into a couple of glasses. I placed Connor's dinner in front of him, sat down across from him, and tackled the food on my plate. We ate in silence.

Connor looked glum. "By the news reports, the vortex looks to have stopped: not going beyond downtown Richmond, but for how long? I wonder if that means the fiends from Hell can't go beyond the gray area, or if they can, are they terrorizing elsewhere at this moment?"

"Maybe we should tell the Army or Marines. Some government agency."

Connor looked at me with disbelief. "Tell them what?"

"That the vortex caught you and drew you up into it, deposited you in Hell, where you met Larry...well, and you know, the whole rigmarole."

"Right. I'll tell the authorities that I became a werewolf at the full moon six months ago, got pulled into the Hell dimension, where I met a demon that looks like an eyeball. Then some blonde human female who got hauled in six months later, helped us to escape." He leaned closer and took both of my hands. "I'll be locked up in a cell, as either they'll think I'm crazy or once they see Larry, he and I will become part of some government cover-up." He added, "And we both will have tests run on us by government scientists. Telling isn't really a good idea."

Angry, I tore my hands out of his as I rose to my feet. "So, all you really care about is saving your skin. You talk the big talk about saving the world. But when there's even the smallest chance you might end up as some experiment, well, forget the world." I stomped away, heading for the front door. "I don't know about you, but I'm furious that Hell can take over my world and make humankind into mindless things or bodies to be possess or food for its fiends. I don't know what I can do, and I may end up a mindless gray pawn or even die, but I will try something.

Connor caught up with me at the door, stopping me. "Okay, okay. Let's do it your way and go talk to the police."

***

We checked on Mabel to see if she had revived. Something swung through the open doorway and knocked Larry into the hallway wall. He bounced off it like a ball. Conner hijacked the lamp from her hands. Tear streaks glistened Mabel's reddened face and her eyes burned with hate. With a scream, she kicked out at Connor's shins, but he grabbed her leg and pushed her back inside the bedroom, locking the door. Pounding and curses erupted from the other side of the door.

"She's got a good pair of lungs on her," said Connor. "Let's go."

"Are we going to leave her locked up inside?" I asked.

"For now, it'll be safer for her."

"I don't know, but it looks like to me that the woman can take care of herself pretty well."

Larry drifted over and bobbed up and down as if nodding that he agreed with me.

The three of us piled back into the old woman's car and drove over to the Chesterfield County Complex. I stared through the windshield up at the night sky. Usually there would be the normal blackness of night, with twinkling stars in the sky, a moon even, but instead, I saw nothing. Connor pulled into a parking space, not far from the police station.

We entered the building and approached a heavyset policeman sitting behind a desk. He was munching on a greasy burger while reading a newspaper. Connor cleared his throat. The man peered over the paper. When he caught sight of Larry, his fuzzy caterpillar eyebrows reared up, as his eyes widened.

He lumbered to his feet, dropping what remained of his burger on the desk, and dragged his gun out of his holster. He pointed it at Larry. "Hold it. Did that thing come from that monstrosity causing problems in Richmond?"

Connor sighed, giving me an "I told you so" look. "Officer, yes, Larry came from the vortex. It leads to a foyer that leads to Hell where he has lived for the last five hundred years."

The officer's gun wobbled as he began to shake. "That thing is five...what did you say? Oh God! The minister of my church is right. We're all going to Hell." His small eyes narrowed. "It's a demon, like in the Bible? Do I need to exorcise it or kill it? Except you can't kill a demon, right?" Something passed over his face. "Wait a minute. You said its name is Larry? What gives it the right to have a human-sounding name?"

Connor peered at the name tag on the officer's shirt. Sgt. Jenkins in black letters stood out in bold relief. "Whatever your parents named you is the same way Larry got named, Sgt. Jenkins." Connor added, "By the way, I'm a werewolf. Not human myself."

Sgt. Jenkins snorted in disbelief. "You don't look like the werewolf type to me. I don't see any hair all over your body."

"And you would know what a werewolf type is supposed to look like? Believe me, I am. Mrs. Viggolone here saw me in all my wolfie glory." Connor's eyes turned red, and his ears started lengthening into sharp points, his pearly whites becoming fangs. He snarled, his voice deeper, "Believe me now?"

Jenkins gulped, took a step back looking indecisive, his gaze switching back and forth between Larry and Connor. His jaw tightened, and he aimed his gun at Connor.

I screamed. "Connor, watch out!" I grabbed his arm, hoping to drag him aside in time. The cop wouldn't have silver bullets in that pistol, but I wasn't going to wait around to see if ordinary ones could harm a werewolf.

As the cop's finger drew the trigger back, he froze. Other officers who had apparently heard all the commotion and came up front became frozen statues at the same time. Spilled coffee from one female officer's cup halted midair.

I looked up and saw that the clock on the wall. Its hands had stopped at 7:30 P.M. Only Connor, Larry, and I could move, though none of us said a word or made a sound.

A soft-spoken voice broke the silence. "Hello." The tone reminded me of rich; velvety chocolate, Christmas morning, and spring flowers all rolled into one.

I whipped around and found myself staring at the most handsome man I had ever seen—after Connor, of course. He had long, platinum blond hair and a pair of soft blue eyes. He wore a long, knee length leather coat over a pair of leather pants, a shirt, and a pair of gleaming cowboy boots—all pure-white.

Connor, still in half werewolf mode, snarled, "Who in the hell are you?"

The other man flashed a sweet smile and replied in gentle tones. "More like 'Who in Heaven are you?' fits me. I'm an angel." His smile widened, revealing brilliant ivories that shone like a halo. "The angel, George."

CHAPTER 3

I always had the impression that angels might be sexless. Effeminate, if nothing else. George didn't appear that way at all. How many times in her life does a woman get her prayers answered and meet two good-looking men? One who's a real animal in every sense of the word, and the other, heavenly as they come? Not often. If ever, in my life.

The angel George crossed the room. The movement recalled a bird winging its way through blue skies. I peered at him, trying to detect if he had wings and that's why he seemed to "fly" to us. But all I saw flapping behind him was his leather coat, its ends rising as if a breeze propelled them. His boot heels click-clacked on the floor.

He smiled, looking down at me from a height that had to be over six feet. "You're Cathleen Viggolone. God forgives you for your divorce."

What's that crack about? A flush of hot anger flared inside me. "God forgives me for some creep who not only cheated on me but divorced me, so he could marry his floozy? Excuse me, but I didn't sleep with some young thing, he did! I. Did. Nothing. To. Be. Forgiven. For, George. And by the way, I go by Cat, though only my friends can call me that. Something you're not getting the choice to do." On those last few words, I poked him hard in his angelic chest and spun around, stomping over to a corner of the police station. Finding an empty chair, I thumped down into it. My arms crossed and not looking at anyone, I muttered under my breath words that would make a truck driver blush, never mind an angel of God. No doubt, more stuff that I would need forgiveness for.

Something touched me. With a frown, I raised my head and looked straight into Larry's iris. He bumped against me in a gentle manner and made a sort of cross between a whine and a chirp. I supposed he meant to give me some sort of comfort. I leaned back and patted him on the top of his...noggin. . .eye?

"Thanks, Larry. I'm sure you don't feel I have anything to be absolved of. You're a good friend, even for a fiend from Hell."

Hurt showed in his big eye.

"Oh, I am sorry, Larry. You're not a fiend."

Larry warbled and rubbed against me like a contented cat.

"I'm sorry for what I said to you."

The angel George stood before me, a single tear slipping out of his right eye. Like everything else about him, the tear shone with light. Behind him stood Connor, completely human once more but with a glowering look etched into the lines of his face.

Connor growled, "You should be...*George*. Didn't a quote in the Bible say, 'Thou shalt not cast stones or aspersions, or something close to that'?"

George looked askance at Connor. "I said I was sorry to Mrs. Viggolone, Mr. Rojas.

"You shouldn't have said such an asinine thing to her to begin with."

George looked up at the sky. "Give me faith, Lord," he whispered, loud enough that we all heard it.

Connor's face became more wolf like as he snarled, "Look here, Heaven's boy—"

I stood up quickly and inserted myself between the two of them like a wall. "It's okay, Connor, it's really okay. We're all not perfect, not even angels from Heaven, I'm sure."

The angel's eyes widened, and his mouth opened, but I covered it with my hand, silencing him from any further comments. I didn't need the werewolf pulverizing him. No, make that me not pulverizing him. Pulverizing him until instead, only his shiny halo remained. Connor's face morphed to human again and I took my hand away.

"You're right, Cat. Besides, we have more important things to worry about than this heavenly messenger."

George did something with his hands then and what looked like a large widescreen television monitor appeared before us. *Angel TV?* I didn't see any sports show or a soap opera, or even a science fiction movie. Though it did show a real live horror story—the hellish vortex in all its nasty gray color.

George jabbed a finger at it. "We need to get there. Now.

I made a half-turn. "Let's get the car."

George grabbed me by my shoulder and pointed to the screen. "No, we can get there faster and much safer by going through this."

I said, "Wait a moment. You want us to go through that?"

"Yes."

"There's no way possible."

He picked me up and threw me at the screen. Shrieking, I covered my head and face with my hands and arms. But instead of striking it, I passed through it and into something like odd, wobbly orange gelatin. The stuff faded away and I landed hard on what appeared to be a concrete sidewalk. Stunned, I lay there when a second later, Connor and Larry dropped down beside me. George arrived from out of nowhere, landing on the ground. Whatever the stuff we passed through, it didn't leave a residue.

I stood, every part of me hurting. "Ouch! Did we have to travel that way?"

George replied, "I got you here and we are only a few feet from the vortex. The easiest and only surefire way to transport the three of you."

I groaned. "I don't think it was an easier way. Sure fire, yes. More hurtful, too. Connor? Larry?"

Connor climbed to his feet. "I'm a werewolf. No bruises or cuts."

Larry floated over to me and bumped softly against me.

I patted him. "Guess you're okay, Larry."

George laughed, the sound like songbirds singing on a summer morning. The angel was starting to rub me the wrong way.

George said, "He's a demon, so of course, he's fine. Supernatural beings are more protected against the slings and arrows of pain and death. Most times."

He reached over and laid a hand against my back. "Mortals and the other living things on Earth feel hurt and can die. Your fragile shell can be torn; it's so simple to leak out your life force. Even your souls are like tissue paper and it doesn't take much to wound them."

Warmth stole over me. I grew drowsy and content. As suddenly as it had enveloped me, the heat vanished. George had withdrawn his touch. The pain was gone.

I laughed, happy and carefree. My body felt great. Not just the pain from landing on the sidewalk, but every other injury I've gotten over the years. Whatever George had done to me must be aphrodisiac in nature, I twirled around like a ballerina on my toes. Even my soul and heart seemed pain free too. Angel medicine should be bottled and prescribed to every human being. I grabbed George and hugged him. "George, I feel marvelous! Being 'touched' by an angel makes me feel great. Why, I even feel frisky, like I was back in my teens again."

George disengaged himself from my embrace. "Doing that to a mortal is potent. I felt you needed to be strong and healthy for the ordeal ahead." He gestured. "Come on, let's get to that vortex and go fight some demons."

He stepped forward and we followed. It only took a couple of minutes until we found ourselves just a few feet away from the gray mist drifting out of the vortex. It didn't move, but hovered there like a force field to keep things out. It also caged all manner of things that massed inside.

Demons, large and small, some horrid, others humanoid, each with just a single difference. Some even rivaled George for angelic beauty. Other monstrosities paced inside that gray field; what had once been humans and animals, I assumed they longer were alive. These undead things saw us standing on the other side of the barrier and they drew close to the edge, growling and trying to get at us. But they couldn't and that made me glad. The way their dead eyes glinted and the way they drooled made me feel like a stuffed turkey ready for their mad version of a Thanksgiving feast.

I took a few steps back. "You expect me to go in there and take them on?" I caught George's eye. "That crap will turn someone like me unnatural like it did to other living people. I want you to understand that I have this allergic reaction to becoming an undead creature. I like being a living human being and I have plans on staying that way for a long time."

A smile graced his lips. "I'm an angel," he replied, taking my arm and making for the grayness.

I resisted. "And that's supposed to make me feel better?"

He said in a patient voice, "I can prevent you from becoming something like that." I must have had a dumbfounded look on my face as he added, "Since I am an angel I do have powers. Remember? How else would what I did to you a couple of minutes earlier work?"

"I see." I frowned. "But if you have all those powers, why don't you and the rest of your angelic brethren just go in there and give those demons some heavenly whoop-ass?"

"Why would we do something with a donkey? Oh, I get it. Look, this may be a version of the Apocalypse—9.0, to be exact. Since the Beginning, written down by God and Lucifer long ago in a contract and signed by both, God's angels are not supposed to engage in any of the lesser apocalypses and do battle. That's only for the last, great one. This time around I lost, ah, won the bet, to come down and get some mortal help to stop this particular one."

Connor butted in. "Are you saying that this isn't the end of the world?"

"It is the end and yet, it isn't." George wrinkled his nose. "It all depends on how it's defined by Heaven and Hell. Technical details, you know."

Connor growled, his teeth sharpening as he grabbed a fistful of leather coat and planted his face close to George's. "Look, Angel Face, are you trying to tell us that this isn't the real thing and that it'll fizzle out, or are you just giving us the runaround? That a planet we live on is the soccer ball between Heaven and Hell?"

"Oh, if Hell wins, the world will end, there's no two ways about it. It's just not the Big One to end the planet for all times. When that one hits, the Earth goes kablooey."

I drew closer. "Kablooey? What does that—" *Oh, no!* "You mean this planet will blow up into smithereens?"

Connor let go of George's coat with a snort of disgust. "Guess we can't count on Pretty Boy's buddies coming to save the Earth." He turned to both Larry and me. "I say we vote and leave the heavenly body here. Let him do some of his mumbo jumbo to protect us from the gray crap changing us into the dead and we'll go inside that vortex to go kick some collective demonic butt."

George shook his head. "Sorry, no can do. I was told I must be part of any saving of the planet—Big G's orders and all. I promise the three of you will be under my Heavenly protection. Nothing, I mean nothing, will bring or do harm to you. We should be able to get to the vortex safely."

I still couldn't believe it. The vortex swirled in front of us like some ominous raven of doom. Stepping through it might mean adventure and saving the world, or again, the end of my life. I cut my gaze to him.

"Are you sure?"

"I swear by my Heavenly Maker. Angels can't lie."

He touched my shoulder, then Conner's, and finally Larry on the top of his eyeball. The four of us slipped through the barrier and into the grayness. Nothing happened to us. A crowd of the undead milled around us like starving wolves circling a herd of sheep, drool dripping from their jagged teeth. Each time one of them would rush one of us, it would run smack into something like an invisible force shield. It would rejoin its buddies. With dull, vacant eyes and unable to get to us, they snarled and banged on that invisible barrier. Ignoring them, we kept going, the vortex one big bull's eye and we the arrows. A monstrous being that I never imagined in my wildest nightmares shot out from the swirling mouth of the swirling miasma. It looked like a cross between a hog and a lizard oozing with slime, with strange looking appendages like twisted wires whipping out from where normally the eyes would be. It roared and stomped its feet. To the left of us, we walked past a twenty-foot version of what reminded me of Rodan from the Japanese movies. It squealed like a pig, as small, symmetrical things with mouths full of jagged teeth tore at its flesh like ravenous piranhas. They darted in and out, avoiding the bigger monster's flapping wings and beak full of serrated teeth. On occasion, the Rodan lookalike would catch one of its harassers by a tongue that whipped out of its bill and speared it with the pointed tip, swallowing the creature whole.

More and more *lusus naturae* spilled out of the vortex and intermingled with the undead. They attacked them and ripped out chunks of flesh with their fangs, claws, and other appendages. The scene looked like something out of a nightmare, a drug-induced delusion, or even a bad B-movie on the late, late show. I waited for our supposed protection to fail as we finally reached the vortex itself.

Connor yelled at George over the roar of the vortex. "What about weapons?"

George gave us all a serene smile. "When we have need of weapons, they will appear when the time is right. Have faith."

I stared into the mouth of the eddy and shivered. "Have faith? I'd still like an M-16 in my hands to back up my devotion."

Suddenly, I couldn't feel the ground beneath my feet. With horror, I saw that I hovered several inches off the pavement. Looking at the vortex, I noticed that it drew nearer. *Oh no, it's not coming closer. I'm floating like a balloon toward it.* The others also headed for the mouth of the storm. George gave me a thumbs-up. Not one hint of fear shone in his eyes, only a calm acceptance of whatever fate had in store for him and us. I envied him his conviction. Of course, with George being an angel, it might take God, angel, or Lucifer to destroy him, while with me being a mere mortal, it wouldn't take much for me to become demon chow.

We entered the mouth, and the gyre spun us to the other side like an insane amusement ride without being strapped in. Our feet descended and planted us back on terrain. We had arrived in the lobby to Hell.

The grayness filled the place like it did before. Not silent like the last time, demons shared it with us. They circled us, snarling, snapping, screeching, and laughing with insanity. We gathered together in a smaller semicircle, back-to-back, as we faced off the creatures. I wondered what weapon might appear to me. The hell beasts stopped making noises and stood aside, craning their heads to watch something approaching.

I squinted at a speck in the distance—a slight dark figure in the mist. The grayness whipped away from it. It didn't look monstrous, but as it drew close enough for me to see, its face filled me with dread. Chilled, I recognized an old boyfriend I had dated back in high school. Tom Lipton may have the looks of an angel, but deep down, he was all creep.

He grinned. "Hello, Cat. Long time no see." His grin grew wider and nastier. "Gotten older too."

"Maybe I'm older, Tom, but at least I'm not siding with Hell. You were a real piece of work back then and have obviously been rewarded for it. You only dated good girls to deflower them and the only reason you had any interest in me, so I broke up with you. I heard that you liked to pull wings off butterflies and pour antifreeze into the drinking bowls of cats and dogs." I shook my head. "And you know what? You and my ex are two of a kind—nasty bits of hell spawn. Loser with a capital L."

He grabbed a handful of my hair and yanked me against him. He grabbed me by the shoulders and dug his fingernails deep into my flesh. Tears welled up in my eyes from the pain. I fought to free myself from him, but his grip tightened.

"Look, bitch, if you hadn't dumped me that night years ago, I wouldn't have sped out of there and smashed into that tree. I wouldn't have died. I should have been the one to dump you, after I got a piece, of course."

Connor appeared behind Tom. "Take your filthy hands off her."

Tom grinned as his head swiveled 180 degrees like Linda Blair in *The Exorcist*. "I see you got yourself a knight in shining armor. Is he as shiny in other departments?"

Connor smashed his fist into Tom's face and then kicked out at Tom's legs. Tom let go of me and I got out of the way. He rotated his entire body around like a snapping rubber band, to align with his head, and he glared at Connor. His skin began to melt like hot candle wax, reshaping itself into a grotesque version of his human features. Yellow eyes glared out of a mug whose flesh had gone from the pink of human skin to green as a lizard's backside. Warts and sharp spurs covered the face and large, sharp horns sprouted from his brow like a bull's. Tom grinned, revealing razor-sharp, reddish fangs and laughed with piggish snorts.

"I can tell by your eyes that I'm not a pretty sight. When you end up in Hell, most times you don't get to keep your pretty boy image."

I put my hands on my hips.

"Tom, I think this change suits you. You've become the real you."

He snarled, "I didn't ask for your opinion, bitch."

He dropped into a crablike position and scuttled toward me. I pedaled back, trying to elude him. Still silent, the other demons cut me off and formed a solid barricade to keep me from escaping Tom, while others formed a solid wall of bodies to keep Conner, George, and Larry from coming to my rescue. Heart pounding, I heard popping noises and groans mixed with growls that rose in crescendo. Out of the corner of my eye, I noticed Connor stripping. His naked flesh metamorphosed, fur sprouting like grass. A snout full of sharp fangs jutted out of his face and claws sprang from fingers and toes at the end of hands and feet that changed into paws.

A cracking sound switched my attention back to Tom. He stood before me, a long black tongue lashing out of his mouth like a bullwhip, cracking loud enough to hurt my eardrums. It wrapped around my neck, and he hauled me against him.

He said, "Come on, honey, give me a kiss."

I screamed and tried to dislodge the tip of the nasty, wet tongue forcing its way into my mouth. The rest of it squeezed the back of my neck tighter, like a boa constrictor. I began to choke. Using his tongue, Tom tugged my lips toward his open mouth. Drool rained out of it. I fought harder, dug my heels into the ground, and pounded my fists against his chest. It didn't help.

Something large and furry leaped onto Tom's back. The tongue loosened its grip and snapped back into Tom's mouth. I escaped his arms and saw what or who had attacked him. *Connor!*

Backing away, I saw that he had latched his jaws onto the back of the fiend's neck. He made growling noises as he clawed at the back, ripping away strips of cloth and green skin.

I clapped, as I said, "I see that my knight in shining armor, or should I say, fur, is giving you the what for. Never threaten a damsel in distress around a werewolf."

Tom screamed, more girly than macho man to me. Where was the badass demon now? Oh, yeah—caught by the badass werewolf.

Snarls and growls rose all around us. I saw that the other demons didn't seem pleased about Tom's predicament. No doubt, they didn't like their "entertainment" ending this way. George and Larry appeared on either side of me. A large, shining, golden sword appeared in George's hand. Larry made noises that I swore sounded like growling. I understood what this meant, and I didn't like it one bit.

"Guess this means we're going to fight. Right?"

George smiled. "Have faith. Good shall triumph over evil."

I stared at the evil that surrounded us. Freaky fiends and nasty, gross beings of all shapes and sizes, crowded the area. More appeared to join the flood of Hell's spawn. It didn't look too good for us.

"Oh well," I said with a shrug, "why not?"

I watched as Demonic Tom escaped Connor and scuttled over to join the multitudes of Hell. Connor joined us. I stared at the drooling uglies and my stomach wrenched.

I felt like a potential superhero who would no doubt get her butt kicked. "You know, I lied. If I had my druthers, I want to die of old age, in my sleep."

George clamped a hand over my mouth, effectively cutting off whatever else I wanted to say. I felt something in my hands and looking down, I saw a long gold staff, sharp points at each end. George withdrew his hand. I turned to look at him and saw with shock, large wings of light springing out of the back of his leather coat. A shimmery glow surrounded him.

He looked incredible.

The demons made murmuring noises. The sound grew thunderous.

George said, "They're going to rush us. Get ready."

I uttered the only appropriate comment for a situation like this as I gripped my staff. "Oh no."

They say that when you're about to die your entire life flashes before you. I saw nothing but the demons as they hollered and as if in slow motion, stampeded toward us.

Most people died in car accidents, by gunshot wounds, cancer, or heart attacks. A lot of human beings passed away from old age, asleep in their beds. Me? I get to die in a new inventive way—being torn to shreds by some demonic entity. Worst case scenario, I wondered about my immortal soul when that happened. Screw it. Forget that stupid Klingon proverb, this did not seem a good day to die.

I gripped the staff and held it before me, ready to take on the first demon to reach me—which happened to be a winged, butt-ugly, toad demon. It flew at me. I swung the staff, and it went through the thing, like a ghost. Everything dissipated.

I blinked. Twice. I stood in a large cavern, alone, and still clutching the staff. A gigantic black stone gate towered before me. It shined with phosphorescence in the darkness.

I muttered, "Am I in Hell?"

"You're not in that part of the Underworld yet, but this is the gate that leads to it and all the rest."

I whirled around, holding out the staff before me. A strange green light, not unlike a chemlight, chased away the darkness. The light bobbed toward me. As it drew closer, I saw a little man holding a lamp. Ordinary-looking, he wore a T-shirt with a smiley face on it, the words "HAVE A NICE DAY" in capital letters underneath. A pair of threadbare jeans hung low on his hips, with a pair of dirty Nikes completing the ensemble. His head was a bald pate surrounded by long, graying, red hair.

An aging hippie? Large, oval, tortoiseshell glasses framed the brown eyes that eclipsed his face.

I held the staff before me like a cross before a vampire. Although, sweating made it hard to keep a good grip on it.

"Who or what are you?" I demanded. "Why am I here? What did you do with my friends?"

He stuck out a pudgy hand. "Hi. I'm Cerbie."

"Cerbie?"

He grinned, revealing big, white teeth. "It's short for Cerberus."

"Wait a minute. Like Cerberus in Greek mythology? The three-headed big dog that guards the gate to the Underworld of Hades?" I peered at him. "You don't look like a big, three-headed dog."

"Here, nothing is as it seems. Even me."

His form began to short circuit like a television picture going out of sync. Suddenly, where a small man had stood, a gigantic dog with three heads towered over me. I dropped the staff and stumbled backwards. Cerberus looked like a poodle gone wrong. *Wow, that's one ugly, pink poodle.*

The middle head still wearing the spectacles, bent down toward me. "Is this more what you expected?"

Drool fell out of its mouth and splat at my feet, creating a big puddle. I took a step back and hoped I kept the distaste I felt off my face. After all, when you're the size of a flea to a gigantic dog, it doesn't do to upset it.

"I expected something more along the lines of a wolf or a German Shepherd. Even a Rottweiler. Something that would induce more fear."

"This form doesn't frighten you?"

I tried to be tactful, difficult, considering three giant-sized pairs of eyes staring at me. I fought my frazzled nerves. Yes, he scared me, but I couldn't let him know that.

"You're gigantic, and that can be scary. But the poodle look is rather too cutesy and the pink color nullifies the terror."

He raised a left eyebrow, no, three left eyebrows.

"Not that cutesy and pink aren't great things to be."

The dog's form did that weird, shaky, TV reception thing again and Cerbie became the man once more. He frowned at the big puddle of drool he'd made and stepped around it. I stood my ground.

"Was that how Cerberus the three-headed dog really looked like in those Greek myths?" I asked. "I hate to tell you, but a giant poodle wouldn't have frightened most people much."

Cerbie sighed. "I always wondered why Hercules had broken down laughing like a madman when he saw me for the first time. My original form was a feathered serpent, but Hades wanted the 'dog look'." He scratched at the top of his bald crown. "Hades' main babe, Persephone, liked dogs. Little, fluffy dogs. He wanted the six months she always spent in the Underworld to be a happy time for her; so, he gave her whatever she wanted. He spoiled that girl something awful." Cerbie sat down on a large rock. "She was one spoiled bitch. If he didn't give her what she wanted she would scream and cry, calling for her mother. Talk about mothers-in-law. Demeter was the original bitchy mother-in-law. Finally, after six hundred years of wedded hell, Hades dumped the bimbo like yesterday's news. She turned around and married Balor, the Celtic god of death. Balor controlled her with his nasty one eye. If you looked into it, you died. Even immortals."

"What happened to Hades?" I asked, as I sat beside him.

"He went back to a life of solitude, judging who would live or die."

"Wait a minute! He's not Lucifer?"

Cerbie laughed. "You thought Hades was the head of the Fallen? Oh, by the gods of Olympus, he's the Angel of

Death. Hades is just one of the many names he's been called by mortals over the centuries. His all-in-black look was never in for a long time, except at funerals, not until the Goth style. Now he can pick up loads of chicks at heavy metal concerts and Goth bars, unless he's there to pick up a soul that died. Nowadays, mortal chicks seem to love moody guys in black."

I stared at the gate. "So, beyond that gate leads to...where?"

"Hell, and Heaven. Also, there's the Land of the Dead, worlds of various myths, like Jotumheim, Svartalfheim, Nidaveillir, Ginnungagap, Alfheim, Niflheim, Muspelheim, Yomi, Diyu, Elysian Fields, Hel, Irkalia, Kyöpelinvuori, Lemuria, She'ol, Avalon, Aztlan, Barzakh, even Faerie. All sorts of worlds and creatures dwell beyond that gate, all that mortals have given names to. And for eons only Death and I could be on the outside, with Death the only one who could visit the mortal world, other than the head Dark Angel, the God Jehovah, and some of Jehovah's angels. But as of late, the big baddies have been cooking up something frightening, making it possible for Hell and the Underworld to forge a passageway into your world."

I got to my feet and wandered over to the gate, pressing my fingers against the stone. It felt like a chunk of ice instead of rock. Beneath its slick surface, something hummed like a million crickets. I jerked my hand back. Not quickly enough. My fingertips almost burned from frostbite.

I looked at Cerbie. "I know. A vortex opened in downtown Richmond and now all manners of demons are on the loose there. Why did you bring me here, Cerbie? Where are my friends? You never did answer any of those questions."

He kicked a rock away and strayed over. His eyes took on the misty glow from his lantern. They gleamed like eerie train lights in a foggy night.

"Your friends managed to get into Hell, from the alcove where you fought. But I didn't bring you here, someone else did. I don't know who that is, and that's the truth. Someone or something wants you to enter through this gate." He pressed something on the front of the gate, and it swung open with a loud groan. "Sorry about the noise, but it's been eons since anyone came this way. Last time someone used it was when Galahad came searching for the Holy Grail. He thought that it had been hidden in the Underworld."

"Then why do you still guard this entrance?"

"Where else would I go? After all, I'm only a myth—" Cerbie's last word echoed over and over as he faded away. The darkness surged back like a suffocating blanket. Beyond the gate, it looked even gloomier than from where I stood. I told myself, "Come on, Cat, get your rear end in gear."

I proceeded between the giant pillars. *It stinks.* A rotting, fishy smell wafted to my nostrils—the odor usually given off by rivers and lakes. Once I made it to the other side of the gate it slammed shut behind me, the sound resonating in the still, fetid air.

God, it's freezing. Wishing I had my coat, I crossed my arms over my breasts and rubbed my hands up and down, trying to bring some warmth to my body. It didn't help much. I took care as I couldn't see past my nose. One misstep and I could trip and fall flat on my face. *Baby steps.* I wanted to keep my arms around me, but instead, I stuck out my hands, making sure I didn't run into anything.

I saw a small ball of light in the distance, bouncing up and down. I headed for it, hoping it would lead me to someone or someplace, hopefully not to my death. But it kept bouncing away, leading me on a wild chase like some will-o'-the-wisp.

My feet ached and the coldness had seeped underneath my clothing to my skin. I thought about my warm bed a zillion lifetimes away. I ran through some water, soaking both my jogging shoes and socks. Something grabbed me and yanked me onto a solid surface.

"Do you have a will to drown yourself?" asked a deep voice behind me.

I wheeled around and saw a barge with a shady figure standing on it. A small flame flared and it lit up the craggy face of a man. He wore a Stetson perched on the top of his head. I sniffed and wiped away the tears drying my cheeks.

"Thanks, Mister—?"

He puffed on his cigarette and took it from between his lips, blowing out smoke. "Call me Charun. No mister to it, either."

"Then this is the River Styx?"

"Yep. I can't understand why you're here. You smell alive to me. Only the newly departed use my mode of transportation." He took a couple more puffs on his cigarette and flicked the burning butt into the murky water lapping at his barge. Suddenly, everything went dark.

I heard a splash as if something large had leaped out of the water, maybe to catch that glowing cigarette butt. A second, louder splash that sounded much closer.

"That's right, I'm not dead. But Cerbie, I mean, Cerberus thought that someone wanted me to get to Hell through this way. So here I am."

A large lantern appeared in one of Charun's hands. It glowed, illuminating him, me, and the immediate area. I saw him all the better for it, a tall rangy man, dressed in black jeans and a black and red plaid western shirt. He also wore snakeskin cowboy boots. Never had I imagined Charun, the Ferryman of the River Styx, dressed like that. He looked like he should be riding off into the sunset; not ferrying souls to the Elysian Fields.

He arched an eyebrow. "What?"

"I just never thought to meet Charun, the Ferryman for the Underworld, dressed like a cowboy."

"I never did like that sinister and gloomy look. One has a right to change his style. Isn't that so?"

He reached over to his ferryboat, which was docked near us, and pressed a button on a box that looked like a radio. Country music blared out of it. The singer, Garth Brooks.

I stepped closer. "Charun, I need to ride your ferry."

"You're not dead and besides, you don't have an obol under your tongue."

"A...what?"

He sighed. "An obol is a Greek coin. I need to be paid before anyone puts one toe on my barge."

"Oh, I see."

I knew I didn't have an obol on me. I didn't think I had a modern coin on me, not even a penny...*Wait a moment.* I dug into my jeans pockets to double check. My fingers touched something small. metallic. round, and I pulled it out. Charun's lantern light revealed it was a penny. I held it out to Charun.

"Will this do?"

The copper on the flat of my palm gleamed in the lamp's light. Charun took it from me and bit down on it, before he peered at it.

"This just might do." He stuck the penny in his mouth, swallowed, and looked at me.

"But you're still alive, not a wraith. Last time I took someone alive across the river was Hercules and he caused quite an uproar. You gonna cause an uproar?"

I crossed my fingers behind my back. I didn't know what would happen to me down here, in the future, and the crossed fingers behind my back cancelled out any potential white lies.

"Oh, no. I would never do anything like that."

He chewed on the corner of his bottom lip. A second later, he nodded. "Okay. Climb on board."

I hesitated.

He snorted. "Get on board already. I may have eternity, but I don't have all day."

Before he changed his mind, I jumped onto the scow. It wobbled, causing ripples in the dark cold water beneath it. I sat down slowly and carefully on a seat I found. No way was I going to upset the boat and find myself in the Styx. I could swim, but being the Underworld, who knew what might inhabit the rivers here.

Charun untied the knot of the rope attached to a large stone pole. He flung the rope into the boat and leaped after it, landing lightly on the deck. The ferry didn't quiver under his weight but remained still. Grabbing a long white pole that looked like it was made of human bone, he used the bottom tip of it to push us away from the dock. He hooked his lamp onto the top of the pole's crook. I couldn't tell which way north, south, east, or west went. I had to trust that the Ferryman knew his way.

"Charun, what's our heading?"

His eyes on the horizon straight ahead, he grunted. "We're heading southeast, toward the Hollywood Fields."

"Hollywood Fields?"

"For every pocket of the mortal world, the cemeteries have their counterpart down here in the Underworld. The nearest one to where Hell has stirred up a hornet's nest would be the equivalent to Hollywood Cemetery in Richmond, Virginia. You'll have to journey through it to get to your destination."

"Does the Underworld have counterparts in the mortal world? Is it just the cemeteries, or are there more collaboration?"

Charun turned his head and stared at me. In the light of the lamp, I saw his eyes had grown large and round; his enlarged pupils inking them with the solid darkness. It drove home to me how non-human he really was. Fighting to not look away, I clutched the end of the seat with a tight grip and stared back.

A lupine grin flashed across his lips. "Many things have their spirit twin down here. And many of those twins are fakes, ready to trip up the fool who dares to venture here before their time of death. Better remember that, mortal."

The flat-bottomed boat docked, scraping onto the ground before large stone gates with a sign "Hollywood Fields" attached. Charun laughed, an eerie bone chilling sound. I shivered as I stood. The ferry rocked, and I fought to keep my balance.

Suddenly, he picked me up and tossed me out onto the dirt before the gate. I landed face down in the muck. Some of the dirt forced its way down my throat and nostrils. "Out with you, foolish mortal."

Coughing, I floundered, my feet tangling with tall, dried grass. I grabbed the edge of the sign and, finding my footing, rose. Charun tossed me something that appeared to be a torch. I picked it up and when I raised it, a dull light flared to life at its tip.

The ferryboat shoved away from the land and as it floated away, Charun shifted into some dark shadowy form, his parting words loud as his lamp blinked out and the boat merged with the darkness.

"Have an interesting journey."

I dusted what filth I could get off my clothing and hair. I spat out what dirt remained in my mouth, and I looked for the latch to open the gate. Unhooking it, the gate swung open on its own, creaking with the sound of rusty cow bells. In the real Hollywood Cemetery, the only time one could visit the place would be in the daytime. Here, in this version, the boneyard was at night. The chilly air caused goosebumps to ripple along my flesh. A pallid, full moon rode the night sky above like a hag on a broomstick, giving off a pathetic light that didn't reveal much of my path.

Different from the beautiful park-like graveyard back in the Mortal Realm, this one gave off the atmosphere of a scary funhouse ride in an amusement park. Where else would I go? With the River Styx behind me and elsewhere unknown, I nibbled at the inside of my cheek and stepped inside. Unlike the paved street that threaded through the cemetery in mortal Richmond, my footsteps crunched on a forest path littered with broken objects. I picked one up, letting light from my torch wash over it.

"Yikes!" I dropped a bone of a human finger. Suddenly, I didn't care to discover what else littered the path.

I walked. Not an easy saunter for a day in the park, but a quicker pace than my regular exercise gait. Fear and the freezing night air were all the motivation I needed. My light flickered. I saw nothing except tombstones and statues. To my right, I noticed a single angel statue, her one hand extended as if offering friendship. In the glow from the torch, the face appeared serene and beautiful. The torchlight and the sad moonlight made a harlequin of dark and light of her marble robes.

Well, maybe there's nothing in this place to really do any harm to me.

Just then, the angel's stone features melted away, becoming a horrible caricature. The angel blinked eyes obsidian as bottomless pits, and it glared at me. It rolled its hand into a tight fist with one finger pointing at me. My heart racing and my mouth dry, I staggered back a few steps.

"A living mortal." she hissed, revealing jagged teeth.

She whipped around on her pedestal and began to wail like a banshee. Her stone hair moved like the snakes on Medusa's head.

"There's something alive in Hollywood!"

Other voices caterwauled, '"Something alive!"' the sound growing in crescendo. Pale, insubstantial things began to pull themselves out of graves and drifted from mausoleums. They drew closer and I realized they were spirits of the dead. Many dressed in various styles from as early as the 1800s to the latest being from my time in the twenty-first century. Some wore Confederate gray and a few in Union blue, the officers grasping swords. They surrounded me, staring with angry, dead eyes and blocking any possible retreat.

Great. It's Night of the Living Dead, only for real. I wonder if they're hungry, too.

I decided to cut my visit short. I saw a small opening between a fat, ghostly woman and a smaller, thin man. Ignoring me, the woman yelled at the man and he inched away from her, shrugging his shoulders. *Ah, another happy marriage.* That worked for me. Their argument gave me opportunity for escape. I took it, and slipped between them, running like something chased me. A quick glance over my shoulder and I saw the ghosts and other dead things surging up the path and from nearby graves. I headed in the opposite direction, away from the angry mob. Right smack into the darkness.

CHAPTER 4

I ran, panic-stricken and breathing heavy, trying not to trip and fall. I almost fell once, but I managed to regain my footing and kept going. I knew what would happen if the ghosts caught me. No way did I want to become the latest addition to this cemetery.

Ghostly hands from a few that caught up to me tried to grab me, but they passed through me like an icy wind. Hands of dirt-encrusted bone broke through the ground and tried to grapple-hook my shoes. I screamed, kicked, and clomped down, breaking finger bones and grinding them back into the graves.

I sprinted past the phosphorous wraith of President John Tyler who lay in an opened tomb. He sat up and rubbed his eyes as if just waking up from a nap. His hands dropping to his lap, he glared at me and called out, "Can't a spirit get some rest in the afterlife?"

Not even bothering to answer him, I sped up and left the angry past president far behind.

My breathing grew ragged as pain clawed through my chest. Blinded by the darkness, I never saw something in my path, and I tripped over it, almost taking a nosedive. I slackened down to a walk when I realized that the ghosts had stopped chasing me. Tired, I flopped down onto a patch of dry grass and sat there cross-legged, fighting to not start bawling. No matter how I wished this to be nothing more than a nightmare, stark reality told me otherwise.

I wanted to do nothing more than rest for a few minutes, but I got back up. The back of my neck prickled. Something stood behind me. Heart hammering and feeling ill. I pun around to meet Confederate President Jefferson Davis's gaze. His shade stood on his gravesite; a large Confederate flag whipped in the night breeze behind him. Both the flag and he shone with a greenish, unearthly light.

"Who are you, madam?" he asked, his voice honey flavored with a Southern accent. He took a step toward me, staring up and down my body. Not sexual by any means, but more like someone appraising livestock and finding it wanting. Would he dare to grab my mouth and yank it open, checking my teeth like a horse buyer would?

Just let him try! I fisted my hands, the nails digging into the flesh of my palms.

He snorted. "So, women wear trousers now. Disgusting."

"At least I don't condone slavery."

Davis's face hardened, his eyes flashing anger. "Why, you little—"

"Begone, Spirit! Back to your grave!"

The new voice sounded familiar and very close. George appeared next to me, his wings spread wide and high. He pointed his sword at Davis, the blade gleaming like a golden light. The spirit slipped back into his grave like mist.

"George!" I squealed and threw my arms around him. "Boy, am I ever so glad to see you." I stepped back and looked around, puzzled. "Where are Connor and Larry?"

He sighed. "They're not with me. When you disappeared, the three of us got transported to Hell and kept fighting. Some demons grabbed Larry and took off. Connor gave chase after them. Alone, I managed to wipe out what remained of the demon horde, though I had to do that by getting back out to the foyer. But I couldn't get back into Hell to find them. That doorway had been sealed against me. An angel can get into Hell maybe once, even twice, but only archangels can enter the pit." His sword vanished. "I'm sorry, I'm only a mere angel, but I did find you. I used my sword and it homed in on you."

"It could find me, but it couldn't track Connor and Larry?"

"You're human. Larry is a demon. As for Connor, he isn't human. He is, in a way, but being a shapeshifter decreases the humanity. My sword can only be used to find or sense mortals and other angels. Besides, both are in Hell and once that way was locked against me, the sword doesn't work." He patted my shoulder. "Have faith; I'm sure we'll locate them."

I shrugged his hand off and jabbed a finger into his chest. "Faith, schmaith! What good is an angel if you can't save the Earth and us with a snap of your fingers?"

"It doesn't work that way. If it did, then the Fallen would never have fallen from grace. We could have turned back time. Come, let's leave this place and begin to search for a way to get into Hell to save Connor and Larry."

Strange golden lights surrounded us, blinking on and off. They sparkled like a million little fairy lights. I grew dizzy from watching them. Suddenly, a flash of brilliant colors obliterated my sight. When the colors faded away, I found that George and I were no longer surrounded by the lights or in the cemetery. Instead, we stood on some road made of black stone. I took a step and the road bubbled. Wondering what it could be made of, I bent over and touched it with a fingertip. It felt slimy and rubbery to the touch. *Yuck. Okay, not stone. Cement? Asphalt?* No, this didn't feel like either of those manmade materials. It didn't seem to be made of any of the usual stuff roads were made of back home. *Duh, you're not on Earth, dummy.* I straightened. "What's this road made of?"

"This is the road to the town of Purgatory, our first stop on the way to Hell. Paved with all the souls of those with bad intentions when alive, it's called Perdition."

I'm standing on people's souls! With a shudder, I stepped off the road and wiped the bottom of my shoes on the grass. It didn't wipe away the nasty feeling that I'd stepped on people.

"I'm not sure I can walk on it. Even if I can get past the point that the pavement is people's souls, it's the bad cliché that it represents."

George took my hands and drew me back onto the road. I shuddered again as the pavement rippled and shifted beneath our feet. A moan rose from it. Damn! Has my stepping on the road hurt someone?

"Cat, it's the only way we're going to get to where we're going."

"But you're an angel; can't you just zap us to where we need to be?"

"Like I said back in Hollywood Fields, it doesn't work that way. Come on, have a little faith, and let's start walking."

I'll scream if he utters one more time, 'have a little faith'.

He walked with his back ramrod straight as if he had a stick up his...*No, not going there*. Meanwhile I tried to keep up with him. Being extra careful I took light steps, trying not to press down on anyone, I winced at every time I heard an odd little sound, wondering if it was some poor soul whimpering in pain.

After a while, the sounds of suffering grew louder and more often, morphing into moans and even screams. This could not be what my mother meant when I was a teenager, that if I didn't mend my ways, I would be walking the road to Hell. At one point, the road squished and splattered onto my shoes. I bent over and touched the liquid on the leather, inspecting my finger at a close angle. That's when I saw the faces looking up at me from inside the road. *Oh God! The eyes!* Eyes stared up at me, some crying, while others glared at me with hate.

I straightened, wiping my finger on my pants. I jogged to catch up with George. The road squished and cried out beneath my feet. I slapped my hands over my ears, hoping, no, praying, to keep out the sounds. They still managed to squirm their way in.

No other place to walk, except on that damned road. George didn't say a thing. His sword vanished, but I was sure if he needed it, it would reappear like magic. He marched on, and I followed in his wake like a frightened, lost puppy. It grew cold and I didn't have anything to keep me warm. I wrapped my arms around myself, tucking my hands beneath my armpits. It didn't help.

I called out, "Hey, George, I know that many things don't work 'that way' for you down here as you said, but how about blinking up a coat for me at least? I'm feeling cold. Surely, that's an easy angel magic trick you should be able to do."

He paused, not looking back. "You should be warm now." He resumed walking.

Something soft and warm enveloped me. I found myself wearing a nice sheepskin coat with a hood, its color pure white. No doubt about it, a coat had been written off that list of "don't work that way down here." Thank goodness for that.

I zipped it up and drew the hood over my head. The beginnings of warmth stole over me. Now if only I could remain safe and feel no pain either, but like that pot of gold at the end of the rainbow, that too, seemed like a million years away. Not until I located Connor and Larry and the vortex had been destroyed, would I ever feel that way again. *Unless I died first. Then, I won't be feeling pain anymore. Death has a way of doing that to you. Damn, I'm a pessimist. I didn't want to die. Not until I'm old and pass away in my sleep.* The pessimist side of me ought to shut up.

Something occurred to me as I stared at the angel ahead of me. I broke into a jog, flinching at every cry of pain that drifted up to me, and caught up to George. "Hey, couldn't you have flown or zapped yourself to

Purgatory? It's only Hell's main door that's closed to you—right?"

He gave me a quick side glance.

"It's me that you're not allowed to use your angelic powers on. I'm on that list of 'doesn't work that way'. Am I right?"

He nodded.

"I knew that must be it." I vaulted in front of him and positioned my hands against his chest. He stopped walking. "Damn—" He gave me a reproachable look at the cuss word. "Sorry, but dang it, George, if you can wing yourself to the place, leave me and do it."

"I can't, Cat."

"But why the—"

He placed a finger, feather-soft on my lips, stopping another word. "Because the Fates want you, or you'd never have been sucked up by the vortex to begin with. I suspect you're a very important key to all of this." He withdrew his finger.

I frowned. "What can I do? I'm an ordinary mortal woman, nothing special. I can't even get my life together sometimes."

He shook his head. "I don't know, but have . . ."

No doubt, my face revealed how I was beginning to despise the faith word and George stopped, sighing. "I'm sure we'll discover the reason why when the time is right." He took my hand and tucked it through his arm. "Now let's get to Purgatory."

We started moving down the road again. George sang a hymn, and I crooned it with him. Calm enveloped me and although I didn't have an angel on my shoulder, I had one at my side. Maybe I might be able to stand traveling to Hell yet.

I couldn't be sure how long we'd been on the road. When I checked my watch, the time on its face had frozen at exactly at the time we had gotten to Richmond. Time didn't work here, at least not in the same way Earth time did.

George stopped and so did I. He let go of my arm. "Welcome to Purgatory, Cat."

I looked up and saw a large slum. Its inhabitants appeared to be the dregs of life in various shades of melancholy. Their clothing and skin dingy, their shoulders drooped, and depression in every detail of their faces. Bitter hopelessness with an added dash of resignation. Life stank for any who ended up here.

George explained Purgatory to me. "This is the place where souls not evil enough for Hell and not repentant for Heaven, end up after they pass away. If after time a soul proves to be penitent enough, he or she may enter Heaven. Otherwise, they're collected by a special squad from Hell that drags them down there."

A rip tore the fabric of the air at that moment, and four winged demons with hideous faces flew in, their horrible shrieks renting the air. The citizens of Purgatory shouted and began to run in all directions. The four demons swooped down and latched onto one soul who tried to hide behind a pile of trash. A teenage boy, he looked like he might have been sixteen or seventeen years old when alive. They flew away with him screaming and kicking, dragging him through the opening that sealed behind them. Those who hadn't been scooped up by the demons resumed their pathetic shuffling and moaning.

I clutched at George's hand. "How ghastly."

"I agree."

"If I survive this, maybe it's time to take stock of my life and sins; go to church, treat my fellow man better, give more to charity, become like a reformed Scrooge and believe in Christmas more—"

George yanked on my hand. "Enough. Come on."

I kept rambling. "Eat less meat and more vegetables; take up volunteering, and all sorts of charitable things."

"Hush, Cat."

I didn't say another word.

As we moved through the town of Purgatory, people avoided us. They made a noticeable wide arc around us and after we passed by, they reemerged into the crowd.

I said, "You would think we're carriers of the plague or something, by the way they're acting."

"No, I'm the problem. Their past sins are still with them, and they feel...queasy because of me."

"Is that because you're an angel?"

He didn't answer.

I turned back to George. "We're not going to stay here, are we?"

He didn't say a word; just walked away.

What's his problem? *And where's he going....*

Something rustled behind me and I twirled around. A short man with a crusty face full of beard and dirt, dressed in a greasy-looking trench coat, and wearing a dirty fedora crammed low over his forehead, stood there. His watery eyes glittered at me from beneath the brim of his hat.

He grinned, revealing stained teeth, the two front ones missing. "Hi, there, sweetie. You must be the new babe in Purgatory. I saw you with that halo boy. What sins kept you from reaching Heaven, and why do you get special treatment, being delivered here by one of those winged messengers?"

"I haven't died yet, if it's any of your business."

He edged closer. "Bet you can't even guess what's got me here, cutie pie."

An overpowering odor wafted up to my nose and I gagged. It smelled like the sewer.

"Your distinctive stink?"

"No, this."

He opened his trench coat. He wore nothing underneath, and his shortcomings were immense.

Suddenly, I found George beside me. "Cover yourself." He took a step toward the man. "Or I'll do it for you."

The little man buttoned up hastily. Eyes cast down, he muttered, "Sorry," and scuttled away, blending into the crowd.

"Thanks, George."

George took hold of my arm. "To answer your earlier question, no, we're not staying here. We're using Purgatory as a direct way into Hell. It's shorter than the other way I know."

Suddenly I understood what he meant and pointed to where the rip had been earlier. "Through a rip like those demons had emerged from earlier?"

A smile crossed his lips. "It is a much easier way into Hell."

His smile seemed off. Not innocent and angelic, but wrong, like a frown upside down. "Doesn't Hell have to open it up?" I withdrew my arm from his grasp and took a step back. "Unless, you can do that, too."

His eyes became black as sin and his smile grew darker as his teeth sharpened. Long spiked claws sprang from his fingertips.

"Oh yes, I can get it to open."

Oh fuck. I stumbled backwards. *The angel has gone darkside on me.*

Terrible screeches filled the air and the citizens of Purgatory screamed in response, the pounding of their feet like stampeding cattle as they ran. The same four-winged demons I saw earlier flew through the open rip that formed in the air. They headed straight for me!

I grabbed at George. "Do something!"

"Why, I am doing something, Cat. I'm sending you to Hell."

I noticed that his wings of light and clothing had changed too. Like his eyes, they turned black. "You're different," I said.

You're such a dumb bimbo, like you hadn't already figure it out.

He laughed, saying with a sneer, "Get her, boys."

The demons seized me. I screamed and tried to break free, kicking out at them and punching their armored skin with my fists.

"Let me go!"

One demon snickered. "Ah, pretty-pretty, I do not think to let you go."

Another snarled. "Finally, a real body and not a soul. Feels really good." It sniffed at my cheek and licked me with an icky forked tongue. "Smells and tastes scrumptious, too."

Its tongue swept along my cheek again. I shuddered, feeling unclean.

George said, "She's not for eating. Just deliver her safely to your Hell Lord. Understand?"

The cheek licker slurped its tongue back inside its snout and grumbled, "Yeah-yeah."

"Sorry about that, Cat, but lower lackeys, especially those from Hell, need to be put in their place on occasion. My, ah, new employer doesn't want you harmed in any way." George laughed.

I hated that laugh.

George continued, "He wants that privilege for himself, or for one of his higher muckety-muck devils. I heard rumors of how you might be the perfect gift for one of his nastiest demon lords. I believe that you'll be his new plaything." He snapped his fingers and the coat he gave me earlier vanished. "You won't need that where you're going. Take her away, boys."

Demon wings beat the air, lifting them and me up, toward the rift in the sky.

George called out: "Enjoy the flight. I'll see you there."

I struggled, but the demons held on to me tight. Looking down, I suddenly realized I didn't want to get free, especially as the town below had become ant-sized. The demons flew me through the tear, and the edges melted together behind us. I found myself in darkness, thick as India ink—oily and wet like blood. A nasty odor of sulfur wafted into my nostrils and my eyes watered.

The temperature intensified, switching between unbearably hot and arctic cold. One moment I sweated and the next, I shivered.

The demons plunged and I saw a glimmering light, growing larger and larger as we drew nearer to it. As it blinded me with its glow, the demons let go and I tumbled down, landing on a hard surface. Groaning, I stood up on shaky legs.

"I see that faker got you too." The voice sounded familiar and male.

Gradually, my sight returned, and I saw Connor. He huddled naked, dirty and miserable, but human nonetheless, chained to a large wooden stake driven into the ground. The demons had Larry collared and chained, although he could rise off the ground, and floated at Conner's side.

"Connor? Larry?"

I dashed over to them. I kneeled next to Connor and tried to free him. As for the lock, I had no key. "That Heavenly snake in the grass fooled me," I said. "Is he a demon in disguise?"

"No, only a disgruntled employee of Heaven," replied George as he stepped into the light. His wings folded together and they dissipated. "In Heaven, all one ever hears about is about Michael, or any of those damn archangels. Hell made me an offer I couldn't refuse. Here at least, I get a promotion and an upgrade in status. As it's been written in that human book, *Paradise Lost,* 'it's better to reign in Hell than to serve in Heaven.' And I am fucking tired of serving those half-assed choir boys." He stalked over to us and I saw that he gripped his sword. Only now its blade gleamed blood red, with skulls etched into the metal.

I stood. "Hell sent you to stop us, didn't they, George?" I spit out his name. "The Powers in control here fear we can save the Earth and humankind. Isn't that right?"

"That's it in a nutshell, sweetheart." He looked at Larry. "The eye demon will be sent to the Pit of Despair, where he'll be weeping endlessly." His gaze swept to Connor. "As for the werewolf, he'll be stuck in his wolf form forever, to become a part of Lord Hearne's pack of soul hunting hounds. I made a deal with the faerie lord to give him a genuine werewolf, in exchange for some services." He smiled and strolled in a circle around me. "As for you—one of the Lords of Hell is very lecherous and needs a new female to play with. His last one didn't like sex. He finally got tired of the bitch and sent her to join her husband that she'd killed. He put them together in a cage. I heard both provide entertainment and a great source for betting on their knock-down, drag-out fights." He laughed. "Being alive and still in your flesh will make it more interesting for Lord Azazel. I gather he hasn't had a living body to use in centuries. He'll drool when he sees you."

"I don't think I'm his type. Tell him that he needs to keep looking for his soul mate. I'm sure she's out there in Hell, somewhere."

Connor thrashed in his chains and snarled, "If that demon touches her, I'll split its body apart and swallow its black heart."

George sighed. "Wolf Boy, the loyal, well-endowed beast, I'm sure your lust for the human is fine and dandy, but get over it, she's not for you. You'll be howling through fields, helping a faerie lord hunt for souls, while Cat here will be finding a new name for pain and pleasure."

A wooden stake rose out of the ground and the metal chains attached to it wiggled up like snakes. They lashed out and clasped my ankles and wrists before I could get away. With loud clicks, each one locked.

"I think what you're wearing has to go. Azazel wouldn't like it."

He snapped his fingers. One second, I wore my jeans and T-shirt, the next, a diaphanous cherry-red gown covered my body. It had slits that reached all the way up to the upper parts of my thighs. Underneath I wore only a red silk thong, nothing else. My cheeks grew warm, and I knew if I could see myself the color of my face would match the gown and thong.

George cocked his head. "Tut-tut. Too bad your body isn't more beauty queen material, and you were younger in mortal years, but still the novelty of being human should be all that Azazel cares about."

Connor snarled, "I swear George, that if I ever get free, I'll pluck your wings bare!"

Larry twittered. I turned and saw him staring out into the darkness beyond. At first, I saw nothing. Then something, or should I say, three separate beings, stepped into the light. Each one appeared larger, more muscular, and more frightening than the one before.

The one in the middle seemed to be almost as big as an elephant, with the trunk of an elephant and gray skin. One watery, black eye sunk in the middle of its face had no visible pupil. Its tree-trunk sized legs ended in bird feet and the arms hung down sinewy and long, ending with buzz saws.

The one to its right looked like a sea serpent. It had seal fins where the hands and feet should be, and it had a pig's face with bug eyes. Its cavern-like mouth opened, revealing dagger-sharp fangs that it gnashed together when it saw us.

But the one to the left of it would have won the Most Grotesque Ugly award. It had a vulture's body covered in black, rough hair instead of feathers. And in place of wings, it had thick arms like a man, that ended in meaty hands clenched in tight fists. A billy goat's head sat upon the shoulders, with protruding eyes and long curling horns, sharp as needles at the ends. It grimaced, revealing dirty, yellow teeth.

George bowed low to this demon. "My Lord Azazel, here are the three you requested. Note that I had the mortal female clothed especially for you."

His voice grated on my nerves. Maybe he talked the talk about wanting to reign in Hell, but he looked and acted like a brown-noser to me.

Azazel lurched over and gave Conner and Larry a cursory glance. The look revealed them not to be worth his attention. He unclenched his hands, took my chin and jerked it up. With a finger, he forced open my mouth, looking inside as he tapped at my teeth. Maybe I should neigh. Light washed over me and blinded me for a second, so I closed my eyes.

Azazel's voice bleated like a goat, before it switched to human speech. "She reminds me of my fourth female. Remember her, Behemoth? Though that one was lumpy all over with fat and not something one normally lusts over. But damn, if copulation with her didn't prove to be the best time I ever had. I hadn't had such a woman since. Whenever we had sex together, she screeched like a buzzard on finding a dead body. I wonder if this mortal will be like that?"

I opened my eyes. Azazel's face filled my vision. Bile rose in my throat, and I fought spewing it.

"You remind me of Jeff," I muttered.

"What did you say, flesh bag?" Azazel demanded.

"You remind me of my ex-husband. He reminded me of a goat, too."

His breath, a combination of rotting vegetation and sour beer, exhaled into my face. "You even have the same breath he had after an all-night bender."

"Sounds like one hell of a pagan god to me. After me, you'll forget him and any other males in your life. I promise, I'll show you a really good time."

Connor's chains rattled as he thrashed. "Get your filthy paws off her, demon."

Azazel didn't take his gaze off me. "Leviathan, eat him."

George sputtered, "But he's for Hearne and his Wild Hunt!"

Azazel snorted. "That Tinkerbell can survive without him. Leviathan, eat damn Fido!"

The sea serpent demon rolled on its belly toward Connor, drooling.

I had to do something, anything, that might stop it from feasting on Connor. I grabbed Azazel by his cheeks and gave him a big, lip-smacking kiss on his disgusting lips.

I drew away and batted my eyelashes in hopes I appeared sexy, while trying not to gag. *Damn, he stinks like a barnyard.* But I held my breath and inched back to the demon. I caressed him. Something moved beneath the feathers on his chest and thoughts of lice and other, horrid things came to mind.

"Azazel, such a great big demon. Who'd want that man after having been kissed by you?" I walked my fingers up his chest and all the way to his mouth. Ignoring how I really felt about the feel of his big, moist, goaty lips, I kissed him again. "Why don't you just send Mr. Connor Rojas back to the earth and we can get on with whatever you have planned for me? And while you're at it, send the eyeball with him. Doesn't that sound like a good idea?"

Azazel smiled, if the flit across his goat lips could be called smile.

"Woman, no matter what I do with Wolfboy, I will still do to you what I have in mind."

I dropped my hand and tried to step away. Azazel muttered something under his breath and my chains fell off. He grabbed me and yanked me roughly to his chest. I snuggled against him and tried not to think about what might be under the feathers. If I showed him how I felt, everything would be lost.

He chuckled. "Even a lord of Hell can be magnanimous, so I will not let your werewolf boyfriend be eaten, at least, not today anyway." I didn't correct him about the boyfriend thing. Azazel snapped at Leviathan. "Leviathan, leave him alone."

The sea serpent demon roared, then pouted like a spoiled kid, and switched its hungry gaze to Larry. Poor Larry whimpered.

Azazel shook his head. "No, forget the ugly little spud, too." He brought his face closer. "To make sure that you don't try to escape me and my *attentions*, I'm sending Wolfie and the eye demon to a place they won't be able to escape from. If you please me, maybe, and I stress, *maybe*, I might send them back to Earth. After all, when Hell has complete control of your world, your furry boyfriend will either become a zombie slave or end up being demon chow, while the eyeball will be my brand-new pet to torture forever." He opened his mouth and a long green tongue snaked out. It slurped all over my face, trailing slime. I tried not to tremble, or worse, faint from the stench coming out of his mouth and the nasty saliva dripping from his tongue.

Azazel laughed. "At the very least, I'll let the two bastards live, even if they'll be imprisoned forever."

He thrust me aside and clapped his hands twice. Larry vanished. Azazel swung toward Connor and as he got ready to clap again, Connor looked at me.

"No matter what, Cat, I'll escape and find you. Just hang in there." He glared at Azazel. "Azazel, I promise that if you harm her in any way, you'll find out how monstrous a werewolf can be." He snarled, his teeth lengthening into fangs.

Azazel laughed as if Conner had told him a funny joke and clapped his hands twice. Connor disappeared.

Great. Alone with Azazel. Well, not really alone. There were the other two demons and George. Somehow though, I doubted that the demon lord would care if he had any witnesses to what he had planned for me. In fact, I wouldn't be surprised if voyeurism placed number one at the top of his list of sexual deviations.

Azazel snapped his fingers. "George."

The former angel-now-demon snapped to attention and stepped over to the demon's side. "Yes, Lord Azazel?" His voice dripped with sweetness, though the turncoat didn't look happy. It appeared that George had found serving in Hell not all he assumed it would be.

"I'm taking, ah, I forgot your name, darling?" Azazel looked at me, his hairy eyebrows raised.

George answered for me. "Cat, short for Cathleen Viggolone."

Azazel glared at George. "Did I ask you? No, I didn't. I asked this human bitch the question. That's one mark off your ascension into high demon-hood." He seized me by the back of my neck and yanked me to him. "Anyway, the honey pot and I are leaving. Have fun in the meantime."

George eyed Leviathan and Behemoth, looking confused. "How?"

"I don't know. Do I have to think of everything? Think of something. Go to Earth and terrorized some mortals or bring them here and play with them."

He beamed at me. "Come on, sweetie, let's go have some FUN."

His arm tightening around me, we vanished from George's and the other two demons' sight.

CHAPTER 5

Azazel left me with a small female demon and departed. We stared at each other.

Slight, she had lime-green, lizard skin; long, straggly, forest green hair; and big gray eyes with no lashes or eyebrows. Pimples sprinkled across her face like a mine field. She darted over to me and clawed at my top with her hands. Hands? They looked more like wizened monkey's paws.

I batted them away. "What are you doing?"

She settled her head down between her shoulders like a turtle in its shell. "Undressing you. Lord Azazel commands it. He wants you dressed in a more fitting style for a debauching." She ambled away and picked up articles of clothing from a nearby chair. She held them up. "See? Very pretty." She clutched a transparent camisole top and pants.

Did the demon lord really expect me to wear that?

"No way, I'm not putting those on." I yanked them out of her hands and tossed them to the ground. "Besides, I don't need your help in dressing me, even if I wanted to wear them." I added, "Which I don't."

The demon's big eyes welled up with tears that bubbled over and down her face. Like boiling water, they scalded Demon Girl's skin wherever the liquid touched. The tears hissed like steam when they hit the floor.

"Please, don't cry. You'll burn your face off." I picked up the camisole top and pants. "See? I'll put these on and you can comb my hair. Okay?"

Demon Girl stopped sobbing. She nodded her head and flashed me an idiotic grin.

I stripped off the things George had magicked on me earlier, leaving only the thong on. I'd rather have taken it off as butt flossing isn't a treat. Except, the thought of Hell Goat seeing more of me than he needed to, made the decision of keeping it on a smart move. I slipped on the new things and searched for shoes. I didn't spy any, not even flip-flops. Hands on hips, I looked at my erstwhile maid from Hell. "Do I get something for my feet?"

Demon Girl blinked, apparently not understanding what I meant. I directed her attention to my bare feet. She giggled like a crazy loon, gestured at her own feet— which were cloven hooves—and giggled even more.

"No, no, not 'I'll show you mine and you show me yours', but did big, bad demon lord Azazel command you to get something for my feet, to go with the sex shop wannabes? His toady made my shoes disappear when he blinked away my own clothing. Don't I get clogs, sandals, something? Anything?"

She sniggered and shoved me into a chair in front of a vanity. For something itsy-bitsy, she had muscle behind her. I found myself facing a large oval mirror and grimaced at my reflection in the glass. Pale, tired, and dirty, the reflection revealed bags under my red, swollen eyes, signs that I hadn't slept for at least twenty-four hours, if not more. It would take a whole truckload of makeup to get me to look halfway presentable again. That, and a week's worth of Zs in my own bed back home. Something I might never get to do again, unless Hell was stopped. Which looked more and more like it might not happen.

Demon Girl wiggled the stubby digits of one of her hands. A large brush appeared out of nowhere. I swore it looked like one used to groom horses. The bristles didn't look too clean. She grasped it as well as she could with her misshapen hand and began to comb out my matted hair. Demon Girl dragged and tugged the brush through the rat's nest, not being careful about it.

I screeched. "Ouch! Enough of the torture!"

Her brushing grew worse, if that could be possible. I suffered the pain and humiliation in silence.

At last, the bitch finished. I peered at my reflection in the mirror and noticed that miraculously a lot of hair remained on my head. She'd done an inferior job though. The hair also appeared greasy. I said, "My hair needs a good washing."

Demon Girl wiggled her extremities again and a large sink full of water appeared. Scum layered the surface and the water bubbled, as if something swam beneath the surface.

I leaped to my feet, knocked over the chair, and blundered away.

"No, forget the hair washing. I can wait until I'm home again. Besides if I let someone other than my hairdresser, well. . ."

Demon Girl snorted, and the sink vanished.

Whew. I picked up the chair and set it up right at the vanity. Once again, the little demon wiggled her fingers and an assortment of makeup appeared, a variety of creams, powders, and liquids in various colors and shades. Demon Girl sneered with what I thought might be a nasty 'I'm going to make you sorry for the hair washing incident' baring of yellowed ivories. In the reflection of the mirror, her eyes narrowed and turned solid black. I knocked the chair to the ground again. No way would I let the bimbo paint my face. Who knew what the powder and paint were made of? It could be mixed with maggot juice and acid toner, for all I knew.

With a makeup brush clutched in one claw and a glob of green paint in the palm of the other, she growled and hunched over, looking ready to attack. I took a stance, ready to fight.

"Enough. Out of here. Now." Azazel appeared out of nowhere and made a slashing gesture with his hand across his throat.

Demon Girl bowed low on the ground and smirked, and scuttled away like a cockroach juiced with bug poison. She faded away, merging with the darkness.

Wonderful. Alone with the goat. Azazel turned to me and flashed a grin at me. That made me nervous. It reminded me of a wolf showing its incisors just before it pounced on the defenseless bunny.

Yeah, I felt like a defenseless bunny. Only this rabbit didn't have a hole in the ground to escape down into.

He picked up the chair and shoved it at me. "Sit."

I didn't argue. I sat.

He waved a hand and a mirror appeared. Smoke filled the glass, covering it from end to end. When the smoke cleared, I saw them: Connor and Larry in a circular room made entirely of stone. No longer naked, Connor wore a hospital gown. I turned back to Azazel.

He chortled. "Did you think I would be that cruel, mortal? Well, yeah, I am that cruel. That's a grubby hospital gown I snatched from a hospital in your world— off some person being operated on when the Hell fog filled the hospital." He snickered. "I wanted you to watch as your boyfriend and the eye demon suffer, before we do the wild thing together."

Uneasy, I shifted my eyes back to the mirror. Connor paced the length and width of the room. Larry floated about twenty feet up from the stone floor to hover at a small round window with thick bars. Larry twittered and peered out.

Connor called out. "Damn it, Larry, get down here and help me figure out how we're going to get out of here." Larry ignored him and continued to look through the bars. Connor stamped a naked foot against the floor and swore a blue streak. "Look, get your eyeball back down here."

Larry drifted down to Connor and faced him, eye-to-eyes. He made a noise that I had never heard from him before. I shuddered at the eeriness of it, a cross between a coyote's howl and a snake's hiss.

It became obvious that Connor never heard it before either. "Larry, what's wrong?" he asked. "Are you sick or something?"

Larry made the sound again and kept doing it, floating back up to the window. Cracks began to form in the metal of the six thick bars at the window and bit by bit, pieces fell into the room.

Larry can do that?

"By Lucifer's forked tongue," said Azazel, upset. "Damn, they'll both be able to escape soon. Come on, plaything, we're beaming ourselves over there."

He slung me over his shoulder, fireman style. We vanished in a puff of smoke before I could scream and materialized outside of the large rock tower. It had no door, and the single window seemed to be the only thing that marred its solid form, and its rods were crumbling.

Azazel dumped me on the ground, still holding one of my arms in a tight grip. My derriere landed on some small sharp rocks that cut into me. Rattled and hurting, I stood and with my free hand, dusted off any rocks still attached to my body.

"Ouch! Eek!" I yelled, shaking off a beetle shaped rock that appeared to have a mouth full of needle-sharp teeth biting one of my fingers.

"What are these. . .rocks?" I flung it away.

Azazel stared at the window with a frown, ignoring me. More of the little imps appeared. Most of them ignored Azazel and me, rolling up the tower's side to the window and adding to the growing cluster. Larry's weird sound hadn't been the reason the metal started to come apart. A few attacked Azazel and me; the demon snapped his claws, and they exploded into dust.

"Great," Azazel snarled, "Stoners! I thought I had the prison and surrounding area sprayed for those imps. I'll never assign that job to my hench demons ever again. Never let stupid minions do what I could have done myself." His grip on my arm tightened as he turned to me. "Maybe you might be of some use to me, other than sex, of course."

"What do you want me to do? Eat those things?"

"I couldn't have said it better myself, girlie girl."

I struggled to get my arm free. "Oh, no, I'm not eating anything. I yanked one off my butt. Okay, I may not have eaten in a long time, but I am not so hungry that I'll stoop to munching on stones."

Pressing his nose to mine, he snarled. "If you don't make a meal of the stoners, I'll send your boyfriend to Hearne right now to become a soul hunting hound of Hell. As for Larry, what can be more torturous for an eye demon than be a ball for some foot demons?" He released my arm. "Besides, I might not be so rough on you when we finally have sex together. Now, which choice will you take, eat the imps, or have everything nasty that can be devised happen to all three of you? It's your decision, no pressure."

No pressure. Like he's giving me a choice. I walked toward the bottom of the tower. "Got any mustard on you?" I asked, looking up at the window.

The bastard laughed.

Larry hovered at the window, still making that weird noise. I waved my hands to get his attention. When that didn't work, I yelled, "Hey, Larry, I'm supposed to eat these *things* to keep you guys from escaping, or we're all in deep...stuff." He acted as if he never heard me.

Great. I looked at the imps chomping on pieces of the bars that had fallen to the ground beside me, and I shuddered. They looked like beetles. I could never understand why on those reality shows people who had to eat bugs did so. I would never have attempted it. Only now I had to. Except they weren't just bugs but also made of boulder. It would be like having stone soup, but without those other delicious ingredients. My stomach churned at the thought of ingesting them. I grabbed one skittering down the wall of the tower. It didn't snap at me, as I lifted it to my opened mouth. Just as I was about to shove it inside a familiar voice bellowed at me.

"Cat, don't do it."

I dropped the imp, and it scuttled back to the tower. I stared up at the window and saw Connor's face pressed close to the stoners and the crumbling bars, the tips of his fingers digging into the ledge. More rock rained down and I dodged it and the tumbling stoners.

Connor called out again. "Let them eat the stone, then Larry and I might be able to escape."

"Azazel says if I don't eat them, he'll still send you to Hearne to become a hound of Hell and as for Larry, something horrible only he'll be able to appreciate." Tears welled up in my eyes. "I'm sorry, really I am." I snatched another stoner and gagged as I stared at the disgusting thing trying to wiggle free.

A rumble reached my ears, and I looked up in time to see the entire window and tower around it collapsing back into the tower room, although a few of the pieces plummeted down to where I stood. I tossed the little fiend to the ground and ducked out of the way.

The opening being somewhat bigger than Connor, Larry managed to pop through the opening. He saw Azazel and with a squeal, rushed down the tower at the demon lord.

Azazel stood there, imperious, giving Larry the finger. "Come on, you stupid eye demon. Think you can take me on alone?"

"Not alone, never alone," called out Connor. He stood outside of the tower.

He ripped off the gown and stood there, nude. His body became like putty, pulling and stretching like incredible plastic. The flesh reshaped itself from human to wolf. Fur sprouted everywhere. Human ears shrunk and disappeared, replaced by large, pointed lupine ears that shot out of the top of his scalp. A snout full of sharp fangs jutted out from where his nose and mouth had been. Connor in full werewolf mode, growled.

I grinned at Azazel. "You're in B-I-G trouble now."

"No, you three are." Azazel snapped his fingers and from out of the darkness, shadowy forms emerged. At first, I saw five. The five became twenty, continuing until more and more shadows clustered around Azazel. In the hellish light, they grew substantial, becoming demons grinding their teeth or suckers, and snarling. Larry floated to one side of me and Connor the werewolf growled at my other side as we faced off the demon horde.

I looked down at my body, clothed in the Fredericks of Hollywood nymph apparel and did what any red-blooded American girl would do when facing down a multitude of demons. I picked up a rock and threw it at the fiends. "You want a piece of me? Well, come and get it!"

CHAPTER 6

The rock bounced off the nose of one of the demons that loomed bigger than a house. The entity didn't move, flashing pointy incisors and glaring with its five pairs of eyes.

Connor, Larry, and I fled. A thunderous noise behind us let us know they pursued us. Connor the wolf ran faster on four paws than then he would have as a man with two feet. Larry floated, keeping pace with Connor. As for me, the poor, out of shape human not dressed for running and barefooted, I pumped my feet as fast as I could. Connor slowed down when he noticed I lagged. It was then I tripped over something and hit the ground hard.

My knees skinned and bleeding, I had also twisted my left foot. Out of breath and every part of my body aching, I struggled to climb to my feet. It didn't matter. Connor and I found ourselves surrounded. His ears swept back flat on his head, and he growled. We were about to prepare for our inevitable death when out of the blue an orb of light appeared. It covered me from head to toe. Its radiance blinded me, and I squeezed my eyes shut. It must have muddled Connor and the demon horde too, for my ears caught the whining of a wolf and inhuman yells. Instead of being frightened of what had me, it felt good, warm, and comforting. Which mystified me.

***

I opened my eyes when I began feeling cold. The light had vanished, along with Connor and the demon horde. I didn't see Larry either. I was alone in some cold, dark place. I got to my feet. The pain in my body subsided and my foot didn't give out from under me but held strong. I took a step. I brushed my hand down at my knees, but I didn't feel any blood or sores at either one. Had that otherworldly light done that?

Is this a tunnel? I called out and my voice echoed back to me. Being pitch black, I couldn't tell if this place stretched forever in both directions. Freezing, I wrapped my arms around myself and tried to gather some warmth. It didn't help. I wished that whoever or whatever had sent me here had seen fit to garb me in warm clothing and not leave me in this flimsy outfit.

I frowned. Which way should I go? Right or left? Did one-way lead to warmth and safety, or did both ways lead to torture and horror, or worse, death? I did the most sensible thing I could think of in the situation. "Eeney meeney miney moe, catch a tiger by the toe, if he hollers, let him go, eeny meeney miney moe." The last word ended with me pointing left. I headed that way.

I pressed the palm of my hand against stone, which I assumed had to be a wall. *I can't even see my hands in front of me, so how can I tell if it's a wall?* I took it one step at a time, wondering what was happening to my world. By the time I found Connor and Larry again and we got back home, there may not be a home to get back to.

The temperature dropped to what felt like subzero temps. The chill went past my skin and caused my bones to ache. "I would sell my soul for warm clothing." I said out loud.

"Be careful what you say down here. That's Hell's specialty—buying souls. You're not far from that awful place either."

"Who's there?" My heart hammered as I stopped and drew close to the wall for support.

A light in the shape of a ball appeared in front of me. "Me." The voice sounded feminine and sweet.

"God, a light that can talk. Are the laws down in this place insane or what?"

The light bobbed up and down like a ball. "Please, do not take the name of the Lord in vain."

"All right, I won't next time." I fought myself from reaching out and touching it. That would be stupid, as it might have scorched me. Instead, a tentacle of its light stretched out and touched my hand before I knew what was happening. It didn't hurt, as a warm tingle spread from my hand to my arm and from there, throughout my body. I thawed and a sense of happiness overcame me. "What are you? An angel? A fairy?"

The light giggled like a mischievous child. "I'm all that makes up the goodness of humankind. A direct opposite of my sisters, Despair and Hate. I am the Light of Goodness."

"Are you the light that snatched me?"

"Even though it was against the rules, I had to save you."

"If you can save me, you can save my world from the apocalypse."

The light's glow dimmed. "No, I can't. Right now, thanks to that angelic traitor, George, I'm stuck here as much as you are. He put me in this place when I realized what he was going to do and tried to warn Heaven. I've been trying to find my way out for days now."

"Excuse me, but you just saved me. I would say that goes against the *rules*, as you call them. So, that means you did get out."

"Sorry. Look, I teleported out long enough to rescue you, before I was boomeranged back here. I'm as much a prisoner in this tunnel as you now are." The light brightened. "Hey, at least you're away from that demonic horde!"

"Yeah, thanks. But Connor and Larry are still with those demons. Why didn't you grab them too, along with me?"

"Because they're not human, a part of mankind. You are." It drifted closer, dimming down its brightness.

"One's a demon, for goodness sake, the other, is a monster. It goes against all that I am."

"Connor may be a werewolf and Larry a demon, but they're my friends and both have put their lives on the line for me. I'm going to find my way out of this tunnel and get back to them. The three of us will find our way back to Earth and do something to save it."

"They may be dead, you know. What I meant is the werewolf may be dead, Larry is a demonic entity, and it will take more than rending him apart to kill him. It would take an angel or Lucifer himself to be able to do that."

"Maybe you're right, but if you're the essence of what is good in humans you know that most of us are an optimistic species, determined to help others, even if they're not human." Of course, there are those who wouldn't give a damn about their fellow human beings, much less something not human.

"I will go with you," the being said. "You'll need a light to see in this darkness. I couldn't find my way out before, but maybe the two of us might be able to."

"Do you have a name?"

"Name? What do you mean by this?"

"Like my name is Cat, short for Cathleen. What are you called?"

It paused, sounding unsure. "I guess goodness..."

"Let me give you a name. Can I do that?"

"Oh yes, give me a name!" I swore if it had hands, the light being would have clapped them.

"Mmmmm...how about...Lisa? If I had ever had a daughter, that's what I always wanted to name her. And you sound like a young girl."

The light bobbed up and down. "L-ee-s-a. I like that. Yes, from now on I'm Lisa."

It floated on ahead, stopped, and came back. I shivered as a frigid breeze caused goosebumps on my body. "Sorry, Cat. I know you must feel the cold in this place. I can do something about that."

Lisa covered me. The tingle I felt earlier had returned and its warmth spread through me and once again, the sense of wellbeing filled my body, heart, and soul. I almost danced a jig in glee. Now if only I could get my hands on some warm clothing and a pair of shoes, along with locating Connor and Larry too, things would start to look up. Hey, we could save the world while we were at it. But I knew I had to take things one step at a time. Priorities. Yeah, priorities. I asked, "What are we waiting for?"

"Stay inside me, Cat. Let me keep you warm."

We headed down the tunnel, me inside her. The tunnel stretched on forever and although free of pain and toasty warm, thanks to Lisa, my stomach growled, reminding me I hadn't eaten in a while. I wondered how long Lisa and I had been traveling. It felt as if we had been on the go for hours, but it couldn't have been more than a half hour the most.

I stopped and Lisa stopped, too. I slipped a hand out and touched the wall.

"That's freaking chilly!" I yanked my hand back inside Lisa. I scrutinized my fingertips to be sure I hadn't gotten frostbite. "Sorry, Lisa, but I need to rest for a few minutes. I can't do a thing about my hunger, but I can sure do something about being tired." I stepped all the way out of her.

Lisa drifted closer. "Cat?

I squatted down, and ensuring my back didn't touch the wall, I rested my eyes by closing them. The heat of her felt hot against my face, as she asked, "Are you scared of spiders?"

I opened my eyes and, blinded by her, I snapped them shut again for a second. "No, I'm not, but they do creep me out and I rather not come across one." I reopened my eyes, shading them from the brightness with my hand. "Can you get your light out of my face? Why are you asking me this?"

"Because there are little black spiders all over the wall," replied Lisa, moving away.

I jumped up and did a turnabout, canvassing the stone. Lisa's light revealed spiders, millions, no, zillions of them. The little buggers crawled up and down, sideways, every which way, on the wall. My scalp itched, and my back felt strange, like a lot of little creepy crawlies scuttled all over it. I touched the top of my head and brought my hand back down where I could examine it better in Lisa's light. About twenty black spiders roamed it.

I screamed. "Get the damn things off me!"

I jiggled like a bowl of gelatin, did the Watusi, anything, to rid me of the nasty things crawling on and biting my skin. I yelled until my voice ended up nothing more than a croak.

Worse, more of them streamed off the wall in a mass like a large, black living carpet toward me. Lisa drifted over me. Many tiny voices surged into my mind, screaming their death throes.

The ones on me dropped off and burned to a crisp even before they hit the ground, hissing like rising steam. The others surging off the wall retreated to the right of the tunnel. They couldn't handle Lisa's light. It incinerated them. Lisa drifted back off me but remained close by my side.

"What are those—?"

Lisa finished for me. "Spiders? They're a part of Hell and cannot stand a touch of anything good, like me. As you saw, they fried at the touch of my light."

"Do you think you can get us out of here?"

The light bobbed up and down. "Yes, I can do that."

"Since I can't rest—even for a moment—we better get going. Sooner or later this tunnel must end. At least, I hope it does. For all I know, those spiders might not be the only things in here."

Lisa laughed. "There's always hope. That's why I exist. Hope is eternal."

As we moved on, I didn't see any more of the arachnids of Hell. I assumed they didn't want to get near Lisa. I kept quiet and Lisa just bobbed in silence alongside me. I looked down and from the light Lisa cast on me, the coldness of the tunnel caused my bare feet to turn blue, along with my hands. Lisa noticed and she covered me completely. I began to feel toasty, a warm prickle that began in my toes and swept through my body. Invigorated, I trudged on and Lisa remained over me. I saw through her as the light didn't blind me anymore. After walking a shorter time than I thought it would take, we reached the end of the tunnel.

Lisa said, "When I was a prisoner by myself, I searched, but never found an end to this tunnel. You brought luck, for this time we did."

Looking over the edge, I saw a long drop. This world had endless hills of snow that stretched into infinity, but right below our drop, gray rocks jutted up. Something not unlike a pale, full moon soared across a purple-black sky. I heard a wind whistling in the air and it caught falling snowflakes, tossing them into Lisa's glow. They melted.

"Do you know what this place is?"

"Niflheim," Lisa answered.

"What? Where?"

"It is one of the nine worlds in Norse mythology and the homeland of a forever, primordial night, cold, mist, and ice. Obviously, it has snow, too."

"It's a real place? I thought myths were fake."

"Much of your human mythology is based somewhat on fact. You met Cerbie, right? Same thing goes for Charun. Heaven and Hell are much more than a Christian conception."

"Wait a moment—you know about Cerbie and Charun?"

"Cerbie's a good friend of mine. I figured that if I plucked you out of that melee you and your friends fought in and transported you to his gate, he'd let you pass through it. I foresaw it. Not long after, I became imprisoned in here."

"You're the reason I was taken away that time? Did your foreseeing including Connor and Larry being taken and yet, you didn't save them?"

"I'm sorry, but rules..."

"Rules, smules! You told me you already broke them when you saved me and brought me here. Maybe a lot of things could have been averted, but you didn't do a damn thing!"

"I'm sorry," she said in a small voice. "You're right, those rules are stupid."

"Yes, look at George. An angel and yet, he betrayed."

Lisa dimmed. "George. He did what Lucifer and his minions did eons ago, betrayed Heaven and all that is good and light. A B-A-D angel."

"Traded his wings and halo for a set of horns and a pitchfork."

"You know, Cat, the horns and pitchfork are a misconception, dreamed up by humans.

"And I guess the devil doesn't dress in red either." I stepped out of Lisa and felt the freezing air of Niflheim dig into my skin. I wanted to get back inside Lisa again, but I fought it. As if she knew my thoughts, Lisa stroked a tendril of her light over me and her warmth stole over me.

"No, Samael, the Lightbringer, or as you know him, Lucifer, doesn't look good in red. His purple skin clashes with it. He prefers blue, actually."

"Like that song, the one about a devil in a blue dress."

"What? Why would Lucifer even want to wear a blue dress?"

"Forget it."

Lisa's glow burned hot. "Cat, look. Behind us."

I looked over my shoulder. Lisa's light showed a mass of something large and black flowing along the ground and walls, heading for us from the dark recesses of the tunnel.

"It's the spiders," said Lisa.

"What can we do?"

"Jump!"

"But there's nothing down there that's soft to land on. I could break something, worse, I could die."

"It's either jump or get eaten alive. I can keep them off you only so long, but with so many, sooner or later some will get past my defenses and get you."

"Putting it that way, breaking a bone doesn't sound half bad. Though that might enable any future horrors to be able to snatch me easier."

"If you do a running jump, you might be able to sail over the rocks and land in some snow."

Yeah, right—what choice did I have? I took a few steps back, took off at a run, and leaped. By some miracle, I landed on a large snowdrift, barely missing contact with a large rock as the momentum pushed me deeper.

Even though I didn't smack into the rock, I still got hurt. A couple of sharp pieces from the ground scraped me, slashing the top of my left hand. I bled, the snow going from white to red. Being so cold here, the flowing blood froze fast, and I began to lose the feeling in my body. I thought it'd felt cold in the tunnel, but that was more like being in Florida and Niflheim was like Antarctica. I wouldn't last long. The cold began to overtake me, and I wanted to lie down and go to sleep. *Where's Lisa?*

Something lifted me out of the snow and cradled me against something warm and furry. I looked up. *Oh God!* Gigantic and with long white hair all over, what held me looked like something out of some paranormal reality show. Big, glowing, red eyes about five feet across peeked out of the hair where the face would be.

Abominable snowman? Sasquatch?

I screamed. "It's Bigfoot! Lisa!"

"Oh, come on, not that again." The monster said in a booming voice.

"Are you going to eat me?"

"No, I don't eat people. Ever since Jack and the Beanstalk, we giants have been getting a bum rap." The voice came out of a very big mouth, loaded with sharp teeth the size of knights' lances. Those ivories looked perfect enough to chew a body in half.

"Well, then what are you going to do with me?"

The giant grinned. "Why I expect you and your bitty light friend here to come home with me to my place and have tea. It's teatime you know." Its grin grew wider. "The tea will warm you up real fine. Besides, I can bandage your wound."

Something thermal touched me and I rolled my head around to see Lisa.

She said, "We would be happy to take tea with you." A coil of her glow swept over my cut and a minute later, it vanished. "As for my friend's cut, there's no need to worry about it anymore. My light healed it."

The giant laughed, a thunderous noise that rumbled deep in its chest and sent bone-jarring vibrations through me. Though it didn't mean me any harm, the giant might still kill me with kindness.

"Why, I'm happy to have you," he laughed. "The name's Harry."

"Hairy, because you're covered in hair?" I asked.

He laughed harder. "No, spelled H-a-r-r-y. That's my name. What's yours?"

"I'm Cat and the light being is Lisa." I added, "Thanks for saving me from freezing to death."

"No problem, new friend. Now, let's go have that tea."

Harry took off, his legs making six feet strides. Lisa floated beside him, managing to keep up with the giant. A light in the distance grew more definite as we drew closer to it. I saw it came from a large castle carved into a mountain. This must be Harry's abode.

Harry halted at a door that appeared at least twenty-five feet high. He unlocked it, pushed it open, and slipped the key somewhere on his person. Who knew fur had pockets? Stepping inside with me, he waited for Lisa to dart through before slamming the door shut. Surprisingly gentle, Harry lowered me to the floor, made of the same gray rock as the castle. I looked around and saw giant-sized furniture of ice, covered with animal skins. Across the room, light filtered from a large archway.

"That leads to my kitchen." I must have looked confused because he added: "Where we're going to have our tea."

He walked through the archway, and we followed. Inside the kitchen, we found a gigantic stove and a fridge, both made of solid blocks of ice. The rules of reality must work differently here as fire would melt the ice back on Earth. I noticed a giant-sized microwave—not unlike the one back in my kitchen. Obviously Niflheim had caught up with the modern world.

How does he cook in that microwave? With dishes and containers made of ice? Wouldn't that make them melt? Then again, things were operated on a different scale here.

Harry saw me eyeing it and he grinned. "A friend back in the mortal realm had one made especially for me. The same friend has gotten me other things I have in my home. Ain't it right dandy?"

"Yeah, it looks really nice. Cooks and everything?"

He grinned, puffing out his furry chest with pride. "Oh yes, in much faster time than the old wood burning stove I had." He walked over to his fridge and yanked open the door. "Let's see, I think I'll make something yummy in my microwave to go with the tea." He looked at Lisa and me. "Oh, the only tea I have is Earl Grey. Will that be fine with both of you?"

I shrugged. "Sounds great to me." I looked at Lisa. "Lisa?"

The light hovered a few inches off the ice floor. "Since I can exist only on is the goodness of mankind, I'll just be enjoying teatime with the both of you. Long as you like it, Cat, anything is fine with me."

Harry slammed shut the fridge door and walked over to a kitchen counter. "Oh, you can't drink or eat with us, Lisa? Wish I had some of that goodness for you to snack on." Disappointment carried in his voice.

Lisa laughed. "Oh, but you do have that goodness, Harry, loads of it. I feel the heat of goodness rising from you. Very strange, to tell you the truth, until I met Cat, I thought anything not from Heaven or not human, wasn't naturally good."

Obviously not offended by what Lisa implied, Harry beamed as he put a ceramic plate of something into the microwave and pressed a button. To my surprise, the thing started cooking. I wondered where Harry got his power?

Harry said, "Well, my mother always said, "Harry, you're a good boy. There ain't anyone can take a candle to you. Glad to know she was right on the mark."

Taking the plate out of the microwave, he put it in the center of the ice table. He placed some napkins down on the table, scooped me up, and settled me on top of one of them. He perched on a chair across from me. I sniffed. Something smelled delicious. I saw it came from some muffins on the plate. Lisa drifted up and settled on the table between Harry and me. She toned down her light not wanting to melt the tabletop. Harry poured himself a giant-sized cup full of hot tea and handed me a thimble that could fit his pinkie full of the same tea.

Harry apologized. "Sorry, but that's the smallest thing I have around here that you can sip out of."

I picked up the thimble, which, to me, was the size of a large pail. "This is...just fine, Harry." His face grew sad. I took a sip, burning my lower lip. "Mmm...it's really great. Nice and hot. I can feel my body defrosting all over."

Using a fork, Harry broke up a huge muffin and handed a crumb over to me. "Try that," he offered. "I made it in the microwave, modifying a recipe of my mother's. The recipe says to bake in the oven, but I modified it to be done faster in the microwave."

He peered at me with an anxious look as I took a bite. What was a crumb to him, was as big as a small cake in my hands. I chewed and the flavor of blueberries exploded in my mouth as the warm morsel melted as it went down my throat.

I smiled. "Wow, that's scrumptious. But where did you get the blueberries, in fact, where did you get any of the ingredients to make blueberry muffins? All I've seen around here is rock, snow, and ice, and more rock, snow and ice. Not a spot to grow anything."

Harry beamed. "I could say it was my friend, but he only shops once in a blue moon for me. Being a giant of Niflheim, well, we know a bit of magic here. I mean, who can stomach eating rock? It gets old after a while. And being a vegetarian, I don't go hunting other beings to eat. Although, I can't say the same for the other inhabitants around here. I magicked me a hothouse in one of my rooms, using full-spectrum fluorescent bulbs my buddy got me from your world to help the blueberries and some other veggies and fruits to grow in soil."

He broke up more pieces into smaller ones and gave them to me. After eating them and drinking the thimble of tea, a yawn escaped me.

Harry eyed me with concern. "Tired, are we? Well, never let it be known that Harry didn't lend a bit of sleeping space for his guests like a good host."

He scooped me up and carried me with thundering steps to what had to be his bedroom. Harry's bed was made of wood and not the ice and rock I expected. Carved with fantastical images and covered with soft, furry animal skins, the bed dominated the room. He gently deposited me on top of one of the two fluffy pillows near the headboard.

I said, scrambling to sit up, "Harry, where did you get this bed?"

He scratched his side. "It used to belong to Odin. I won it from him in a card game. The old god likes his gaming. He loses plenty too, but does that stop him gambling? Naw. A good thing for me that day. It's truly a bed fit for a god, and I get to sleep in it every night."

I yawned again. "I can't take your bed from you."

Unable to keep my eyes open, I heard Harry tell me that it was okay with him that I use the bed. Or should I say, the pillow? He and Lisa whispered 'Goodnight' to me and Harry switched off the light. They left the room. I curled into the soft pillow, warm and safe for the first time in days.

CHAPTER 7

I dreamed, and in it, Connor and I went to my favorite movie theater back in Midlothian, not far up Route 288 from where I lived. We held hands and hung out in front of the concession stand, waiting as some pimpled-faced teenaged boy got us a tub of popcorn and two large sodas. The odor of fresh popcorn mixed with butter smelled enticing. I protested to Connor that I had to watch my figure. He leaned over and said with a grin, "Let me watch it for you." Right in front of theater goers, the teenage workers behind the concession stand, and the ticket taker, Connor kissed me. It went from a sweet tickle on the lips to thrusting his tongue deep inside my mouth. As the kiss grew more passionate, his hands roamed all over and Connor tore my clothing off, piece by piece, tossing them to the floor. People surrounded us in a circle and chanted, "More, more, more." Surreal and beyond weird, in normal circumstances I would have never allowed this to happen. In a blink, both of us were naked.

A large king-sized bed appeared and suddenly Connor and I were stretched out on it. The people kept chanting, louder and louder, until the sound echoed back from the ceiling. Money exchanged hands with bets placed on positions and other erotic things as they surrounded the bed. Our lovemaking morphed into the wild, rough stuff. I struggled and screamed at him to stop but couldn't as I found my hands handcuffed to the bedposts.

Connor paused and rose onto his knees and stared down at me. He grinned like the Cheshire cat, his flash of teeth suddenly insincere. I recoiled, as he stroked my cheek with a fingertip.

He said, "Cat, you're such a big tease. You know, you're not that great. So, why not take what you can get? Quit being such a prissy-faced twit and more like a tart, and let's get it on."

I began to believe this couldn't be Connor. "You're not the man I thought you to be."

His face melted and became Azazel's. "No, I'm not, but hey, who's perfect? Let a demon show you some real loving." He attacked.

I shrieked and fought. The people changed into demons and crowded closer, chanting, "More, more, more. . ."

I woke up with a start, my breath caught. I sat up, entangled in fur, drenched in sweat. My shaking eased as I realized I lay on a pillow. *Harry's bed*! *I'm in Harry's bed. Phew! A dream.*

Nothing more. And yet...uneasiness filled me.

Not thinking, I disentangled from the edge of one of the large furs Harry must have covered me with, slipped off the pillow, and climbed off the mattress. Big mistake. Being a bed fit for a god or giant, I fell. Scrambling, I grabbed the fur coverings which thankfully went all the way to the floor and slid the rest of the way down, though I still crash-landed. I managed to find the way to the kitchen. Harry sat at the table, sipping hot tea and talking with Lisa. The light floated in the air, keeping off anything made of ice.

"Lisa!" I called out, as I held onto the edge of the doorway. "We need to get going."

She floated down to me. "Is something wrong?"

"Yes, I had a nightmare, but that's not the problem. It's the feeling I got after I woke up. I really need to get to Connor and Larry. As fast as I can."

Harry put down his cup. "You'll need to dress warm. Those things you're wearing aren't made for warmth, nor decency, truth be told. I have some doll clothes that my little niece left here when she last visited."

"Doll's clothing?"

Harry stood. "Don't worry your pretty head about my niece missing any of those frippets for her doll. She won't miss any of it as she has more toys than she plays with."

He left the room, returning a minute later, clutching human-sized clothing made of fur in his hand. He handed them over, motioning for me to head back to the bedroom to strip and change. I tottered back to the bedroom, where I stripped off the filmy garments and slipped on a pair of pants and top made of soft, piebald fur. I toed my feet into the black furry boots, and then shrugged into a coat with a hood, the same color as the boots, but shaggy like a bear's winter coat. Black furry gloves completed the ensemble.

I stared at my reflection in the giant mirror that elongated from ceiling to the floor. *Oh, God, I'm an Eskimo version of a curvier Barbie.*

I trekked back to the kitchen where Harry and Lisa waited for me.

"How do I look?" I asked in a cheerful voice.

Harry answered, "Nice, very nice."

"They fit," I said, "which is all that should matter anyway."

I looked up at Lisa, who floated like balloon ten feet above me. "Ready to go?"

"Ready."

Harry handed me a doll size basket filled with what looked like pieces of bread and one large M&M type candy. He gave me a piece of paper that he'd drawn a map on. It pinpointed which areas of Niflheim to avoid, like the cave of the ice dragons. "The map should help you get to the border that divides this land and the next."

I said, "You're not showing us the way?"

He shook his head. "I would have taken you both, but my niece is visiting me in a couple of hours. Her mother—

my sister—will be with her, so I can't. But the map is very detailed and will steer you in the right direction."

Harry stood in the doorway. Illuminated by the living room light, he watched as we trudged away. I waved goodbye. Lisa bobbed ahead of me to guide the way and I followed her. According to the map, we had to keep south, and don't veer off, or we would never get out of this frozen world. I peeked back over my shoulder for the last time. Harry and his place had become a speck, blending in with the snow that had started to fall. As the snow transformed into a blizzard, I couldn't see anything, just unending, pristine white.

Lisa came back to slip over me, keeping me drier and warmer than the garments would have done alone. She also kept things lit five feet in front of me. Her light also melted any snowflakes making it easy for me to see. We didn't talk in this freezing world of silence. I began to think that Harry might be wrong and nothing besides him lived here. What self-respecting ice dragon or any other kind of creature would want to exist in this Antarctica of the Underworld?

Something howled several yards behind us. I stopped, causing Lisa to do so as well. "What's that?" I asked, crushing the map in my hands. My heart hammered against my ribs.

The sound came again, this time right behind us. I wheeled around and peered into the falling snow, and I couldn't even see evidence of my own footprints, let alone anything else. The thing howled again, right in front, and I turned.

I squinted but saw...nothing. If I asked Lisa to expand and brighten her light, it would melt the snow and make the source of my fear visible. I didn't ask. I didn't really want to see it. Okay, ice dragons didn't howl, did they? What other kinds of dangers did the map mention? I stared down at it, using Lisa's light to scan the parchment. I almost missed the word. *Fenrir.* I jerked my head up to gaze straight ahead. The thing howled for the fourth, fifth, and the sixth time. It sounded like it was in front, to the right, behind us, and then to the left of us. *Frak, is it circling Lisa and me?*

Fenrir, Fenrir. What in the world did Fenrir mean? I racked my brain, trying to remember why that word seemed so familiar. A...name! A dim spark in my memory, made me recall it being attached to a wolf, or something like that from...Norse mythology. I reflected over the Norse mythology I hadn't read since college. A he, or a she? What kind of wolf, or something with a wolf?

There had been a story about a wolf that suckled twins—no, that came from Roman mythology. I almost jumped out of my skin, when another howl rented the air. Then it came to me, who or what Fenrir was. One of three children of Loki and the giantess, Angrboda, prophesied to be the cause of the end of the world, or Ragnarok, as the Norse called it. Supposedly, it would break free of the chain the gods bound it with on the day of Ragnarok.

The vortex. Of course. Hell is taking over my world. Armageddon. Ragnarok. Both end of the world scenarios pretty much the same, no matter what spin on myth or legend.

Something snarled, much closer. Breaking free of my thoughts, I stared straight into a pair of large, red eyes. The biggest damn wolf I ever saw stood outside Lisa's protective light. It loomed as big as an elephant, from its nose to the tip of its tail. Soon as the falling snowflakes touched its fur, they liquified with a spit and hiss. Drool dripped from the beast's open jaws, full of large, sharp-edged fangs. The drool smoked and sizzled when it hit the snowy ground.

Note to self: do not to let mutt-face lick my face.

Alarmed, Lisa said, "The drool is poisonous acid, so stay within my light. Hold your breath as much as you can, for if you breathe in the odor, you'll die that way, too."

"Don't worry, I'll stay within your light." *Nothing would drag me outside to meet Fido.*

Damn, and here I thought Connor was big for a wolf, but compared to Fenrir he was a Chihuahua to a Shetland pony. Fenrir stalked us with a lowered head and stiff movements. It growled, halted, and grew quiet, then it thrust its snout as close to Lisa's light as it dared. Its eyes gleamed.

"Come out and play," said the wolf with a raspy chuckle. "Let's play 'fetch'. You throw yourself at me and I'll catch you, eating you in the bargain."

Canis lupus could talk, and in English, too!

I crossed my arms. "Right, dog breath. I'm just itching to play your version of Red Rover. Go find a tree to mark, or whatever a wolf likes to do."

Fenrir sat down, tucking the tip of its tail over its paws. "I can wait you out. I'll keep following you. Sooner or later, you'll screw up. And when you do—it'll be din-din time."

It chuckled, a real downright dirty-down-to-your-socks kind.

Chills raced down my spine.

Lisa and I started moving again. The wolf rose off its haunches and trailed us. It had to know about Ragnarok. After all, Fenrir was no longer chained to a rock, and that meant only one terrible thing.

"Hey, Fenrir, if you've gotten loose, then it must mean it's Ragnarok or Armageddon, right? You got a score to settle with Odin and the others. Truth?"

The wolf padded alongside us. It seemed to have no problem sloshing through the accumulated snow on the ground.

"You got it in a nutshell, takeout. Between me, Hell, and some other baddies, there won't be much for any god to worry about, not even the one you believe in. Now fast food, don't you think it'd go easier for you if you got away from that goody-two-shoes of a light and crawl into my mouth? Better me eating you than some demon having you, or becoming zombie bait."

"I'll take my chances and not play Red Riding Hood to your Big Bad Wolf."

Fenrir guffawed. "I heard that story. What big teeth you got, Grandma. The better to eat you with!" It laughed harder, as if it understood the sick joke.

"Go fetch a stick or something. Go find a Frost giant to play with."

I tramped faster and Lisa increased her speed to keep up.

With no effort at all, the wolf stayed right beside us. "If you think I'm terrible wait till you meet the Frost giants, Bubba and DeeDee. They're quite a couple. They think that any mortal fool who crosses their lands is food for their pot. And then there are the ice dragons, Mogal, Jantum, and Jerry. Three dinosaur sized lizards with freezing cold breaths you don't want to meet. If you got to be eaten, I'm the better choice."

"That's supposed to make me feel better? I'm supposed to give it all up and crawl down your throat? Go away."

Lisa and I kept plowing through the snow. Fenrir still stalked us, remaining silent. I hoped we hadn't gotten off track and prayed that soon we would reach the borders of Niflheim and escape. Maybe Fenrir would follow, but from the map, it looked to be a warmer place on the other side, easier to escape Loki's monster child without the complications of snow and ice.

I gripped the map, tearing a tiny hole in it. With Fenrir loose, and that version of the end of the world proven true, I wondered about the other myths connected to the end of the world. Which of those would I face? Mulling over unbelievable things made me think about Connor and Larry. Connor's face appeared in my mind's eye. Among everything that happened since the vortex sucked me up, getting to know him had to be one of the good things. Okay, so he grew hairy at the full moon. Nobody's perfect all the time. As for Larry, it had to be hard going against your own kind, but he did because of his inner goodness.

Determination to get away from all this and find Connor, and Larry too, kept me going. No way would I let the end of the world get me down, not without a good fight anyway. Although what I could do, remained to be seen.

Wait a moment. Fenrir.

I stopped and stared at the wolf pacing back and forth. Could I trick a monster? "Fenrir, you weren't always here? Right?"

The wolf stopped moving and narrowed its eyes. "No, I'd been chained for a thousand years to some stupid rock, in some cave on the other side of Niflheim."

"How did you get away?"

Fenrir sat down and laughed. "If you think that I'm going to let you find a way to chain me up again, you're mistaken. This monster is free and is planning to stay that way."

"Are you worried a tiny morsel like me can chain up something like you? It couldn't hurt to tell me. I mean, I'm not some Norse hero, or a god."

The wolf cocked its head to one side. "Mmm...I guess the walking TV dinner might be right. Some demon lord who called himself Azazel set me free. The demon promised that if I helped him bring forth Ragnarok—though he called it Armageddon—he would serve Odin to me on a silver platter." Fenrir paused and turned to stare off into the distance.

I looked in the same direction, trying to see what he saw. But the snow-filled air made it difficult to see anything. "What are you looking at?"

The wolf swung his gaze at me and for a few seconds, didn't say a word. Then Fenrir drew as close as it dared to Lisa's light. "We have company."

"Company?" I repeated, peering through the falling snow again, but all I saw were big, fat flakes. "Lisa, can you see or feel anything?"

"Fenrir is right. Dark things are approaching."

"Dark? That doesn't sound like anything we want to meet," I said, my heart battering as if trying to escape my chest.

The ground shook as if something massive stomped upon it. Either that, or an 8.0 earthquake on the Richter scale. Neither prospect seemed endearing to me at that moment.

The snow stopped and the clouds in the sky drifted away. A full moon gave off an eerie, ice-blue glow in the velvet black. A few stars danced around it. I could have been back on Earth and not on barren ice in the Underworld. Through Lisa's glow, I watched as two gargantuan figures approached. Each time their feet touched the ground it shook. They stopped several feet away.

The ruff on the back of Fenrir's neck rose and the wolf bared his fangs in a parody of a grin. "Why, if it isn't the rednecks, Bubba and DeeDee."

Frost giants. Just what Lisa and I needed. More monsters.

One of the figures got down on its knees and laughed. "Well, howdy, if it ain't ol' Fenrir! How'd you git loose, youse ol' mangy cur?"

Fenrir walked toward it, stiff-legged and growling. "A demon from Hell let me loose to help bring on Ragnarok, you big, stupid popsicle."

The other giant spoke in a feminine voice. "Ah thought things were gittin' kinda peculiar around here." She pointed at me. "Who's the itty bitty inside that there glowin' light over yonder?"

"It's none of your business," I retorted, trying to muster bravado in my voice, though inside I quaked.

The giantess laughed. The sound caused an avalanche of snow to slide down a nearby mountain. "The itty bitty talks. Ah never ate a talkin' meal before."

"This itty bitty isn't going to be eaten, especially by something with a pea for a brain."

The male giant guffawed. "Hey, Dee, she says youse has a pea brain."

The other cuffed him across an ear. "Shut up! If ah'm a pea brain, youse is an ice doodle."

Bubba's face grew red, and he jumped up, his eyes sparking with anger. He threw himself at his twin and they fought. The ground shook, causing a few more avalanches. As they rolled all over the ground, they got Fenrir mixed up into the fight.

Lisa and I bolted.

I ran, as much as one could on the snow and ice without slipping. Lisa kept pace with me, keeping me warm as we headed south. If I remembered my map, the Frost giants lived closest to the border between Niflheim and the next land. I couldn't remember what kind of place it would be, but it had to be better than here. The potential to be eaten or killed, and even freezing to death, lingered like a specter over me.

Something howled in the distance behind Lisa and me. I glanced over my shoulder and saw Fenrir loping not too far behind us. The wolf would be upon us any second now. Looking straight ahead, I spotted the border. A large sign, ice sickles hanging down on one side, announced: 'You're now leaving Niflheim. Have a nice day.' *Nice day, my petunias.*

Lisa and I sped past the sign and ran full tilt into a land full of warmth and sunlight. Fenrir bounded across the border close behind us. I tripped and fell. Lisa floated off me.

I rolled over onto my back and found Fenrir standing over me, saliva dripping from its mouth. A few drops of that drool fell upon me and scalded any bare skin. Lucky for me, that wasn't much exposed due to the clothing I wore. I yipped, flipped over onto my hands and knees, and scrambled away. The wolf hunted me.

No next chapter to my life. I was about to become Purina Dog Chow for some oversized canine. I sweated in the fur coat, whether with fear or from the warmer climate, I couldn't tell.

"Hi, what's goin' on?"

A childish voice piped in, just as Fenrir lowered its opened jaws over my head. The monstrous wolf looked to the right of me, and it fell to the ground, and cowered like some fraidy-cat nerd about to be whipped by the schoolyard bully, terror in its eyes. I got to my feet and looked to see what terrible thing turned this monster of legend into a whining puppy.

What the—The most adorable bunny sat in front of us. Its fur shone white as if it had been bleached, with not one particle of dirt marring it. It had a fluffy cottontail and a twitching pink nose. The bunny's eyes were big and round, pink and full of innocence. Nothing terrifying at all.

Fenrir lay on its back, revealing belly and throat as if groveling to the alpha of its pack. I couldn't understand how something so cute and sweet could inspire the dread that the giant canine showed.

The bunny hopped over onto Fenrir's chest and wiggled its nose over the throat. It seemed like a tiny mote of white against the brown fur.

"Little bunny, don't go near that monstrosity," I cautioned. "It'll have you for dinner."

The bunny cast a glance back at me for a second before it returned its attention back to Fenrir. Whimpers slipped past the wolf's fangs, growing louder by the minute.

I said, "Why, you nothing but a big fake, a cowardly bully. And here I thought all this time you were some terrifying abomination and you're nothing but a—"

The bunny opened its mouth wide and with loud, gut-wrenching screeches, it leaped upon Fenrir and tore out the wolf's throat. Chunks of fur, flesh, and blood flew everywhere, and over the pristine white of the bunny's fur and face. I saw the hint of the pearly whites in the rabbit's mouth, which it used to tear and chew Fenrir's flesh. I shrieked and stumbled, tripping over something and slamming to the ground hard.

"Oh, God, oh God!" I cried out, as I scrambled to my feet and when I did, I saw what I'd tripped over. A skull on the dirt. A human skull. A skull covered with dried blood.

"Hell bunnies." The soft whisper curled into my ear.

Something warm touched me and I looked aside, afraid of what I would see. But I only saw Lisa.

"Remember, Cat, nothing down here is what it seems. Not even cute, little bunnies. You should have realized that by now. What is cute and adorable is really depraved and evil. This is the Underworld, where Hell, mythology, and Faerie reign supreme."

I stared at the sweet little bunny burying its face into Fenrir. It had killed the whopping big wolf and now gorged on its flesh.

"Oh, I can see that. Where fuzzy bunnies are *Monty Python* horrors."

"*Monty Python*?" Lisa sounded puzzled.

"Just remembering a movie." I started to tiptoe away and whispered. "Come on, Lisa, let's sneak past the mini exterminator."

The 'killer rabbit' stopped feasting on Fenrir and looked at Lisa and me.

It unnerved me, seeing those pink eyes wide-eyed with innocence in a once alabaster face covered in blood and gore. The bunny licked its lips, sending a small pink tongue to circle around to catch the dripping blood.

I cringed.

The bunny hopped forward. "My name is Cutie Pie. Can I eat you?" it asked in a sugary voice.

I reversed a couple of steps. "Wouldn't you like to be like other rabbits and exist on a vegetarian diet? Like carrots? They say red meat isn't good for you."

The bunny reared up and wiggled its nose. "Vegetarian? I like meat. Meat is good. Killing is good. Let me kill you. Pretty, pretty, please, with sugar on top?"

I bolted. I didn't check to see if Lisa stayed with me. Besides, the rabbit didn't eat light, only meat. Like me! Looking over my shoulder, I saw the fluffy Hell spawn in hot pursuit. With its hops eating up the distance between us, it wouldn't be long before I would look like Fenrir; my bones picked clean.

Lisa drew up beside me. I said, "Lisa, I never thought my death for me would be caused by an adorable rabbit."

"It won't be if you do as I say. Dart into those bushes over there and wait."

I noticed the bushes and thrashed through them, the branches slapping me. Crouching down and hiding, and slowing my jagged breathing down to a minimum, I still had to be nosy. I parted some leaves and peeked through a small hole in the bush.

Lisa hovered a couple of inches above the ground. The bunny hopped up to her. It rose on its haunches, sniffing the air. It would have looked adorable except for the gore. It looked more frightening than Fenrir ever did.

"Light?" said the bunny. "You smell bad, light. Bad, bad light."

Lisa drifted closer and the rabbit reeled back in alarm, hopping away. "Bunny, you're not nice or huggable," said Lisa with a gentle voice, "but pure evil." She overlaid the bunny. "I thank you for stopping Fenrir, and I'm sorry, but I can't let you kill and eat my friend, Cat. You must be punished."

The rabbit screamed, flaying within Lisa's light; Lisa had become a cage it couldn't escape from.

The bunny's fur began to smoke, catching fire. Rich, red flames enveloped it, consuming its life. When the fire died, nothing remained, not even a lone cinder. Lisa glided upwards.

"You can come out now, Cat. The bunny's gone."

I stepped out from behind the shrubbery. "Lisa, what did you do?"

"Nothing. I am good and the bunny is evil. Evil can't exist inside the light of goodness. It would either be changed to the side of good or burn away like a stick of dry wood."

"Why couldn't you have done that to Fenrir?"

"Because I'm as big as you are and Fenrir is much too big for me to contain."

"I'm sorry. At least you stopped the Easter Bunny's evil twin."

"I didn't stop it. Its own evilness stopped it." Lisa flickered.

"Come, we have many miles to travel. You need to find your friends and stop the apocalypse. And there are more of those bunnies here."

Since it felt warmer, I took off the coat and hung it on the bush. I wished I could find cooler clothing so I could take off the furry things I wore now, but there was nothing I could do. We continued along the path. Lisa bobbed, while I walked. On occasion, we did run into more of those charming, little bunnies and either ran away from them or Lisa enveloped the tiny fiends and they burned up. It seemed that this place had not only cute demon bunnies, but also other deadly creatures. You wanted to hug them, regardless of the risk of having your throat torn out. We encountered fluffy, hellacious kittens, monstrous canaries like insane versions of that little cartoon bird, and playful puppies that wanted to feed on me and gnaw on my bones like chew toys.

We finally reached the border and stepped over. Or should I say, we bolted over, being pursued by a horde of ravenous bunnies at the time. The little hellions screeched to a halt, blinking pink eyes. None wanted to follow us. I noticed the sign, lit up with bright, garish lights, and in big, bold letters:

WELCOME TO HELL,
WE'LL TAKE YOUR SOUL,
NEW OR USED.

CHAPTER 8

I didn't see Connor or Larry anywhere. No one else either. Not a demon or spirit in sight. Desolate and humid, the place had no color, just washed-out drab everywhere. If a soul had to be sent somewhere to be miserable for eternity, this would be it.

"Lisa, how do we go about searching for Connor and Larry?

Help me out. I'm kind of lost in the directions department here."

"I won't be going with you, Cat."

I turned. She hovered close to the border. "What do you mean? Of course, you're going with me. How else would I survive this place without you?"

"If I go with you, it will cause a catalytic reaction. In your world, goodness can coexist with evil. Down here in Hell, only evil can exist. Goodness belongs in Heaven only.

"But that's good. We can nip this end of the world business in the bud then."

"Yes, but that means the end of you, Connor, and Larry too. Besides the fact, it would be against laws of the balance of good and evil, for me to destroy Hell. This place is needed and always will be needed for evil to be contained. With no balance, it would affect your world."

Yeah, I guess I can see why she couldn't go. I didn't like having the cards stacked against me in getting Connor and Larry out of Hell.

Lisa floated back over the border. "Goodbye. I'm heading back to visit Harry. He said I could when I mentioned to him that I couldn't enter Hell with you.

We'll meet again. Good luck...luck...luck..." Lisa grew smaller and smaller, until she faded from my sight.

Uncertain what to do next, I leaned against a rock and thought things out. Without Lisa as my guide and companion and without any resources to keep me safe, I stood in the last place a mortal shouldn't be. The last land had cutesy killers that reigned supreme. Hell, no doubt made that place look like a Sunday Mass in church. I'd rather face a dozen killer bunnies then Azazel or any of the other nasty demons that occupied this place. Killer bunnies are nothing more than warm fuzzies. Okay, fuzzies with sharp teeth, but still better than what waited for me in Hell. Stab the fuzzy in its heart or cut off its head and it died. Demons could only be exorcised, and I didn't carry a priest or a psychic in my pocket.

Connor and Larry were my reason for being here in the first place. Either would help save me if I needed it. I had to do the same for them. Taking a deep breath, I left the rock and stepped onto a path that led deeper into Hell. *Okay, so far so good.* I hadn't run into any nasty being nor had anything jump out at me from behind rocks or any spot on either side of the path. *You've only gotten maybe ten feet from the border. Give it time, you'll run into one of those fiends sooner or later.*

The atmosphere hung heavy and oppressive. Soon I dragged my feet, wondering why I even wanted to make any attempt to save the world. What did it matter anyway? Who cared? Look at all the wars we keep having back home. Besides that, what about the kids selling drugs, stealing, fornication, murder, and other equally nasty stuff. Earth already had set its heading to Hell. Armageddon just made it a real fact.

Feeling dejected, I thought, *I'm right. Why go on? I'll just take a seat on that rock over there—*

Cat, you can make a difference. You've gotten this far. Besides, think of Connor and Larry. You can do it. Repeat over and over: 'Hell no. I will go. Fight the good fight and mo.'

No, I'm not...hey, where'd that voice come from? I swept my gaze around the area.

Me.

The voice sounded too cheerful for my depressed state. Although, I doubted a demonic spirit would be playing with me by encouraging me.

I crossed my arms, as I played along and thought, *Me, as in whom?*

You, yourself. Your conscious.

I'm arguing with myself? Now, I knew I had to be losing it. My adventure in the Underworld must be getting to me.

"Excuse me, but why would I listen to some voice that claims to be my conscience? You might be the voice of some nasty entity who crawled inside my head and is trying to trick me. I bet they can do telepathy, or something like that. This is Hell, for goodness' sake. Now, get out of my head!"

The voice no longer talked to me inside my head, but spoke out loud as if whoever it was, stood in front of me. "Look, if I'm a demon, I sure wouldn't be giving you a pep talk and a cheerleading song to sing. Think about this. I would convince you that life isn't worth a damn and slip a pistol into your hand to shoot yourself with. Now, am I right or not?"

It couldn't be me, not outside of my head. I jumped to my feet, looking around. "I guess, maybe." Excuse me, but had I just agreed with the voice? "I'm short of a few marbles," I said.

"You're not going insane. I'm your conscience. The laws of physics down here enable me to kinda become real. Now, go find Connor and Larry, and save the world."

"But—"

"Now!"

"All right, all right. Boy, you're a bossy conscience. Where were you when I was about to marry Jeff?"

"Look, you never listened to me before when I was just your woman's intuition. I tried to warn you, but lust and blind love put rose-colored glasses over your eyes and shoved ear plugs in your ears so I gave up. Figured you had to learn some lessons. Besides, this isn't about 'do I marry that dirtbag or not,' but concerns the entire Earth. It affects your life and soul much more than a lousy marriage."

"On blind faith, I'm supposed to believe that you're really my conscience and do as you say? That you're not some denizen of Hell out to get me? Ouch!" I grabbed my head with a hand. "Hey, that hurt my head."

"Get moving, Viggolone, or I swear I'll give you something worse than a headache."

I headed down the path. My conscience didn't bother me again. Or whatever the hell it really was. I took a left onto another path and continued, only deviating when I ran into a flare-up of lava fire and the occasional, bothersome imp, much easier to handle than demons. My spirits rose as I remembered handling worse. Black Friday sales, my ex-mother-in-law, and PMS. What was Hell, after all, but another bothersome salesman calling just as I was about to sit down to dinner. Hell spawn proved to be a lot easier to fight off than a pushy salesman. Azazel was prettier than my ex-mother-in-law, too.

An hour later, I heard running footsteps behind me.

Phew. What in the world is that smell? An unpleasant odor permeated the air. Not sulfur, but...some cheap men's cologne?

I tensed and looped around to see what I had to fight or run from.

Shocked, I saw my divorce lawyer, Mr. Timmons, as he huffed and puffed toward me like the pudgy penguin he resembled. The jerk had screwed me over my divorce, siding with my ex. After the divorce was finalized, he bedded one of his other clients. He never got to enjoy her, because he choked to death on a chicken leg he had been eating. It seemed he had ended up in Hell.

"Hey, Mrs. Viggolone," he blurted out. "Need a lawyer? Hell is hell for women down here."

"No," I answered, sprinting away. "Just keep away from me."

I ran, outstripping him. Down here, and with his spirit still as overweight and soft as he had been in life, he couldn't catch me.

He yelled. Skidding to a halt, I whipped around and saw a big demon popped out of thin air. It snatched him and slung Timmons over its shoulder. The lawyer didn't look happy.

"Come on, Mr. Timmons, time for another court trial," said the fiend.

"But I never win, and damn it, I never get paid either," said Timmons with a drawn-out whine. "What kind of lawyer takes charity cases anyway?" Resignation on his face, he sagged over the creature's shoulder and let it carry him away. With a resounding pop, both vanished.

There is justice in the afterlife.

No reason to remain, so I moved on. I never saw so much bleak, endless landscape, empty and gray. Except for Timmons and the malignant spirit that took him, I hadn't run into anything else, but I decided to flop down on a nearby, big rock to take a breather and take stock of what to do next. That's when I saw a large, windowless building made of black, smooth stone a short distance away.

Deciding I should check it out, I got up. As I drew nearer, I heard voices from within. Among these voices, I heard the caw of a crow that grew louder until it became a shrill scream. Against my better judgment, I fingered along the stone until I discovered an almost undetectable door. With a click, it swung open, and I slipped through the doorway. It appeared no one worried about locking the place up.

Inside, shadows flared up and shrunk on the gray walls, contorting like some nightmarish, black kaleidoscopic, thanks to a sickly yellow light that didn't appear to shine from any discernible location. My hand pressed against one of these walls, I saw what made the shadows. Demons of all sizes and shapes surrounded something smaller, dancing and shaking, laughing and screeching. I swam through the sea of bodies and managed to get to the center. Thank goodness, they were too involved to notice the idiot human among them. I held my breath and peered between two noxious smelling bodies.

Larry!

The poor eyeball wore a metal collar fettered to a large, heavy chain hammered into the floor. He wept, tears splashing down to the floor. The other beings laughed and poked at him, using sharp sticks, knives, rocks, or their claws or tentacles.

I grew angry and stepped in front of Larry, clenching my hands into fists. "Stop it. Leave Larry alone."

They stopped it all right. Eyes tightened, eye stalks jiggled, and other unmentionable things swung at the interloper, the fool with the big mouth. I'd become the mouse who had blundered into a room full of hungry felines. I gulped, fear tightening my nerves. Suddenly, they stopped all their noise, and the silence grew deafening. The crowd pressed inward.

"Bet you're all wondering why I told you to stop harassing this helpless little guy? Well, I'm wondering too. Guess I know how to stick my big foot in my stupid mouth and shove deep."

The horde sounded off. Some snarled, others growled or twittered, while others made sounds I couldn't even begin to describe. They drew closer. I eased away until my back pressed against a wall. Larry had grown silent and hovered off the ground, his chain not letting him go higher than three feet. He yanked on it. The part of the chain connected to the stone floor began to crumble loose, bit by bit. *Is Larry that strong*? I just needed to keep the others from leaping on me and tearing me apart, and give him enough time to free himself. I prayed that it wouldn't take too long.

"Guys and girls," I said. "And those of asexual persuasion, let's talk this out."

A few snickered. One got close enough to flick out a long tongue, slurping it sloppily up my right arm. Yuck! I shook off the dripping drool, marking the wall with it.

"You don't want me or the eye. I'm too fat, and I'm sure he's really not all that tasty, either."

One small imp darted up to me and poked me in my side.

I squealed, "Hey, cut that out! That hurts!"

I swung at it, but it dodged. It grinned as it looked back at the others. "The mortal's plump enough. I get one of the legs."

Another creature, big and fat, knocked the little one aside, sending it crashing into the wall. "Go to Hell, one leg is one too many for you, imp."

The imp scrabbled to its hoary feet and giggled. "Can't go to Hell, I'm already here. Hey, fatty, you don't need any part of her. You gotta enough fat in you to last for all eternity." It cackled and skipped out of the bigger one's way as it lunged.

"Great," I muttered. "I'm the turkey they're fighting over.

Next, it'll be who gets the wishbone."

Suddenly, and without warning, a long metal chain swung and smacked into the demons, sending some flying and knocking others to the floor. Larry had gotten free, but he still wore the collar attached to the chain he used as a weapon. Sharply trumpeting, he swerved the chain left to right, then from right to left.

"Come on, Larry, let's go." I called out.

I hightailed out of the building, Larry right on my heels. The end of his chain almost didn't make it out before the door slammed shut. Looking around, I found a big boulder, and huffing and puffing, my muscles straining, and with Larry's help, we rolled it against the door. Lodged tight, it kept the obscenity yelling residents of Hell inside. I hoped it would be quite a while before they could break out.

Since it might be in both our interests to free Larry of the chain, I spied a small, sharp rock and plucked it off the ground. I pounded at the last link connected to the collar until it busted. Knowing I didn't have enough time to try and get the collar off, I ran over to check to make sure the door was still barred.

I came back to Larry. "Larry, where's Connor?"

He whirred, quit, and began to shake in a very odd manner. It took me a few seconds to figure out that meant. He had shrugged.

"You don't know where he is, do you?"

I saw the rock had moved a couple of inches. That meant that the things inside might soon free themselves. How much time did we have before they got out? I didn't plan to stay around to find out. "Larry, we need to leave."

We jogged. Well, I did, Larry floated beside me. After a while, we slowed down when we realized nothing pursued us. Now able to take a breather or two, we stopped. My lungs burned and my side ached. I settled on a convenient rock. Larry hovered at eye level with me. "Larry, tell me the last time you saw Connor?"

Larry chortled what seemed like a series of bird calls of every kind. He hovered up and down like a mad, out of control helicopter. I reached out and grabbed hold of him.

"Whoa there. Slow down. It's hard for me to make sense of your language. I took Spanish 101 back in college, not Eyeball from Hell."

He continued to jabber. It was all meaningless jumbles at first. Slowly, I began to understand some of the gobbledygook he spouted and that shook me. As I understood, he and Connor had been separated and taken to different spots of Hell. He never saw which way Connor had been taken, but he swore that after he'd been chained up, one of his jailors snickered that maybe the werewolf had been sent to the deepest pit of Hell.

I stood. "The deepest pit of Hell? Do you have any knowledge of where this place might be?"

Suddenly, Larry possessed my body. He made me sketch something in the dirt with my fingers. Three minutes later, he popped out of my body. "Never do that again, hear me?" I said. "I know you wanted to make the map, but never, ever, possessed me again. Are we crystal clear?"

Larry whined and lowered himself to the ground beside the map. I squatted, but not near Larry, and peered at a stick figure and a circle that had to be us standing at one end. At the opposite end, I saw a child's depiction of what could be a pit. Larry twittered, and somehow, I understood he meant that it wasn't far away from where we were. I got to my feet and erased the picture using the toe of my shoe.

Larry drifted ahead of me and I followed. Everything seemed quiet, like we walked in a park on a Sunday afternoon. This being Hell, I doubted we would see a great view along the way or hear songbirds.

The temperature had been hot and humid earlier, but it'd been dropping for a while now. It felt good after the heat, but it kept dropping until it reached winter conditions. I shivered as the cold penetrated me, and I wrapped my arms around myself to keep warm. I wished I still had the coat Harry had given me. Ice crusted over everything, and my breath frosted the air. I turned and saw Larry shaking, an icicle dangling off him.

Goosebumps? Did I see goosebumps popping out all over him? I looked down at my arms. Tiny bumps prickled along the skin there.

It grew darker. *Great. Freezing cold, now darkness. What next?*

Something roared. I paused, and with my heartbeats growing rapid, I peered back over my shoulder. In the fading light, I saw the terrible thing that pursued us. "Larry...RUN!"

We skedaddled out of there. Immense, it carried a large club and swung it over its head as it lumbered after us. I didn't have much time to really get a good look at it, but it had an ugly mug with one big, red eye stuck in the middle of its face, above a bulbous nose. Like a cyclops. At that point, it had grown too dark to see much else. The same darkness made it also increasingly difficult for me to see where I headed. Larry trumpeted and bumped against me hard, shoving me off the path. I almost fell.

"What the—?" I looked at where he bumped me toward and managed to spy the darkened mouth of a cave. "I see it, Larry."

Another loud roar sounded close behind us. Larry flew into the cave. I didn't care what waited for us, but I took Larry's cue and ducked inside. I pressed my back against the rock wall of the cave and slid down to the ground. Larry thumped down beside me. Thankfully, the opening proved to be large enough for both of us to squeeze through, but not the big ugly. It hit the cave entrance, but it couldn't get in. It roared and kept battering itself and its club against the rock overhang. Rocks and dirt loosened and clattered down to the cave floor, raining on us. I coughed as grit went up into my nose and into my mouth. Making myself as small as possible, I curled into a ball against the wall of the cave. Larry whimpered and lay against my side. The Cyclops used both of its hands and grabbed at the edges of the cave's mouth. Sounds like the cracking of thunder filled the air as the rock walls began to crumble. Dust rose in choking amounts. I huddled there, cold and frightened. A squealing Larry crawled into my arms. I closed my eyes and waited for the inevitable.

The Cyclops screamed, a high-pitched and unnatural sound that echoed in the darkness. It stopped trying to wrench apart the opening. Instead, other noises drifted into the cave from outside, horrible, chilling.

I opened my eyes. I scooted inch by inch on my hands and knees to the cave's entrance. I knew it was stupid, but I had to see what it was that could take on a cyclops. I peeked out.

A green light lit up the Cyclops as it hunched over, its head bowed down. A female Cyclops towered over it, wearing an apron and carrying a rolling pin in one hand and a lantern.in the other. The green light came from that lantern. She wore pink curlers rolled up in her hair and stomped her feet encased in pink bunny bedroom slippers. Her voice boomed. More debris clattered down. I ducked back inside. When it stopped, I stuck my head out again.

The female said, "Get on home. I only asked you to go find me some milk. But no, you had to get all big and bad and try to beat up some little people. Well, I got news for you. You're giving up eating little people like you promised. We're vegetarians now. Get your butt home."

The Cyclops mumbled something unintelligent and shuffled off, dragging his club through the dirt behind him. Mrs. Cyclops strutted after him, her big behind swinging back and forth like a giant-sized watermelon.

Everything cleared, I crawled out of the cave and rose. I chuckled. "That monster has his own monster—his wife." I looked back at the opening and saw Larry hovering in the opening. "Larry, it's okay to come out. They're gone. We better get going."

"Now, why did you really think it's okay?"

Startled, I saw Azazel, his shoulder propped against the rock and with a big smirk plastered on his face. Behind him stood a couple of demonic henchmen, hideous and menacing, and both wearing fedoras and trench coats.

I demanded, "Where's Connor?"

His mocking smile grew wider. "Now, that's no way to talk to your potential lover boy."

"You're not a potential anything to me."

Larry floated out of the cave and got between us, glaring and growling at him.

Azazel's eyes became narrow slits. "Call off the mutt, or I'll let my guys work him over."

"Back off, Larry. You don't want the idiot boys to touch you. They don't appear all that clean to me."

Larry didn't obey but kept blocking Azazel from me while staring down the demon lord. Azazel began to look bored.

"This is getting monotonous. Time for us to go."

He snapped his fingers and we all blinked out.

***

Larry and I materialized in some room. It smelled rancid like a restroom in some seedy gas station. Filth covered everything. My skin itched, an allergic reaction to maybe what disgusting things might be in here with Larry and me. That's when I spied something huddling in the corner, snarling. I froze.

Azazel had put us in a room with some new terror. It rose and howled, then rushed us. But just as its jaws snapped at us it was jerked back by the chain bolted to the wall behind it. A metal collar surrounded its neck, and it choked itself as it went for us again. But the chain held true. Big and furry, snarling, flecks of saliva around its snout. I examined its wild eyes and realized something familiar about them. *No.*

"Larry, we found Connor."

CHAPTER 9

The werewolf's jaws snapped as it struggled to get at Larry and me, until either he'd grown tired or given up. His chain pulled taut, he didn't make any more sudden movements or sounds but lay down. Cautious, I took a step. Connor still didn't move a muscle, staring at me. Encouraged by that, I took a couple more steps, holding out a hand and wondered if he would snap at it. I edged closer and closer until my fingertips wiggled just within a hairbreadth of Connor's well-defined, sharp fangs. He opened his jaws a few inches. His hot breath fanned my face.

"Connor." *Good, Cat, make it easy for the werewolf to eat your face.*

I ignored the insidious thought. I tensed when he sniffed at my fingertips and widened his jaws, flashing more length of his incisors gleaming with drool. I sweated. *Yeah, right, get close to the werewolf. This must be the dumbest idea ever.*

Instead, he rolled out his tongue and licked my fingers, wagging his tail. I sagged in relief and threw my arms around Connor. He woofed in my ear. I pulled back and recognized the man I knew in them. The psychotic werewolf had departed. I laughed as I hugged him. "Welcome back, Connor."

He snuffled against my face. I withdrew and got to my feet. I kept one hand in his fur, stroking him.

"We need to get you free of this chain."

I frowned, musing over how to do that. Larry's chain had been weak, making it easy for him to break free. This one had been securely attached to the wall and wouldn't be as simple to destroy. Whoever chained Connor used something strong enough to hold a werewolf. I peered closer at the collar around his neck and noticed a bloody sore festering where the collar around his neck had worn away fur and skin. No wonder he had been so nasty earlier.

"Larry, I'm sure this collar is made of silver and it's burning away the fur beneath it and eating into Connor's skin."

Larry glided closer, peering with his big eye. He chirped, then whirred. Next, he burst out with a series of odd sounds, each one different. I figured he had to be telling me an idea of how to free Connor, I couldn't make head or tails of it. Frustrated, he zipped off and left me and Connor alone.

I called after him. "Hey, Larry, come back. Where are you going?"

He'd abandoned us.

Upset, I slid down to the ground next to Connor. He lay on his side, with his head in my lap and his weight leaning against me as he whined under his breath. Suddenly, Larry was back. He had returned with a strange-looking creature, thin as a rail and with pallid skin. It had a pig's head with thick, voluminous lips at the end of the snout. It chewed gum and blew bubbles that popped before they got immense. Connor rose to his feet and growled.

I leaped up. "Larry, we didn't want the demons to know we're trying to free Connor and escape. Now they'll know."

"Nope, missy." The demon spat his gum out into a corner. "I can free the furball here."

"And why would you do that?"

"The name's Abraxas. Larry helped me, by saving me. I mean, I know we of Hell are basically spirit and can't die and all. But the big boss had gotten mad at me and magicked me away to this part of Hell where they chained me for a thousand years and this big buzzard would fly down and tear my heart out of my chest. Over and over, for centuries. At least, it felt that long to me. Anyway, I thought I would go mad from the unending torture, when Larry and this big furball came from out of nowhere. He told the wolf to catch and eat the bird, which it did. Afterwards, they set me free. I told Larry anytime he needed a favor, I would do it if I could. Lucky for furball here, after they saved me, I learned some tricks to save my ass if I ever got myself chained up again. I can summon up a tool or two I can use to free him."

He uttered a few words in a mysterious language I never heard before and a pair of big pliers appeared in his hands. He positioned them at the part of the chain bonded to the collar. Connor whined and whimpered. It took a few minutes, but with a snap, the silver collar and the links dropped to the terrain. Connor staggered to his feet but collapsed on his haunches. I knelt beside him and pulled him to me, being careful of the sores ringing his neck. I watched as Abraxas did the same thing for Larry and freed him of his metal collar. With tears in my eyes, I thanked him.

Abraxas blushed. "Aw, it's nothin'. Besides now that my favor with Larry has been done, I suggest you all get outta here. Because now I can either try to stop you from escaping or sound the alarm. I'll give you a five-minute running start, but nothin' more." An awful grin flittered across Abraxas's lips.

I knew that he'd been more generous than his kind would be. The three of us scrammed. Easy for Larry and me, not so easy for Connor. The poison from the silver had gotten into his bloodstream, and he couldn't lope as fast as he normally could. He whined and stumbled. The venomous, malodorous wounds on his neck were bleeding, sapping away his energy. Connor staggered and tumbled to the ground. He tried to rise using his forelegs, but instead he crashed back down in a jumble of limbs. I dropped to my knees beside him.

I curled my hands underneath him and tried to help him up. *Damn, but he's heavy.* I tried again, but I couldn't lift him. It sucked being a mere human during times like this.

Larry drifted down until he rested over Connor. He chirped a few times, and I realized what he must be saying.

"You want me to try and help him up, maybe even get Connor to make another attempt at rising, and you'll get under him and lift him up? Am I, right?"

Larry whooped.

I whispered into Connor's ear. "Come on, Conner, try and get up again. I'll help, but we need to get you up on your feet long enough for Larry to slip underneath you. Can you do that?" He turned his wolfish face to me and whined. I hoped that meant a yes. It better be a yes.

Gritting my teeth, I slipped my hands under him and encouraged him as he struggled to rise, fighting to remain upright, allowing Larry to dart beneath his belly. Connor's legs buckled, but the feisty little eyeball hoisted all his weight and levitated, although unstable at first. I saw that Connor was out cold. When Larry grew steadier, he elevated to my eye level and chirped again. It took me a couple of seconds, but it hit me what he tried to imply.

"Okay, okay, Larry. We need to leave this place and find someone to help Connor, either in Hell, or back on Earth."

I grabbed a handful of Connor's fur and trotted alongside Larry and his burden. My pace picked up as Larry sped up. Legs hurting and struggling to breathe, I cursed myself for not running more often. Earsplitting shrieks erupted behind us. I looked over my shoulder and saw a devilish horde hot on our trail.

I yelled, "Larry, demons!"

He picked up speed. I hotfooted, but he had the advantage of flying. I let go of Connor's fur and just worried about keeping up. My lungs screamed in agony as I sucked in fetid air. A cramp in one of my legs made me want to cry. Thoughts of what unmentionable things the fiends chasing us could do—would do—if they captured us, kept me focused. I longed for home. Had Earth been taken over by Hell or just Richmond? I thought of my friends, my co-workers at the DMV, and yes, even the jerk ex-husband. Tears blinded me. Connor had wanted to save the world and look what happened to him. I wiped the tears away. *I want to go home. I wish there was a way to make this all go away. Make it a dream.*

A soft, feminine voice spoke in my head. *You can, Cat. Oh, it won't make the apocalypse go away, you can't do that. You'll not wake up tomorrow morning and find it had only been a nightmare. But you are close enough to a portal that your friends and you can use to find your way home.*

"Lisa?" I said out loud.

Yes, it's me.

I looked around but didn't see her. "I don't see you anywhere. Where are you?"

I am not with you, Cat, but I can see all that is happening to you. Look to your right.

Something swirled in different shades of gray several feet to my right. A vortex! Tinier than the one that made its appearance in Richmond, but it would do in a pinch. I never thought I would feel so happy to see one of those things again. "Larry, there's a vortex on the right. It'll take us back to Earth."

He stopped and whipped around. For the first time since I met him, the eyeball blinked! Twice. I didn't know how he did that as he didn't have an eyelid. *Hell magic?* Then he giggled and raced for the vortex.

The horde behind us roared with thunderous rage. I took a quick glance back and saw they'd gotten closer, their claws, tentacles, and unidentifiable appendages reaching for me. I sprinted after Larry, huffing and puffing. Connor still lay unconscious on top of him, Larry zipped through the whirling mass. But, just as I put my right hand through it, something clutched me from behind. I whipped around and kicked out, sending my foot into the soft belly of some gelatinous thing. It felt nasty and the creature made an obscene sound. But my kick proved enough to send it reeling back into another demon, one that looked suspiciously like the one that had helped us free Connor earlier. Both tumbled to the ground, bringing a few others down with them in a domino effect. The multitude of others behind them surged over them, eager to get at me. Not even thinking about it, I dived into the mouth of the vortex. All sounds muffled, iridescent lights flashed all around me. Dizzy, I stared down at my hands and saw that they left blurred trails of motion. Everything became too much for me, as a migraine headache exploded behind my eyes. Praying that I would make it home, I blacked out.

***

I regained consciousness and realized I lay on a kind of surface, but I didn't get up. Not yet. I closed my eyes as waves of dizziness shimmered through me. When it all stopped spinning, I opened my eyes, sat up, and saw the house. I had made it home.

Had everything been nothing more than a dream? Maybe, I had tripped and hit my head since a headache was piercing my brain. Something chirped above me. I looked up and saw Larry hovering over me, minus Connor. He descended until he hung eye level with me. I still wore the doll's clothes Harry had given me, the fur filthy and plastered to my skin.

I winced. "No, not a nightmare."

Larry looked confused.

I stood and brushed off any dirt. "Ignore the crazy person, Larry."

The pressure deepened in my noggin with every word I spoke. I assumed it to be the result of traveling by this particular vortex.

"Remind me next time to travel another way from Hell to Earth." I rubbed my temples. "Since we're home again, let's get inside. Everything seems fine here, for the moment anyway. I hope I still have aspirin or other medication in my medicine cabinet because the pounding in my head is a killer."

I approached my front door, Larry beside me. It stood ajar. I balked, and I jerked around to look at Larry. The pain jabbed at my head and colorful spots danced before my eyesight. I waited for the wooziness to dissipate before I said anything to him.

"You opened my door? You took Connor into my house?"

He chirped. That better be a yes. Bone tired, and the headache not helping matters, I didn't care if the planet blew up right then and there. I wanted relief from the throbbing and to be able to get off my feet, but Connor needed medical attention first. I stomped up the front steps and through the doorway. Larry followed, and the door closed behind him with a click. *That's creepy. How did he do that?* Although he is a demon. *Duh*! Either he can do magic or has psychic powers.

I didn't see Connor anywhere, either in wolf or human form.

"Larry, where did you put Connor? I need to check his neck."

Larry flew from the living room, down the hallway and into my bedroom. I traipsed after him. The old lady we had left locked in the bedroom before driving to the police station was nowhere in sight. Maybe she'd freed herself and escaped. I hoped nothing bad happened to her. Naked and pale, Connor sprawled across my bed. He peeled his eyelids a crack. I could see his agony; his tanned skin looked pasty. His beard fuzzed his cheeks, chin, and upper lip. Dirt crusted all over his body. I worried about infection from the still bleeding sores around his neck. I'd assumed from all the films and books that werewolves could heal quick. Maybe being in Hell had changed that, or maybe the folklore was nothing more than hogwash.

"I tried to show you a good time, Cat," whispered Connor with a smirk. He coughed a couple of times. "You think being a werewolf I would have healed by now.

I examined the damage from the sores surrounding his neck. "I'm sure Hell has a whole new set of rules on how quick even a werewolf can heal from wounds. I really think we need to get a doctor to look at you, Connor. This doesn't look too good, and all I have in my medicine cabinet is salve, cheap plastic bandages, things like that. Nothing that might actually help."

Connor struggled into a sitting position. He swung his legs over the edge of the mattress and tried to stand, dragging the blanket off the bed and wrapping it around his lower half as he did, hiding his nether regions. I raised my eyes to the ceiling and muttered under my breath about him worrying about his nakedness at a time like this after I've already seen it all.

"What?" He asked.

My gaze met his. "Nothing. We need to get you to a doctor."

"I'm healing. It just took a little longer than usual."

"What?"

"Look, I'm healing. Check my neck now."

Shocked, I saw that his wounds no longer bled. They had scabbed over, but the scabs had dropped off to reveal pink skin. Connor hobbled to the bathroom, trailing some of the blanket that stayed firmly in place around himself.

He paused at the doorway. "I need a shower, Cat. Besides, getting to a doctor might not be the smart thing to do right now. And I'm not saying because I'm a shapeshifter. Your neighborhood is quiet as a tomb. Something's not right."

He dropped the blanket and entered the bathroom, shutting the door behind him. I had to agree with him about the neighborhood. Leaving Larry alone in the bedroom, I wandered through my house and went outside. No noise or movement of any kind in my neighborhood, not even birds chirping. I ran next door to my neighbors, Jim and Patsy Lemming, and pounded on their door. No one answered, and I didn't dare snoop in their windows. I ran back home. The stillness coupled with Richmond humidity made it feel like a vast sauna. Connor was right. I didn't see any of the grayness, zombies, or monsters, but I didn't see any sign of life either. That scared me more than anything else.

I ducked into the house and slammed the door behind me, locking it. My back against the wood, I slid down to the floor and huddled there.

My headache worsened.

CHAPTER 10

As a little girl, I used to wake up screaming from nightmares. Daddy would rush in on the heels of my screams, take me in his arms, and rock me back to sleep as he sang a lullaby. He told me monsters didn't exist. He said they were the result of eating too much junk food before bedtime or watching a scary movie, nothing more. I had fallen asleep while on the floor and one of those dreams had shocked me awake. The scream lessened to a tiny whistle. The throbbing behind my eyes told me the headache hadn't lessened or left.

I sat up and whispered, "Well, Daddy, you're wrong. Monsters do exist. But you know what pisses me off even more? You're not here to soothe me or rock me back to sleep with some lullaby. At least you and Mom passed away before all this happened. Because to be honest, I think this might have been more than the two of you could handle. I want to keep my memories of a father able to take anything on remain intact. My beliefs have been shattered enough."

I got off the floor and headed to my bedroom. I passed Larry, as he sat on the couch and stared at the flat screen television. Somehow, he'd managed to turn it on, though only static crackled from it.

The bedroom door clicked shut behind me. I heard sounds of running water coming from behind the closed door of the bathroom. That let me know that Connor still showered. I crossed the room to the closet and chewing my bottom lip, I slid it open and rifled through hung clothing and empty hangers, searching for something to wear. Something apocalyptic? Post- apocalyptic? Whatever.

I grabbed a hanger holding a pair of black jeans, embroidered, gold vines trailing down the legs, plus another hanger with a T-shirt, the words, 'HAVE A NICE DAY' under a smiling happy face screen printed on the front.

Staring at the words and that round, smiling face, I giggled and couldn't stop even when I began hiccupping. Who else but a nutty person would dare to wear such a shirt today when the world they knew may be almost gone?

I tossed the shirt and pants on the bed, before I grabbed a pair of clean socks from the top drawer of the dresser. I grimaced when I saw that the socks had smiley faces embroidered on them. *Have a nice fucking day. Right.* Dropping to my knees, I rummaged under the bed and dug out a pair of black, leather tennis shoes.

The bathroom door swung open. I ripped off the fur clothing Harry had given me, stomped past Connor at the sink, and stuffed it all into the large wastebasket in the bathroom. Connor wore a towel around his hips and had almost finished shaving. He set the razor on the sink.

"Any clothes I can put on?" he asked, staring at my nude body.

"There's a garbage bag full of Jeff's old clothes in the closet. That's where I got the men's clothes I gave you when we came back the first time."

He wandered into the bedroom. Turning on the shower, I stepped under the warm water and scrubbed away the remnants of Hell. I felt dirty, violated even. I kept washing my skin until it gleamed pink, almost raw. I stepped out and dried myself. Before I left the bathroom, I swallowed a couple of painkillers for the headache.

The contents of the garbage bag that held the men's clothing lay strewn on top of the bed. I didn't see Connor.

I'd have to talk to him about making a mess. With a shrug, I dressed and returned to the living room.

I found Connor with Larry on the couch in the living room, both waiting for me. The television had been turned off. Connor looked gorgeous in a pair of jeans and a navy-blue T-shirt. I admired his physique, all the way down to his bare feet. *Bare feet?*

I arched an eyebrow. "No shoes?"

He shrugged. "I lost that pair you gave me, and I couldn't find any in that bag. Heck, as a werewolf, I'm used to being barefooted." He got off the couch and tramped over to the front door, his limp gone. "Anyway, we need to go to the vortex and see how bad things are. Lack of footwear is the least of my worries."

How bad things are? One didn't need much imagination to guess how awful the situation had grown downtown.

I said, "Shouldn't we rest up? Get our energy back?"

He stopped and looked at me. "Do you think that Lucifer and his minions are taking a siesta?" He threw open the door and stepped outside.

Larry lifted off the couch and flew after Connor. I sighed and joined them.

We drove down I-95 in a car we'd stolen. Connor labeled it as borrowing it from my neighbors. What was one more crime in all the things I had done or been involved in since the vortex appeared? Jim and Patsy had probably become undead monsters since we've been in Hell and eating their way through living people, or if they hadn't, had long since settled in some zombie's belly.

I stared out of the passenger window. The gray fog drifted along the highway, and it covered everything. We seemed to be the only car moving on the road. Other vehicles dotted the area like bizarre art objects. They had been either abandoned or deserted after crashing into other vehicles or the guard rails. I looked inside the crashed ones, but I didn't see any dead bodies, so I assumed the victims had been rescued by first responders or walked away.

They could have been eaten. The grayness could have transformed them into undead.

Eaten, saved by emergency crews, or just walked away, nothing mattered except driving around the increasingly growing clutter of cars and trucks. Worse, the grayness thickened, and it became difficult to see through it. After we almost ran into another parked car, Connor drew over to the side of the highway and cut off the engine.

He said, "It'll be easier to go from here on foot."

I stared at the grayness as it pushed against the windshield as if wanting to get inside the car. I trembled.

"Walk through that stuff? Won't we end up as monsters too? Or to be more accurate, won't I as the only human in here become a slobbering, flesh-eating thing?" I looked at Connor. "Not that I'm not saying that you can't become a zombie, though I doubt Larry will." Larry squealed. "Sorry, Larry, I didn't mean for that to sound so...oh, I don't know what I meant by that."

Larry bleeped and I took that as acceptance of my apology. I watched as Connor didn't say a word, but unbuckled and got out of the car. He stood there, waiting. I heard the seat belt buckle behind me unsnap and Larry slipped over from the back seat into the driver's seat, joining Connor. Nothing appeared to be happening to them. The grayness inched its way in through the opening. I grabbed the door handle and opened my door, almost falling out. Maybe I could have stayed inside, but how long before something came along and got me. Besides, the grayness had half-filled the car by now. I stood in it and some of it shifted pass me into the open doorway on the passenger's side. A tendril of it brushed against my left hand and I didn't develop an incredible hunger for flesh of the living either. The stuff felt disgusting, oily. Maybe it had lost the power to change me.

Or maybe, someone didn't want it to make me a zombie. Maybe someone has other plans for me. It felt like a hand squeezed my heart at the thought. Who would have plans for me and why?

The three of us hiked down the highway toward downtown. Instead of touching me like it had for that second back at the car, the gray stuff stayed several inches away from us, although like a macabre bubble it surrounded us. I wondered if we could go anywhere. I turned right, thinking to head down an off ramp that appeared. Suddenly the Hell fog became a solid wall blocking me. Afraid to test the boundaries, I trotted back over to rejoin Connor and Larry. It went back to being nothing more than formless, drifting...stuff. Except I knew that it herded us like cattle to where it wanted us to go.

We trudged on in that chilling, lonely world. More cars, trucks, and motorcycles scattered across the pavement, their drivers missing. Like apparitions, buildings would loom in the grayness, unfriendly sentries on each side of the highway. The buildings would vanish, ghostly silhouettes in the mist, and you wonder if you hadn't imagined them.

Had we even made it out of Hell? What happened to all those things that had piled out of the vortex? What about the people made into zombies? And what about those who survived the car crashes or took off on foot like we had? Surely, I'm not the last human?

The problem was, I never saw another living person. Only the occasional building and the abandoned vehicles kept us company. My feet complained like two old women. I wanted to give into them and sit down, but I forged on, trailing behind Connor who walked with ease and a tireless Larry.

Yeah, I'd like to be a demon and be able to fly. Do demons even get tired? Damn, I could go for cup of coffee and a long soak in a tub of hot water right now, then a good long sleep in my bed. Like that would happen.

Okay, counting my blessings: I'm alive and not a zombie. I hadn't been eaten. Not yet, anyway. Azazel didn't get to make me his main babe. I stared at Connor's sexy posterior, enjoying the sight. There are a few nice perks to this end of the world stuff. Even Larry's a perk. Things could be worse.

Suddenly, tall skyscrapers reared up out of the noxious pea soup from Hell, and I knew we'd made it to downtown. Something roared, sounding not far from us. Okay, it's double times worse.

Another wail came from behind us, followed by another and another until the uproar surrounded us.

Triple worse.

CHAPTER 11

Why did we always have to be stuck right dab in the middle of the horror? Forget the coffee. I had a sudden yearning for something much stronger that would burn a path down my throat. Liquid fire that would keep at bay the fears and the insanity of the situation.

Connor turned and whispered, "I'm going to shift into my wolf form, and when I do, I'll get the attention of whatever is surrounding us. When that happens, take off and keep heading down the exit to downtown. Make sure Larry goes with you."

"You're kidding? You're going to take on those things?"

"Just keep going, even if it sounds like those 'things' are killing me. Worry more about getting Larry and yourself to safety. I'll get away and come looking for you later. I know your scent, so I'll be able to track you."

Larry drifted over to us and winced every time something bellowed. He pressed against me and whimpered.

Connor turned to him. "Larry, you go with Cat. Okay? I want both of you away from here and to find someplace safe to hide. I'll find you. I know your scents. I'll be able to find you."

It looked like Larry might argue as I saw something like defiance glimmer in his iris. A second later, he slumped and bleated.

Connor nodded at Larry. "Good. Now, get going."

He walked away but came back. He leaned over and kissed me on the lips. I stared at him, surprised. Should I kiss him back? Unsure of what to do, I decided to go the safe route and hugged him.

"Good luck, Connor," I whispered.

Frown lines formed in his forehead, but they smoothed away, and he smiled, before he stalked off into the vapor. Not long after, I heard a wolf howl, followed by numerous roars. Right after all that, the sounds of fighting reached my ears.

Instead of doing as Connor had instructed, I tiptoed closer to the sounds; Larry right beside me. The bleak mist parted for us, revealing the combatants. My werewolf paced the pavement on his hind legs, snarling. Not even bothering to take off his clothes, the shift had shredded them into tatters now hanging off him in ribbons. As if he knew, he paused and turned his head to stare in my direction. His eyes glinted, and I knew with anger at me for not doing as he'd asked. Out of nowhere, a terrible creature beefed up like an incredibly massive bull on steroids, attacked him. It slung a massive paw edged with sharp claws at Connor's head. I gasped. The claws dug into Connor's skin, and he yelped. The creature grabbed him and began to drag him toward it. Rather than trying to escape its clutches, Connor sank his fangs into the upper part of one of his adversary's arms.

Enraged, it tried to shake him off. But Connor held on and kicked his hind feet at its stomach, digging into the flesh and tearing out hunks of it. With a roar, the brute managed to free itself of the werewolf and it flung him away. Connor landed hard on the pavement, the air knocked out of him. He lay there, not moving.

"Connor!"

The monstrosity switched its attention from the unconscious shifter to me. The others looked too. None of them made a noise.

The calm before the storm.

Dumb, dumb, dumb, I really should have listened to Connor.

I had nothing to fight the creature with, and even if I did, it might not do me any good. Look what it had done to a werewolf. I got ready to bolt when Larry darted in front of me, ready to rush the freak.

"Forget it, Larry, let's leave."

Out of the corner of my eye I saw Connor regaining consciousness, getting up by his front paws first; his hind feet second. He shook his head and rose all the way up on his hind paws. His opponent approaching us caught sight of him, halted, and roared again. Out of the crowd another joined him. It had tentacles that lashed at the air. If one had been bad enough to hurt a werewolf, what could two of them do?

They charged him. Connor sidestepped, they bulldozed by him, and he attacked them. He got the first one by its throat and hung on with his mouth, trying to crush its windpipe and maybe be lucky enough to kill it. But the other one grabbed him from behind with a tentacle and yanked him away from the first fiend, but not before he'd ripped out its throat. The first one dropped to its knees, applying pressure at the open wound. It stared at Connor as he howled and tried to bite at his second attacker. The first one laughed, green goo bubbling out of its mouth. With horror, I saw the wound closing. It withdrew its paw, revealing a throat like new.

Of course, indestructible monsters. These creatures either came from Hell and if not demonic, from any of the numerous worlds of magic and the supernatural that the vortex led to.

It lurched to its feet and clicking its claws, red eyes glowing, it went to join its monstrous partner. Connor was trapped in the second one's grip. He glanced at me and yelled in human speech, "Run, Cat. Now!"

I didn't argue, even though I didn't want to leave him. I escaped, Larry flying right behind me. We ran down the off ramp. Screams filled the air, and I couldn't see where I was going, blinded by the thick gray enveloping us. At least it didn't do anything to me. As the din faded, I realized I hadn't been meant for monster food either. That scared me more than anything else, because I believed the fiends chasing Larry and me could have easily caught up to us. Sooner or later, whatever dues I owed some deity or fiend, would be collected.

Jagged pain lanced my lungs, I stopped running, gasping, When the agony subsided enough, I walked past empty buildings. Larry kept pace alongside. Downtown seemed another world, silent and eerie. Not a single zombie, demon or any other monstrous creature came at us. If it was like this in Richmond, had this happened to the rest of the United States, even the world?

Of course, dummy. Did you think it just happened to Richmond, as the apocalypse couldn't happen to a nicer town?

I heard the clatter of an empty can being kicked. It came from inside the building I stood in front of. I saw a clothing store, or it had been before Armageddon. It appeared to be an empty place, except that sound denied that.

"Larry, did you hear that?"

He nudged my shoulder and nodded. I clenched both fists against my thighs and didn't move a muscle.

"So, I didn't imagine it. Should we chance a look or just keep on going?" Glancing at Larry, I saw shaking side-to-side. His rendition of no. "Yeah, wouldn't it be stupid for us to enter that place?" I stared at the building. "Major stupid."

Just as we began to walk away, shadowy shapes emerged out of the shifting gray stuff and cut us off. One of the shapes grabbed Larry and yanked him into its embrace.

"Go ahead," I said. "You might as well eat me."

"Now why would we do that?" asked a petite woman with skin the shade of mocha as she stepped away from the shapes.

I dropped my jaw, then blurted out, "You're human!"

"That I am," she agreed. "We all are."

Her eyebrows knitted together like caterpillars kissing as she stared at Larry. "Damnable things like that are

inhabiting Richmond now. Humans are in the minority."
She shrugged. "Follow me."

I trailed after the woman and the other humans into the building. Inside, a huge, burly man held Larry in a tight grip. He carried my friend over to a large cage, like one used for large dogs. It was obvious he didn't care if he hurt Larry or not, as the man shoved him into the kennel and slammed the door shut, locking it. Larry whimpered and pressed himself against the bars.

"What are you doing to Larry?"

The woman looked at Larry and snorted. "You gave one of those hellish things a name?"

"No, his parents did."

The woman and the others in the room snickered. She stopped after a few minutes and walked over to the cage, stopping about a foot away as if she feared Larry might get through the bars. Dropping down into a crouch, she studied him for a couple of seconds before she pointed at him.

"Are you trying to tell me that horrible thing has parents?"

"Yeah, he does. And if it wasn't for him backing my ass up many times, I would be dead now, or worse."

She gave Larry a thoughtful look as he chirped and pushed up against the cage bars. Pursing her lips, she stood and swept her gaze back to me and nodded.

"Yes, I agree that there are more wretched things than death these days. What's this about Hell?"

"Where do you think all those unholy things came from when they came out of that vortex? Hell has decided that it's time for the apocalypse. It's the ultimate showdown with Heaven, and with Earth as the prize."

She pushed a chair at me. "Sit."

I sat. Even though the chair was made of rusty metal, it felt good to finally get off my feet. She grabbed another chair, turned it around, and sat down facing me. Her hands draped over the chair back, she stared at me for a second before she spoke.

"Since that thing showed up two weeks ago, this gray stuff has spread throughout Richmond and the surrounding counties, even covering the whole state. That's the last we heard. Any phone calls or texts we've sent, no one has replied. There's no television or radio, and forget the Internet—seems anything that runs on electricity has died. We tried running laptops and tablets off batteries but received nothing but a weird static. Had to shut them off, as we couldn't recharge the batteries, once they ran down. Need electricity for that, too."

That time I spent in Hell and those other places, had it really only been two weeks?

The woman got up and paced the room. The others watched her. She stood maybe no more than five feet four, if that, her black hair cut short in a cap of tight curls and her eyes a shade of chocolate, fringed by thick lashes. Even though I judged her to be maybe in her fifties, maybe a little older, she was beautiful.

She stopped in front of me and crossed her arms. "The name's Crystal Henning. Before all this happened, I worked in real estate. I have gathered as many humans as I can find and lead them." She laughed, raking a hand through her hair. "I used to live in Woodlake in a nice home. Now I bunk out here with everyone else, sleeping in a sleeping bag." She grabbed me by the shoulders and peered into my eyes. "We're homeless, thanks to creatures like your Larry back there."

She glared at Larry over her shoulder, and he backed away from the bars, whimpering. Then she dropped her hands and sat down in the other chair. "Since you seem to be friends with one of the monsters and know what caused this vortex, tell me everything. And I mean everything. I want to know what's going on. I need to understand why it's happening. Talk."

I told them what happened to me up to that point. Crystal's face remained set and she didn't blink, not even when I got to the pretty incredible parts in my story. But then, I had no doubt she had some off the wall stuff she could tell me. When I finished, she sighed.

"If you told me this story before all this happened, I'd have told you to go get some help. But I've seen things, God, I had to do things no sane person would do. I assumed something more scientific caused the vortex. Maybe I could believe in another dimension. An alien invasion. But this is all a plan for Hell to take Earth over? And where's Heaven in all this? I haven't seen any warrior angels down here."

I looked her straight in the eye. "There's one angel. The angel, George."

"The angel...George? Never heard that name in the Bible. What load of crap are you feeding me?"

I shook my head. "I'm not feeding you anything. He is called George and he is an angel. Well, he had been an angel. Now he's on Hell's side and I guess he'd be considered a fallen angel. He's part of what's behind this mess."

"Let me understand this. And I'm sure the rest in this room would like to understand it better, too. Some former angel is part of the reason for the vortex opening and all those hellish things escaping into our world?"

"In a nutshell, yeah, that about sums it up. He said that it's better to rule in Hell then serve in Heaven—like that quote from *Dante's Inferno*."

Crystal rose to her feet and left the room. The others didn't join her, they started talking to each other and ignoring me. I strolled through the doorway and found myself in a hallway, but no Crystal in sight. Eventually, I heard something that sounded like laughter, but very low, from a few doors away. I stood in the doorway and watched as her laughter got higher and higher, out of control, and soon Crystal was sobbing. She hunched over, her arms folded across her stomach. The poor woman. I'm sure my tale made the craziness she'd been going through even worse. I went to her and put my arms around her, hugging her and whispering comforting words as I patted her back. I thought that this should be me, breaking down; instead, here I was consoling someone else. My little jaunt through Hell and beyond had made me more resilient than I realized.

Her tears subsided after a while and she withdrew. She wiped away the tearstains on her face. "Sorry about that. I don't know what came over me."

"Don't worry," I said with a shrug. "Even a stronger person would have broken down with all the unnatural things going on. No one can be a super person."

"Yeah, I guess." She grimaced. "I better wash my face, then we head back to the main room. I couldn't break down in front of those people. They look to me as a leader of sorts.

I didn't know what else to say to her. After all, just because I caught her breaking down and I gave her comfort, didn't mean we were bosom buddies. After she freshened up in a nearby restroom, Crystal and I returned to the others.

She walked over to Larry's prison and not touching the bars, stared down at him. Not tearing her gaze away from him, she spoke. "One cannot let go, not for a second. You need to be vigilant, on your toes, or a monster will eat you. That's what happened to a friend of mine, Janie. She just lost it, right on the corner of Broad and Eighth. Kept screaming. Something came out of the gray mist, snatched her up in its pincers, cut her in half and gobbled her down. It went after me, but I was damn lucky that Jim here ran out of a nearby building and yanked me inside. He made sure I kept quiet and still. After a while, the thing wandered off."

She turned and smiled at a pale, nerdy guy with wire frame glasses slipping down his nose, his green eyes blinking like an owl's. I assumed this must be Jim. He blushed and shrugged. It was a very telling moment between the two of them, as he might not be the type to attract her under normal circumstances. He blushed and looked more suited to playing video games, not fighting

Hell creatures or romancing a tough-as-nails real estate lady. But hey, what do I know? I noticed the gun he gripped and the malignant look he flashed Larry. Maybe I should rethink about the geek knowing how to kill demons. I joined Crystal at Larry's cage.

I asked, "What about Larry here?"

She snorted. "That thing? We'll have to get rid of it, try and kill it."

Larry squealed like a stuck pig.

A chill filled me at what she just said. He was my friend, someone who helped me. "Don't kill Larry. He's not one of the bad guys, He helped me. And since he's a demon, he might have useful information." I dug my nails into the palms of my hands. If she didn't listen, did anything to—

Crystal said, "How can that be useful? So far, I haven't heard it speak in English and no one here can comprehend the oddball noises it makes." She looked at him again. "Except maybe you."

"He's not a killer demon or monster. Larry's more a victim than anything else. Give him a chance. Please?"

"This goes against my better judgment." She gestured to Jim and another man. "Jim, Carl, free the ugly beastie."

For the first time since I heard all the sounds he made, Larry snorted. Guess he didn't care for the moniker. The cage door unlatched, he slipped out and remained by my side, keeping his gaze on Crystal. I patted him. "It's all right, Larry. Give them time. Remember how long it took me to get use to you and Connor."

He whistled.

"You might try and apologize to Larry," I said. "He didn't care for being called an 'ugly beastie'."

He levitated until he faced Crystal, eye-to-eyes. She looked apprehensive, like she believed he might rush her and eat her face off. At last, the tension broke and she apologized. "Sorry. You're not that ugly."

He chortled, spewing off a bunch of whistles and snorts.

"I could be wrong, but I think he said you aren't so ugly yourself. But don't quote me on that. I'm just starting to learn to speak "Larry".

Instead of getting angry, Crystal started laughing. The rest of the room joined in. Relieved that I hadn't made it worse for Larry, I listened with amazement as a series of giggles erupted from him.

Later that night, we all sat around a large table, eating Top Ramen noodles and drinking from bottles of water. Larry rested on a nearby bunk. He had shut his eye to take a nap or something. I realized he did have an eyelid, but where he hid it, I didn't know. Hungry, I scooped up more noodles from my bowl. Though I wasn't eating five-star restaurant gourmet food, this tasted like the best damn meal I had in a long while. I chewed on the noodles and didn't join in the conversation, just ate and listened as the others talked. They discuss plans for the next day, who'd take over watch tonight, and about their former lives before the vortex had come. No shock about being right about Jim's former life. He had been a computer programmer for a big bank downtown. Layton had been a cook in a fast-food place. One beautiful, tall girl, Jen, the daughter of a rich CEO, had just a few months before I graduated high school. Another young man, David, had gone to Virginia Commonwealth University and had been majoring in theatre before all this happened. Many of the others had similar stories. Not one had been prepared for this nightmare, no one was a readymade survivalist. Rich, poor, everyone now equals. Being a former DMV worker no longer seemed so bad. I survived, and that was the only thing that mattered. I settled down to less listening and finishing my food.

Finished with my dinner, I put the bowl down when Crystal turned to me. She said, "Sorry, we don't have much to offer in the way of food."

"Hey, this is the best meal I've had in a long time."

"Yeah, I suppose you didn't get anything that great to eat in Hell."

I took a swig from my bottle of water and shrugged. Just as I took another swallow, a loud explosion from outside shook the room. I choked on the water and sputtered it out, dropping the bottle. Water splashed across the table.

"What the hell is that?" asked Carl, as he leaped to his feet.

CHAPTER 12

The men sprang to their feet and thundered to the door, grabbing guns along the way. They paused, waiting, as one brawny, older guy unlocked it and opened it a crack to peer outside. Whispering an all clear, he motioned the rest to follow him. One by one, they streamed outside. One of the women rushed over to close and lock the door behind them.

Crystal joined me at the table. Time slowed down to a crawl. My heart in my throat, I got up and slipped over to the entrance. Except, it didn't help my nervousness, so I trekked back to the table. Still feeling jittery, I didn't sit down but stared at the door. I felt a light touch at my hand.

"Sit down," said Crystal.

"I can't. What's happening out there? Will they be all right? Don't you want to know?"

"Sure. We all do. When they return, we'll learn what made that din." I must have shown something in my face, as she added, "Yes, my nerves are all tied in knots and I'm keeping my fingers crossed, but I know the men are being careful out there."

Halfway sitting down in the chair, I paused as the locks clicked and the men piled in, the door slamming shut after the last one. Between them, I could see a few of them carrying something wrapped up in netting. I couldn't make out what they captured, but it snarled and fought as they struggled with it, making it as far as the middle of the room. Crystal elevated to her feet and shouted. "Put it in the cage in the other room!"

They had another cage? Not far behind them and Crystal, I followed and watched as they carried/dragged their prisoner out of the room and down a hallway until they came to a locked door. Crystal unhooked some keys hanging off her belt and after a quick search, inserted one in the keyhole and unlocked it. It swung open with a creak and after she hit the light switch and light flooded the room, she backed away as the men forced the snarling thing inside. Minutes later, they headed back to the main room.

One of them remained at the locked door—Les. A large man with a big belly and a ring of red hair surrounding his bald pate, I remember overhearing he'd been a prison guard before the vortex. He said, "The thing is locked up."

Crystal turned to me and asked, "Do you want to see what they caught?"

Les unlocked the door and entered. Crystal and I walked inside, hard on his heels.

He said, "The noise came from some kind of bomb. This ungodly monster was comatose when the others crouching over it saw us and took off, vanishing into that damn fog. We knew better than to touch it. I mean, it might have been playing possum. The other things could have left it as a trap for all we knew. It's a good thing that Tom remembered to grab the net, he threw it over the beast. It didn't move, so we knew it was knocked out. We had to work quickly, before it started to wake up."

The cage almost filled the room. I wondered where they'd gotten it from, and how they maneuvered it into here. Why even have it—unless they'd bagged other monsters or demons before. I drew closer and stared between the bars. A werewolf. Suddenly, it shot up to its hind feet and charged. Frightened, I stumbled back with a squeal. Instead of snarling, it grasped the bars with its furry paws and stared at me, silent.

"No!" I recognized the eyes, before it blurred from animal to man. Connor. No longer a beast, a naked man instead.

He spoke, his voice rusty. "Cat."

I pleaded with Les. "That's Connor. Let him out."

The man shook his head. "Are you nuts, lady? That's something unnatural. Even worse, it might be a demon pretending to be able to become a human being. I'm not letting that thing loose to tear my throat out."

I turned to Crystal. "Crystal, let me inside. I'll show you that Connor won't do any harm to anyone here."

She shook her head. "What the hell is he?"

"A werewolf, but he's one of the good guys. Let me prove it." I put a hand on her shoulder. "Trust me."

She sighed. "It's your funeral." She nodded at Les. "Unlock the cage door, Les."

Mumbling under his breath, he unlocked the cage door, backing away as he pulled a gun out of his back pocket. "I'm not opening it. You do it. It's your life."

I opened the cage door a crack and slid inside. Les locked up behind me. I rushed to Connor. Despite being dirty and covered in scratches, he grinned. I hugged him and asked, "What happened?"

He shrugged. "I fought the demons but more showed up and I took off. I caught your scent and tracked you while trying to evade the horde behind me. Unfortunately for me, they tracked my spoor, too."

"That noise we heard. The loud boom. What was it?"

"One of the demons actually had a bomb. He threw it at me and I couldn't get away fast enough when it landed beside me and went off, knocking me unconscious." He swept his gaze toward Crystal. "I'm sure they would have killed me if your men hadn't gotten to me. Thanks. I'm sorry about my reaction to them, when I regained consciousness inside here, too."

"See Crystal, he is on our side."

Indecision darkened her eyes. I knew she worried about him not being human, but surely, she remembered that Larry wasn't either. The eye demon had already proved to be harmless to her and her people. She sighed. "Let him go, Les."

He opened his mouth as if to argue but backed away from the opening. Not looking happy, he watched with a resigned look as Connor and I walked out of the cage. Although he didn't put away his gun when he stomped out of the room.

I asked, "Crystal, can Connor wash up somewhere and do you have some extra clothing?"

As if a naked man was her guest every day, Crystal led Connor to a bathroom. She found a pair of jeans and a flannel shirt, along with socks and a pair of work boots, and handed them over to him. The clothes belonged to someone they must have lost, looking about Connor's size. We left him alone to take a shower and headed back to the main room.

Larry sat on the cot, awake. He gazed at the humans gathered around the table talking. They grew silent when we entered the room.

"Anyone got some silver to kill the werewolf?" asked Jim. I guess Les had told the others about Connor, how he changed back to human and what I called him. It didn't matter that he hadn't harmed me, they lumped him with the fiends from Hell.

I grew angry. "No one's going to harm one hair on Connor's body."

Jim snorted. "Connor? The freak has a name?" He glowered at Larry. "Of course, you also brought that other inhuman creature here among us and it has a name, too." He spat out the last word with disgust.

"None of you has been injured by Connor," I retorted. "Larry, either. And calling them names doesn't change that fact."

Crystal spoke up. "She's right about that. The werewolf so far hasn't harmed us and is now taking a shower. Looking as human as the rest of us here. I gave him some of Jack's clothes.

Jim jumped up, his hands in fists. "You gave him some of Jack Kenner's clothes? Jack just died last week, eaten by a one-eyed monstrosity, not unlike that damn thing over there, only bigger!"

Crystal banged her fist on the table, rattling empty, dirty plates and utensils. A crust of bread rolled off a plate and onto the table. "Enough! So far, he's shown he isn't going to hurt us." She looked at me. "Although, if he does, I'll be the first person here to put a silver bullet in his heart. Is that clear?" Some of the others grumbled, but they subsided, and conversation turned to other topics.

Crystal grabbed my arm and led me over to Larry. She said, "I meant what I said, Cat. First time any of your unnatural buddies decide to attack anyone here, the first bullet will come from me. Is that understood?"

"Real clear. But I promise you, neither will do anything. If not for Connor and Larry, I wouldn't be alive today.

Larry floated off the cot and purred, bumping against my side. I gave him a hug. "Thanks, Larry."

The table conversation died, and I saw why. Connor strode into the room, dressed in the clothes Crystal gave him. The shirt tugged a bit tight across his chest, but otherwise everything fit. Though I assumed he'd dried his hair with a towel, it still looked damp and like he had used his fingers to comb it out. Ignoring all the eyes on him, he wandered over to us. The conversation picked up again, but this time in low whispers.

No doubt it would take time before everyone felt safe around Connor. He patted Larry, who purred and bunted him like a cat. The eye demon floated back over to the cot and settled down on the mattress. Connor stuck his hands in his jeans pockets and stood there in a self-conscious manner, scraping the toe of his right boot against the floor. With a small sigh, he stopped the scraping and stuck out a hand at Crystal. "We have never been introduced. I'm Connor Rojas."

Crystal took his hand and shook it. "Crystal Henning."

"Nice of you to take in someone, no make that two someones, of the supernatural persuasion. I can sense by the air around here that I'm not a very popular person at the moment." The whispering halted and Connor switched his focus to the others, especially to Jim. Jim stared back, a defiant gleam in his eyes. Connor returned his attention to Crystal.

"Well, Cat claims you're fine, but I have something to say." Crystal withdrew her hand and wiped it on her pants. That spoke volumes. Connor shifted and stuck his hands back in his pockets.

"One wrong move, and believe me, I know what can kill a werewolf. I've read the books and seen the movies. There are plenty of silver things around here that we can melt down into a bullet. As for one-eyed here, I'm sure I can find a way to exorcise him back to Hell. So, neither of you better prove Cat wrong. Do we have an understanding here?"

"Loud and clear," replied Connor.

Larry stared at Crystal, remaining quiet. It was obvious he understood her all too well. I fixed Connor a bowl of ramen noodle soup and he carried it over to the cot and sat down next to Larry. Eating, he kept his eyes on the others as he slurped noodles into his mouth.

As Connor swallowed a mouthful of noodles, something banged on the door hard, knocking it off its hinges. The door fell to the floor with a crash, and something most foul entered. The former Angel George. Not in his new dark Goth look, once again he wore white, and looked as pure as a newborn baby. In my opinion, a newborn baby cobra.

The slimy bastard oozed his way further in. "Does anyone need divine intervention here?"

No one moved, though I swore I heard the clicks of several guns being readied. It appeared the others did not trust him either.

I spoke up. "Don't listen to him, Crystal. That's the former angel turned turncoat demon I told you about.

He minced over to me. "Oh my, you poor dear. I see that nasty demon and werewolf has gotten you all mixed up." He grabbed my hand and squeezed, his grip almost crushing it. I tried to yank my hand out of his, but he held all the tighter. Tears filled my eyes.

Something hit the floor and shattered. Connor leaped up, remnants of his bowl scattered around his feet. He glared at George. "Get your filthy hands off her."

George let go of me and I hastened over to Connor, rubbing my hand. No longer caring, George looked bored with whatever game he played.

"All right," he said with a nasty laugh. "Heaven is not here to save your pathetic mortal asses."

He swept his hand over himself from head toe, replacing white with black. The halo blinked away, and the wings shone with dark light. He laughed at all the weapons cocked and pointed at him.

"Why don't you be the good, little mortal wimps you are and just give up. My demonic bad boys are waiting outside and would love to come in and tear you from limb from limb. On a personal note, I do appreciate good old-fashioned carnage myself." He winked out and reappeared by the opened doorway. "But my new boss wants me to take some souls without any bashing of heads. I guess we've been sending way too many up to my former boss and Big L doesn't like that. He had this bet with God that mortals are nothing more than crybabies. That if put to the test; you'll give up your immortal souls and go to Hell rather than fight it out hoping help from Heaven arrives."

Snapping his fingers, one of the chairs by the table flew over to him. He whipped it around and swung a leg over, sitting down.

"You know you won't win. Earth and its mortals have been bones of contention ever since Adam and Eve. This is Armageddon, so get over it. Now what do you say, guys? With a snap of my fingers, I can get the contracts to you and all you need is to sign your signature in blood. It has to be your blood, of course."

The room had fallen silent. I swore I could hear everyone thinking. "Don't give into his lies," I cried out. "He gave up being an angel just because like a spoiled brat, things in Heaven didn't go his way."

Connor added, his tone quiet, "I may be inhuman, but at least I can't lay the destruction of mankind and Earth at my feet."

George rose lazily and yawned. "Oh, shut up. You don't have much choice. Look how I got in here without a problem. Give up your souls the easy way or be prepared to have them taken." His eyes turned obsidian and a sword of black metal appeared in his hand. "I vote for the not so easy way. I'd like to skewer this sword of darkness through your hairless monkey bodies."

Les ran up to him. "I give up." He dropped to his knees.

George smiled down at him. The smile chilled me to the bones. "Oh, you do, do you? Too late. I retract the offer."

With a war cry, he swung his sword in an arc, separating Les' head from his neck. Shock still in the eyes, the head dropped to the floor and rolled away. The body spurted blood and collapsed.

George licked the blood off the sword and smacked his lips. "Mmm...too much cholesterol in him," said George with a smirk. "Now, who's next? Better get it over with now. Otherwise, I'll call in my demons and you'll live long enough to watch them gnaw on your innards after they tear open your stomachs. It's not a pretty sight."

Larry screamed, flying at George. But the dark angel swung his sword like a bat and knocked the eye demon to the other side of the room. Larry slammed into a wall and slid to the floor, knocked out.

George grinned, staring past me. "Come on, Wolfboy. Let's see if you can huff and puff me away."

Connor! I whirled around and saw that he began to shift, his clothes shredding. Within seconds, the snarling werewolf stood there, before leaping over me at George.

"Connor, no!"

Too late, George propelled his sword outward, and Connor ran right into the tip. George gave another thrust, impaling the sword deeper into Connor's chest, right where his heart would be.

"Bastard!" I screamed, rushing him.

With a laugh, he pushed Connor away and grabbed me. "Ah, eager to be in my arms again, I see." His grin widened until it split at the sides of his mouth.

I struggled against his hold, wanting only to check on Connor. Staring down at him, I watched his eyes glaze over. He didn't move. *Connor's dead.* I began to cry.

"Let her go, you hellish imp." Crystal held a rifle in her hands and the others gathered behind her, weapons of all kinds in their hands aimed at George.

"Oh, this is so boring," replied George, yawning. "Do you think that a bunch of hairless apes can kill an angel? A dark angel? Just because it happens on TV, that doesn't mean you can do so in reality." He dropped me to the floor, next to Connor's body. "I'm going to rip every one of your hearts out of your chest cavities and ground them to dust beneath the heel of my boot. Unless my minions get you first. Dinner time, guys."

Unimaginable terrors crowded into the room, each one bigger than the one before it. They had sharp claws, teeth, pinchers, and other terrible appendages defying description. I scrambled to get up and skated in both Les's and Connor's blood, hitting the floor.

Crystal and her people formed a circle; most of them faced the demons while she and a few others kept their gaze on George. The sword slipped from his hand as he began to sway. I watched in horror as he morphed. With a cry, he shot up until the top of his head met the ceiling. A snout not unlike a crocodile's opened where his mouth had been, perfect teeth becoming jagged incisors. Black leathery flesh—hard as armor—replaced his soft skin while his demon wings remained tripled in size. Nails edged with claws as reptilian skin covered his hands, while the shoes on his feet split apart and his feet changed the same as the rest of him, elongating and toes ending in claws. Enormous and gruesome, he looked like what I always imagined dragons look like.

I rolled away as a claw at the edge of one of his toes missed me by inches. I managed to tow Connor's body after me.

I heard gun fire, swords slicing in the air, and snapping jaws. Fear filled me as I wondered if the demons would win this time. Heads rolled and the bodies were blood fountains dowsing the fighters, floor, walls, and ceiling. Men and women kept shooting, bullets having little effect. I lugged Connor's body over to lie beside a still unconscious Larry. I would do anything to keep his body from being flattened. I searched for something to use as a weapon, when I saw George's sword on the floor, but as I was almost within fingertip of it, it vanished.

I'd be damned if I ended up back in Hell. Maybe I would be dead within seconds of taking on George the dragon, but at least I would have tried. I grabbed the only things I could find, a butter knife and a fork, and brandishing them, charged George's foot. "Come on, you ugly behemoth. Don't tell me you're afraid of me."

George clicked his claws and demons and humans froze in place, reminding me of a little boy's action figures. George swiveled his long serpentine neck down so that his face hovered only a few inches away from mine.

I flinched when I saw the mock grin on his lizard lips. "You got to be kidding, right?" he said. "Baby, I'm going to play with you like a cat plays with the mouse it caught. I have plans for you. Let's see if you don't mind a little demon sex." A lecherous gleam appeared in his dark eyes.

He's like a gecko on crack if he thinks that.

I gripped my weapons tighter and slashed them in the air. "Don't call me baby! And if you think you're going to even get close enough to lay even a kiss on me, you're going to be sorry. Come on big, bad, and ugly as sin."

"Back away, Cat." It sounded like Connor's voice. But George had killed him.

Keeping one eye on the dragon, I saw Connor in human form and up on his feet. He clutched George's sword in one hand. The only evidence of his chest wound was a dried, red stain.

Unlike the others in the room, he hadn't become a statue. George was shocked as I was to see Connor. Maybe being unconscious negated George's magic spell. Wondering if Larry had awakened, I looked over and saw the eye demon still out.

Connor approached the dragon. "Georgie Porgie, you should know better. The only way to kill a werewolf is silver. You should have gotten rid of this sword when you metamorphosed. I'm going to take you down."

The sword had disappeared, I thought. *Who sent it back*?

George cocked his head and flashed a crocodile smile, flicking out a forked tongue. "Oh, the irony; St. Connor and a dragon named George."

Uttering a war cry, Connor sprinted at George. Everyone else unfroze and resumed battling.

CHAPTER 13

George swung his tail around and power punched it into Connor's chest, knocking him across the room like he was nothing more than an irritating gnat. The dragon lowered his head and lunged at the fallen Connor, gnashing his choppers. At the last minute, Connor scrambled out of the way on skidding feet and George's snout rammed into the wall. Larry became conscious at that moment and rolled away, stopping when he got to me. He curled against my legs, whimpering.

Everyone stopped fighting and scattered as George craned his head all the way up to the ceiling. He smashed both head and neck through the dry wall. Chunks of stone, plaster, and wood rained down. Larry and I ducked underneath the table. I hoped it would hold. Those alive either tried to join us or ran out of the building. George began to flap his massive wings and flew through what remained of the ceiling, causing the rest of it to crash to the floor. We had to get away or we would be crushed. I dashed. The others and Larry followed me, and we fled out the front door. A furry blur juggernauted past me. Connor, transformed.

The grayness did not touch the other survivors with me. I only wondered why for a moment, my gaze drawn to the sky. George was rising higher, many of the fiends hanging onto his tail. A vortex formed and he flew into it. It closed behind him with a rumble. Not every demon made it and a few bodies tumbled back down into the collapsing building. None came out.

I felt a soft touch at my back, and I turned, seeing Crystal. We headed back into the building. Piles of trash scattered everywhere in the room, covering dead bodies. From the doorway at the other side of the main room, we heard shouts. Still the werewolf, Connor used his inhuman strength and dug a tunnel through the mess. Freed, the others swarmed out.

Crystal called everyone to huddle around her, although she had a couple of men with weapons keeping watch. "We need to leave and find another place. Don't any of you remember, before all power died, when we heard over the radio about another group hiding in Carytown? Maybe we should head that way, see if they are still there."

One woman said, "But the mist—"

"We stood outside since that infernal fiend and his army destroyed the building, and the fog didn't come near us. I doubt that means anything good in the long run, but for now that might give us the edge to find a new place to barricade ourselves in."

Deciding we needed to sift through the ruins for much needed weapons, food, and equipment, Crystal did warn us to be careful as the building might still collapse on us. Uncovering what we needed, we packed what we could into backpacks. Connor became human again and after finding a package of wipes and using them to clean himself, he stripped the clothing off the body of a man his size who had been killed by a demon and dressed. Nobody said anything or tried to stop him.

He taught me how to load and shoot a pistol after I admitted to him I didn't know how, as everyone picked their weapon of choice. I prayed in silence that the mist wouldn't change the dead into revenants as we walked away.

I wondered if it was daytime, hard to tell though. We marched in single file, a former Marine, Bubba, clutching a rifle as he led us, and with Connor guarding the rear. Nothing attacked us and even the fog retreated, letting us pass. I tightened the grip on the pistol Connor taught me to use and kept it close. Could it be that Hell wanted us to reach our destination? Whatever its reasons, I kept my eyes and ears open.

We traveled nonstop for a long time. We kept in sight of each other always, for our own safety, not stopping to eat and with Crystal only allowing the occasional potty break. I could feel blisters forming on the bottom of my feet and they went from irritating to downright agonizing.

We passed the Science Museum of Virginia across the street before the gray mist darkened, hiding the building. Making it to Boulevard, we turned left and walked until we stood across the street from the Virginia Museum of Fine Arts. I wondered about the time and tapped Crystal on the shoulder.

"I wonder how late it is?"

She shrugged. "I don't know, but maybe we should stop and find a place to get some sleep." She called a halt to the others. "Bubba, Jim, check that building out. The Bed and Breakfast, not the one next to it. It will have beds. Oh boy, would I love to sleep on a mattress tonight for a change instead of camping out on floors or in chairs like we did back at the other place we used. But make sure all windows and doors are secure and nothing hellish is waiting inside."

The two men went inside and came back out ten minutes later. Jim gave a thumb's up.

"It's safe," said Bubba.

Everyone piled inside, when I heard a scream coming from the museum that stopped me in my tracks. More screams joined that one, followed by loud grunts.

Connor grabbed me by the arm. "Come on. If you're wondering what that is, I smell zombie."

Chills racing up my spine, I let him lead me inside. Crystal closed the door behind us and secured all the locks.

Some spread the sleeping bags they brought with them in the main front room, saying they preferred that. Maybe because they would be closest to the front door we had barricaded? A couple of others like me, Connor, and Larry, checked out two bedrooms. We didn't want any surprises that night. Yes, demons can most likely teleport their way in, but I doubt the undead had those options or the brains to think of finding their way in. I hoped not.

Bubba took first watch and after a small dinner of canned food and water, everyone settled down for the night.

Connor, Larry, and I found a comfortable room. Larry floated over to the large dresser and lowered himself on the top of it, his eye toward the wall. Soon after, he snored.

Suddenly self-conscious, I fingered a strand of hair and sat down on the edge of the bed. I watched as Connor crossed over to the door, locked it, and came back. Not looking at him, I felt his weight press down into the mattress and the bedsprings squeak. I listened to the thuds of his boots hitting the rug-covered hardwood floor.

"Cat, it's okay. I'll sleep on one side of the bed, or I can stretch out on the floor. I'll even keep my clothes on."

I faced him. His eyes appeared larger and they glowed. With concern, and maybe something else? Something leaning toward lust?

I shifted, feeling something deep within my womb. There it was. Lust. I just hoped it was mutual on his side.

He asked, "Do you want me to find another room?"

I shook my head. "No, this is a king-sized bed. It should be big enough for both of us."

He smiled. "I wondered what might be wrong." He glanced over at the snoring Larry who still faced the wall. "You don't have any issues with Larry in here, do you?"

I teased, "Because Larry is an eyeball? Now, that doesn't mean he's not attractive, but I'm just not into eyeballs or demons even."

His grin grew wider. "Oh, but a werewolf is a different proposition?" He leaned his head over and kissed me. *Oh, yeah*. His lips hard and yet soft. Mmmmm...not bad at all.

He pushed me down and leaned over me, planting both hands on each side of my head, and kissed me again. Somehow, we ended up with our clothes scattered across the floor and both of us under the covers, doing much more than kissing.

Oh my, he found all my erogenous zones.

Werewolves were not bad in the sack.

Afterwards, we lay side-by-side in silence.

He stared up at the ceiling. "I haven't always been like this."

I sat up, drawing the sheet over my breasts. Silly since he had seen all of me in the most intimate way possible. "What do you mean?"

He looked at me. "A werewolf."

I didn't say anything but waited for him to go on.

He continued. "Back in high school, I was just a guy, a geek actually. Only human."

"A geek? You? Are you pulling my leg or something?"

"No, I'm not. Never cared much for sports, well, maybe baseball, but I never wanted to try out for it. I loved books; loved to read. Read them all the time. It bothered my older brother, so when he met this girl at a college frat party one night he set her up with me as my prom date."

He sat up, fluffed his pillow, and leaned back against it. I nodded to let him know to go on with his tale.

"Anyway, to make a long story short, she and I left the prom early and she convinced me to take her to this area where teenagers parked to make out. Only I found out she had no plans of making out with me, she wanted to eat me."

He must have seen my puzzled look.

"She was a werewolf. Somehow, I escaped her, surviving, but she still managed to bite me. I ended up in the hospital, but in a day, I healed with not a sign of a scratch or bite." He let out a breath. "I left town four weeks before high school graduation. I had to. From books on werewolves I read, I knew what I would become at the next full moon."

"Oh Connor, I'm sorry."

He reached out and tucked a strand of loose hair behind my ear. "What do you have to be sorry about?"

I had to know. "What happened to that female werewolf?"

His face hardened and his eyes turned dark. "I hunted her down and killed her."

I didn't know how to answer that.

He looked at me. "Cat, understand, I would never harm you. Do you believe me?"

I nodded, because I did. "I do."

He closed his eyes. I laid my head on his chest and held him close. Soon, Connor's breathing became rhythmic, and I knew he'd fallen asleep. I listened to his heartbeat until it lulled me to slumber not long after.

I woke up and stretched, and found I was alone in bed. I sat up and I didn't see the wallpapered walls or even Larry on the dresser nearby.

"Hello, sweet thing," said George, leaning against a wall and smoking a cigarette.

I screamed.

***

I never felt more uncomfortable than having George look me up and down, his gaze lingering on my intimate places. He snapped his fingers and I found myself dressed.

Bastard. Dirty-minded creep. Okay, he's a devil now, but for eons he'd been an angel, for goodness sakes. Aren't they supposed to not care about things like that? As if he had read my thoughts, he grinned and patted the right side of my face. I didn't care if he turned me into something or cut my head off with his sword, if he had patted my breasts instead, I would have slapped his smug face.

A television materialized out of nowhere, a horror movie showing on the screen. I looked at George. "How did you get electricity? And you want me to watch some zombie horror flick?"

An oily grin flitted over his mouth. "Oh, it's not a horror film. Take a closer look."

He snapped his fingers. The picture zoomed in. I peered at the multitude of glassy-eyed, drooling things everywhere. I even saw a couple of what had been dogs in life before the grayness got to them. Some gnashed their teeth, others pranced, and all of them keened a long howl. The sound grew deafening. The gray fog covered everything, even the building they surrounded.

I took a closer look. I gasped. "Oh no, that's the B&B." Zombies surrounded the building. The screen switched to a new view. I saw one of them inside with Connor. I looked away, closed my eyes, and covered my ears with my hands.

However, George wouldn't allow it, and grasped my hands with his, pulling them away. He whispered into my ear. "Don't you want to see what Connor is going to do with that ravenous zombie at his throat?"

I popped open my eyes. A zombie with a distorted and disfigured face had Connor trapped beneath it. The disgusting thing nuzzled his bared throat. It licked him there with a maggoty green tongue. Connor had his hands under its chest, trying in desperation to shove it away. It looked like zombie strength was besting werewolf power. Across the room and nailed to the wall, Larry hung upside down like a macabre picture.

"George, stop it. End all this madness." I stared into his eyes and his face blurred as tears welled up in my eyes. "You can, right?"

He laughed and loosened his hold on me. "Now why would I do that? Even if I could?"

"You're a devil now. I know I'm new to all this, but I do remember that part about devils making deals for souls."

He let go of me. Almost skipping over to a chair, he threw himself in it and, clasping his hands behind his head, smiled.

"Are you offering me yours?"

I climbed off the mattress and walked up to the smug SOB. My hands on the arm rests of the chair, I brought my face down to his. We touched nose-to-nose. "With conditions."

George rubbed his chin, looking thoughtful. "Mmm...conditions, huh? And what are these conditions?"

"Let Larry and Connor go free. Call off your zombie horde and send them someplace else to dine." I grabbed his hands, stopping him from rubbing that damn chin. "Leave the Earth, put everything back to right, and I'll go with you without any argument."

"You'd sell your immortal soul for the world? Go to Hell?"

"You think I'm not scared, that I have some big damn hero issues? Honestly, I'm scared shitless. But no matter how things have been on Earth, no one deserves what happened here. As for Connor—"

I slid to the floor. Tears ran down my cheeks. I'm not hero material, but last night Connor had made me feel that maybe, I might have a little hero inside me. He had a lot of hero in him. I'd began to care for him. Not sure if that meant love, but it just might be.

I thought I had loved Jeff, instead I realized too late, that it had been nothing more than a moment of lust disguised as love. Who knows? Maybe, in more normal circumstances, something could have grown between Connor and me. But with a zombie about to gnaw a hole in his neck, Larry hung up like a side of beef, George zapping in more undead into the hotel to feast on the survivors, and Earth in the middle of Armageddon, I had no other choice. For Connor, Larry, and all those people still alive in this horrible mess.

I scrubbed away the wet stains on my cheeks and stood. Hands clenched in fists, I thrust out my chin. "What do I have to do? Sign in blood?"

"Nothing that melodramatic—not like I'd offered last time. You really can't believe all that's written by mortals, especially the Bible. I can think of something much simpler to seal our bargain. Something that will be more enjoyable for both of us." George got out of the chair and held out a hand. I placed mine in his.

With a jerk, he tripped me, and I fell against him. Our lips locked and he kissed me, soft at first, rougher the next. It repulsed me. He began to nibble my lips, trailing from there down to my neck and bit. Something changed, and I felt wobbly, out of it. He drew away and I saw his eyes twinkling. *Twinkle, twinkle, little stars.*

I asked, my words slurred, "What did you do to me?"

"Sweetheart, there's still enough angel inside me to do that with my bite. Think of it as sorta like angel dust."

I swung out at him. "Bastard!" The room spun around like a merry-go-round out of control. George's voice filled my ears, growing heavier and slower, until it became ringing. I needed to lie down until everything calmed down. Instead, I did the next best thing.

I blacked out.

***

As I regained consciousness, a voice penetrated my brain, soft at first, then growing louder and louder. Still groggy, I opened my eyes, blinked a couple of times, and tried to sit up. Except I couldn't, it felt like something heavy sat or lay on top of my stomach. Glancing down, I saw something. It looked familiar.

"Larry?"

It stared back at me, its brown eye unblinking. *Brown eye*? *Wait a moment, Larry's is blue.* "Just who are you?" How stupid. If Larry could only create sounds, did I really think that this creature could speak? That it would say, "Hey, I'm Bozo", or something like that? Guess that made me the Bozo here.

"Gracie, get off the merchandise. I said watch her, not use her as a bench."

I veered my head toward the voice, which proved to be a big mistake. Waves of dizziness rolled through my head. When they subsided, I caught sight of George touching ground. His dark wings closed and settled against his back and vanished.

Dropping to one knee beside me, he grinned. "I see that you're awake. And I see that you've met Gracie. Sorry about Gracie, but she's great at guarding and really gets into her job. If you had tried to get away, let's just say, you'd been eyed to death."

I groaned. The damn eye hadn't left when George ordered her to go.

"Gracie, off," he commanded again.

The eye demon soared up like a helicopter into the air. It glided over to a nearby chair and lowered itself down onto the seat. George shrugged as he turned back to me, saying, "Lower cast demons. What can I say?"

"Where am I?" I stumbled over each word like an inebriated sailor. *Oh yeah, George's bite.*

George sat in a chair. "My place." He laughed. "Well, not really my place. That's in Hell. In a manner of speaking, I appropriated a whole building here, just for myself."

I sat up, being careful not to move too quickly, but realized my hands had been chained to the headboard. Like a dizzy girl could get up and run away. I waited until the sparkling dots dancing in my vision dissipated before I looked around the room.

I said, "Where..."

"...are you? You're in one of the bedrooms in the Governor's Mansion."

The bastard had taken over the Governor's Mansion? How dare he! Not caring about the waves of dizziness that might result if I moved and forgetting that I was chained up like a pet dog; I tried to swing my legs off the bed. The chain yanked me back on the mattress, this time I laid at the edge of the mattress, lopsided, my legs hanging off the bed.

When my world stopped tilting again, I glared at the snickering dark angel who leaped to his feet. "How dare you? Add in stealing the Governor's Mansion, what you did to me and my friends, and causing the apocalypse, I'm going to kick your demonic butt."

George grabbed my arms, suddenly serious. "This does not belong to your Commonwealth anymore. Remember, Virginia, the United States, and Earth are no longer humanity's world." His fingers bit deep into my flesh.

"You son of a bitch!" I cried out.

His eyes transformed from blue to black as coal. His fingernails grew into claws that cut, making me bleed.

"You're my prisoner, mortal bitch, and I can do what I want. If you want to quibble about who this place belongs to now, I'll just throw your sorry ass back outside and right into the midst of some hungry, undead former citizens of your state. After all, you're not that special. Your soul is the same as the next mortal's. I actually think it would be amusing to watch you being torn apart and devoured."

I squirmed and tried to look away.

George snarled, "Don't you dare look away!"

I stared at him. Not one shred of the angel remained in him. He no longer pussy footed around. The evil rose off him like a rancid stink. He let his demon out, pure and simple. My stomach roiled as coldness filled me

He let go of me. I had to get out of here and get back somehow, someway, to the others.

George said, "Gracie, I'm going out. Watch our...guest, and make sure she doesn't find a way to get her chains off and escape. Although, I doubt she'll be able to do that."

He blinked out of the room. The eye demon flew off the chair, growling like a rabid dog. It wasn't big, or had arms or legs, but something told me that this little imp could do a lot of damage. It coasted toward me, slow and steady, taking its time.

I tugged at and jiggled the chains. Nothing. Tied tighter than a junkyard dog. For the first time as Gracie drew closer, I noticed the redness in her sclera. *There are no eye drops in Hell.*

Gracie had gotten almost eye level with me. I shimmied backwards, drawing my legs onto the bed, until I pressed against the headboard. If eye demons could smile, I imagined that Gracie wore a big shit-eating grin. She made for me like a bullet shot out of a rifle. I tried to leap up onto my feet on the bed, tangling with the chains, and that's when it happened. The chains broke. How, I didn't care. Only one thing mattered. Freedom to get the hell out of there, like all the devils of Hell pursued me. Or, one of them anyway.

I rolled off the bed and made tracks for the closed bedroom door. Behind me the air whooshed. And whirling around I saw the malevolence in Gracie's eye. She meant to tear me limb from limb. Yeah, she didn't have hands or teeth, but I didn't plan to find out how she would have accomplished that. I grabbed the doorknob. The door hadn't been locked and I flung it open, scrambling outside and slamming it shut behind me. My hands on the wood and breathing hard, I waited. Nothing from the other side. I giggled.

It didn't have hands. No way to open that door. Score one for me.

My breath caught as something passed through the wood like a ghost. Shadowy, in a definite round shape, it hovered in the hallway. Gracie! I almost pissed my pants. *Shit. Larry never did that. Why hadn't he ever done that?*

Larry needed to show me everything he could do so the next time I ran into another eye demon, I'd know what to expect. That's if I ever got out of here alive. I bolted. I found the stairs, clattered down the steps, and sailed across the downstairs floor to freedom. I threw open the front door (thank God, not locked either), and I zipped outside. The door remained wide open, but did I care? That demon could pass through solid objects. My life hung in the balance.

The gray mist didn't bother me. As before, it kept its distance. I didn't care. Beating feet, I sneaked a peak over my shoulder and saw Larry's evil twin still hot on my trail.

I stumbled over rocks and broken pavement, almost rammed into abandoned cars, and worried about running into the clutches of something even worse than Gracie. Tears burned my eyes, my sides ached, but I kept going.

"STOP!"

I skidded to a stop. Something slammed into my back. I screamed and spun around.

I saw Gracie on the ground. She began to quiver like a demented bowl of jelly. Was the damn fiend scared? Great, if something frightened her, then that meant nothing but trouble for me.

Out of nowhere, a glowing ball about my size appeared and moved in front of the eye demon. The glow grew blindingly bright. Hotter, too, as waves of heat radiated from it. It darted over Gracie before she could have escaped. The glare flared a brilliant platinum, that I felt like I stared into the sun. I closed my eyes. An awful squealing like a pig being butchered reached my ears. In mid squeal—nothing, and I opened my eyes. The object drifted mere inches in front of me and its radiance made me shut my eyes. I said, "Well, go ahead. Eat me, dissolve me; however, you'll kill someone like me."

"I am not going to eat you. Yuck."

Where have I heard that voice before? I opened my eyes and saw that it's toned down its light to something my sight could handle.

"Cat? Are you, all right?"

Oh, God. . .

The light winced, at least it seemed that way. "Please, don't even think the name of God in vain."

"Lisa? Is that you?" I touched it. My hand passed through and tingled in a pleasant manner. No dissolving flesh or anything close.

She bobbed. "Of course, it's me, silly."

I asked, "Does this mean Heaven is going to step in finally?"

"No. I'm just the scout sent ahead." She covered me and I felt warm and safe. "I can take you back to your friends."

"How—"

Within seconds, we soared over Richmond. My stomach dropped to my toes as I stared down at the grayness covering the buildings, and streets, and freeways below. I never had been much for traveling by plane, not with my fear of heights. But when you traveled by plane, you did it inside a solid material contraption. *Now, only insubstantial light stood between me and a terrifying drop to death.*

"I am not insubstantial, you know."

I forgot she could hear my thoughts. "I'm sorry, but what you are, isn't solid. Not how I think of density anyway."

Lisa eluded a flying imp. "Human perspectives. I'm not made from photons, but from goodness, remember?"

The imp made a turnabout and arrowed for us. Lisa shot out a thin wall of herself and the demon flew right smack into it. The wall sparked like a bug light and obliterated it. A slight breeze appeared out of nowhere and caught the ash, tossing and scattering it in all directions.

Just as suddenly as Lisa had taken off with me, she had me back in the building where I had spent the night with Connor and the others. She dumped me right dab in the middle of a battle in the main room. From one side of the room Crystal and four others shot at a crowd of zombies. The bullets didn't hurt the undead, and they kept on coming. It looked like zombies: ten, humans: zero until Lisa touched each zombie, liquefying them before our eyes. If she had a face, I would have kissed her.

Jim swung his weapon at Lisa. "What the hell is that thing? If it can take out those zombies like that, I don't want it near me."

I leaped in front of Lisa. "Hold on. Lisa's my friend."

Jim kept his gun on us both. "Damn you, girl, you're human. Why can't you have human buddies like the rest of us? It's just not natural. What's next? Group hugs with zombies?"

Hands on my hips, I said, "Are you joking? Hug a zombie and you'll get your face bitten off. Lisa is the Light of Goodness. She's from Heaven."

Lisa bobbed. "I have been sent to see what is happening so far."

A suspicious look crossed over Jim's face. He didn't lower his rifle. "So, you're some Heavenly intervention sent to save us?"

"I'm good, but not that good. No, I can't stop all this horror and put things to right. That takes a higher power."

"Well, I'm not putting down this rifle either."

Crystal tapped Jim on the shoulder. "Jim, lay down your rifle. Please." He did as she asked but kept it at his side. Crystal gestured at a table and chairs nearby. "Have a seat, Cat," she said.

It appeared that the dead hadn't destroyed everything. I threw myself into a chair. Groaning, I felt every little bit of ache in my muscles and bones. Crystal sat opposite of me.

I asked, "What happened to most of the others, Crystal? I only see a few of you."

"They're dead."

Oh, dear God! Did that include... "Connor and Larry?"

"My opinion, good riddance to any inhuman thing," growled Jim as he stomped over to the other side of the room. No doubt he included me in the inhuman equation.

Crystal shook her head. "With those creatures attacking, we didn't have time to worry about them or you either."

"I understand. It's a kill or be killed world these days."

Crystal pointed at Lisa. "What about...what did you call it?"

Lisa moved over to Crystal, her pale glow now a shimmering crimson. Guess she could get angry too. "I am Lisa. Cat named me. I am the Light of Heavenly Goodness. The Archangel Michael sent me to check out what was happening on Earth. He's getting itchy wings, wants to come down here with his guys and kick some demon booty, but the big G is holding a tight rein on him. I have to report on what is left of humanity and make a decision if their souls are worth saving."

Crystal jumped to her feet, sending her chair crashing to the floor with a loud bang. "What you're saying is that God won't step in? That he has you casing us out?"

I stood. "George is right? This is all about a bet? Let's see how the mortals react?"

"Sorry, Cat," said Lisa. "I hate to say it, but yeah, George told the truth. Believe me, it doesn't make me happy either."

A nasty smell wafted over to us. I twirled around and saw that George had appeared. Next to him stood a big demon that looked like I imagined a troll would look like. It detained a struggling furry creature. Connor! George held a leash attached to a metal collar around Larry who looked ashamed.

Connor bit his captor's arm, and it yowled, releasing him. He loped over to me and Crystal. He stood on his hind legs, ferocious with teeth bared, ready to rip apart anything that dared come near us.

One of the men cocked his weapon, ran forward, and prepared to shoot, but George shook a finger at him. With horror, I watched as the man's rifle exploded in his face and blew off his head. The body lurched, spraying blood, before it hit the floor.

Moving away, distaste evident on his face and dragging Larry with him, George stalked over to a part of the wall and leaned against it. "Does this mean that Heaven is finally ready to poke its nose in the fracas?"

Lisa retorted, "No. I've been sent here to check out the situation."

Spying a chair, George grabbed it and whipped it around. He tied Larry's leash to it. Swinging a leg over, he sat down, his hands hanging over the back, and stared at me with resignation. "Now, do you see why I defected? I mean, why aren't they stepping in and putting a stop to Hell's takeover? No, they send this measly shade of a lamp to find out how humanity is doing. The Big G is more interested in a bet with Lucifer, then how his children, who he claims to love so much, are suffering."

Lisa glowed red. "Excuse me, I am not some measly shade of a lamp! I am the Light of Goodness, you misbegotten winged frou-frou. And yes, Heaven is concerned. They just don't want to march right in and maybe cause the destruction of the rest of this world."

"Sure, sure. And I'm just your basic good guy. Not."

Lisa darted over to me. "Don't listen to the whiney brat there, Cat. To show the good faith of Heaven, I am joining your side." The red glow morphed to a bright white. "Let's kick some...what do you humans say—"

I coughed, clearing my throat. "Demon ass."

"What?"

I said it louder, feeling heat on my cheeks and the back of my neck. "Ass. Demon ass."

Her glow flickered. "That's it—I'm going to kick some demon donkey. Okay, let's start with this jackass." She bulleted straight for George. "Come on, let's see what you got, sulfur breath."

Disbelief in his eyes, George rose to his feet and booted the chair away. Both the chair and poor Larry struck the wall. The chair splintered and Larry slid down the wall to the floor, dazed.

"Did you call me sulfur breath, light bright?"

She skidded to a stop and guffawed. "If the smell is obvious...Enough of this name calling, let's get down and dirty. For me that might be hard, but I'll do what I must do. For you, it should be as simple as a walk in the park."

With a roar, George charged her. He got inside her, but he couldn't get completely out of her. Kicking and thrashing, his yelling muffled, the Light of Goodness zipped up into the air. They both disappeared as they faded through the ceiling.

The humans pointed their weapons at George's buddy who was left behind. Snarling, it retreated until it couldn't go any further, as the wall stopped it. Even though it tried, it appeared to have a problem passing through the drywall. The fiend saw the hapless Larry lying on his side nearby and it inched over to him, slow and deliberate.

Before anyone could shoot, it dived for Larry, grabbed him, and used him as a shield.

It threatened, "I got me a hostage, and I will damage it."

Jim snorted, then laughed. "And that will stop me from shooting? In my opinion, that will give us two less worries in the universe."

A single, big tear fell from Larry.

CHAPTER 14

Troll boy looked confused. "But he's one of yours."

Jim raised his gun and sighted it at both entities. The troll demon dropped Larry and tried to bolt, by staying close to the wall. Larry rolled over to Connor, who changed to human form and worked at freeing his friend from the collar. I went to help. Both of us removed the chain but couldn't release the collar. Screeching, Larry rocketed after the other denizen of Hell and smashed into it.

"Two for one sounds pretty good to me," said Jim, as he aimed.

Connor tackled Jim and the gun went off, the bullet hitting the wall and missing the battling hellions by a few inches. After he snatched the gun from Jim, he tossed it to me. I fumbled the catch, and the gun fell to the floor. Lucky for me and the others, it didn't go off. I picked it up. Connor altered back to the wolf and rushed the troll, knocking Larry aside. Connor began to power punch it, but it karate flexed out a leg and sent him flying through the room to slam into me. Both of us struck the floor and the back of my head bounced off it. I saw glittering stars.

Connor leaped off me to go for the hell beast again. Anguished screams cleaved the air, and I blinked and tried to focus. I got off the floorboards, shaky, bruised, and feeling sick, my head throbbing.

The devil shouted, as it tried to hold onto a thrashing shapeshifter while also clashing with Larry. Finally, it threw the werewolf my way again, but I dodged, and Connor smacked the floor snout first, but he picked himself up. The demon hopped around on one leg, spewing obscenities.

I asked, "What happened?"

Crystal replied, "I think Larry did something to its leg. I would say he bit it, but he has no mouth."

Larry helicoptered off the floor, flying at his antagonist again. He circled the ugly's head. A chain appeared. I assumed Larry could do magic like other demons, but this was the first time I'd seen him do something like this.

The chain snaked around the other's neck several times, until the chain covered its neck and the bottom of the entity's face. Larry zipped away, bringing the end of the chain with him, too. The evil creature struggled as it choked, not able to breathe. Did they even breathe oxygen?

It must, at least while here in the mortal realm. Its puke green face became a vivid shade of hot pink, the color deepening as the chain pulled taut.

Fury shone red in his eyes as Connor lowered his head like a charging bull, T-boning the demon right in the middle and sending it into the wall. The wall cracked on impact and as the monster worked to rise, Connor sank his fangs into the bad boy's stomach. Unable to watch, I covered my eyes. Horrible sounds wafted over to me, but I refused to sneak a peek.

Curiosity got the better of me. I took my hands away. No longer a werewolf, but human once more, Connor bent over and gagged from green slime covering his mouth and face. Larry dropped to the floor, exhausted. The troll sat propped up against the wall, lifeless. A hole in its middle and the chain wrapped around its neck, it stunk worse than when it had been alive. Connor stopped retching and backed away from the body, wiping the gross stuff off his mouth. Suddenly, the body dissipated and became black smoke that faded away.

Jim walked over and looked down at Larry, a small saw in his hand.

I called out. "No, Larry just risked his life for us. He saved our butts."

Looking irritated, he replied, "Hell no, I'm not going to kill the critter. I'm gonna free the little bugger from this collar."

He dropped to his knees and began to cut away at the metal. Larry lay there, quiet as Jim sawed gently at the collar. The collar came undone and dropped to the floor with a loud clang. Larry rushed over to me, and I hugged him.

David led Connor out of the room. The man came back alone minutes later. Crystal had a woman, Jen, plus David, picked up and throw away the broken chair, while the rest of us went to pack up our stuff. No one said anything, but we all sensed we wouldn't be staying here.

A half hour later, Connor walked into the room, dressed and cleaned up, his hair damp. He grinned as he headed over to me.

"Damn, feels good to get what's left of the demon blood out of my stomach. I had to rinse the taste out of my mouth. Several times." He wrinkled his face. "I still have an unpleasant aftertaste."

Crystal gathered the rest of us together. "We're going to have to leave this place, try and make it to Carytown. I don't know about you and your friends, Cat, but I lost enough people this day to monsters. I don't want to lose anyone else."

Glancing down at Larry and seeing him nod, then Connor, too, I said, "Larry, Connor, and I will go with you."

"Listen up, everyone, gather everything you can carry, and let's get this show on the road as soon as Connor and Jim get back from putting the dead in another room."

They deposited those who had died in a room in another part of the building and locked the door. If any of them rose from the dead, the locked door would keep them secure long enough until hopefully we had gotten far enough away.

Sneaking a peek out the door, Crystal motioned with a hand and said, "The coast looks clear. For now, anyway."

She stepped outside and we followed out single file. Gray fog enveloped the area like pea soup, but drew away from us like we were infected with plague. I tightened my grip on my rifle, suspecting either George had escaped or destroyed Lisa.

We crossed Boulevard and turned left, trudging along the sidewalk, keeping our eyes open for anything dangerous. On occasion, wild laughter erupted or eerie howls escaped from buildings we passed. It made us pick up the pace. Otherwise, our surroundings mirrored a graveyard on Sunday morning. Where are the mobs of zombies with drool dripping out of their mouths? Here were some humans, plus a werewolf and a demon for goodness sakes, and we didn't look like takeout food?

Every part of me hurt and I was running out of energy. Connor's hand stole into mine and he smiled. That encouraged me to keep going.

We reached the corner of Cary and Boulevard and turned right. Good. That made our destination closer. A few blocks later without mishap, we stopped in front of the World of Mirth toy store in Carytown. A dirty flyer about the Carytown Watermelon Festival held every August skittered along the sidewalk. It merged with the ever-present fog, vanishing. Inside one of the store's windows, I stared at a forlorn teddy bear sitting in a red rocking chair.

Crystal allowed us to take a breather, although she had Jim and Connor stationed with rifles at ready.

I never saw Carytown look so empty of life. No people strolling in lively conversation along the sidewalks nor the usual stream of cars rolling down the street. All of that missing hit me like a punch in the gut.

I sat on the edge of the curb and flexed my sore feet. Crystal plunked down next to me, and we rested for a few precious seconds. All too soon, she got up and extended a hand. I sighed and let her help me stand.

Crystal said, "Jim, David, you two go search each building, knocking and rattling the doors. I'm not sure where this other group might be hiding. I'm not sure if they're still alive even."

I looked down and saw Larry staring up at me. I flashed him a weak grin. "I'm okay, Larry. Guess I'm just tired and even a little worried." He whined. "Well, okay, maybe worrying a lot."

Connor came over and wrapped an arm around my shoulders.

"Don't worry, Cat. Things will turn out fine. You'll see."

"I wished life could go back to the way it'd been before all this. I'll never bitch about my life again." When I realized what I said and how Connor might take it wrong, I added, "But not about you or—I glanced at Larry— Larry. You both are the only good things about this mess."

Jim and David returned. They shook their heads at Crystal. Connor moved away, his hand giving me one last caress. He stopped in front of an Indian restaurant two blocks away. Jim followed him and joined him there.

Crystal stared off into space, her eyebrows knitted together like one long line. Not looking at me, she said, "I'm tired. Sometimes I just want to lie down on the sidewalk here and let one of those demons get me. Get it over with. You know?"

I nodded, even though I knew she didn't see it. "I know what you're talking about. It seems that everything is falling apart and no matter what we do, nothing helps."

Tears in her eyes, she turned to me. "All this for a bet between Heaven and Hell? Why? Did we do something stupid? Piss off God?"

I held out my arms and she fell into them, crying. It seemed situations like this can make bedfellows of the most unlikely people. A thousand years ago, before the vortex opened over Richmond, Crystal and I would have never met. Oh, we might have seen each other as we strolled past each other at the mall or at some event, but we would have not gone up to each other and introduced ourselves. Both of us were far different to be friends of that Richmond from that once upon a time. Now, with not too many human beings left in the world, we had to become friends. Humans against demons and other supernatural creatures. Who thought that we would become a minority on our own planet?

Crystal pulled away, wiping her eyes with the back of her hand. "Sorry. I don't know what came over me."

I gave her a smile. "Stress. A human being can only take so much before breaking down. And that's normal stress, not the end of the world kind we're facing here."

"Hey, guess what?" said Jim, excited. "Connor and I found those people we're looking for. They'd been hiding out in an Indian restaurant."

Jim told us on the way that they saw someone come out through the back door after a teenager digging in the trash, and once they got the man's attention, told him about their group. He led us to the building, where Connor waited. He opened a door and everyone piled inside. I watched as a tall man wrenched a curtain across and boosted a table against the door. Looking around, I noticed the boarded-up windows.

"I'm Terry," acknowledged the man. He took us to the back where seven people sat around a table, eating and drinking tea. Only an overweight man with a dark cocoa skin tone sat alone eating at the counter by the stove. He never looked up.

"Here they are, Jefferson," said Terry who joined the others, accepting a cup of tea.

Crystal stepped forward and stuck out her hand. "Hi, I'm Crystal Henning." Jefferson ignored her hand and kept eating, so she dropped it and spoke to the others. "The others with me are Jim, David, Jen, Cat, Connor, and the eyeball is Larry."

A skinny kid with a bad case of acne who looked about sixteen and wore a sweatshirt and pants so big that several teenagers could live in them, got to his feet and ambled over to Larry. He sniffed and wiped his nose with the back of his hand. Using that same hand, he poked at the eyeball. "Hey, that's like one of those things that has been hassling us. Cool. It feels squishy and stuff."

Larry chattered like a monkey at him and came over to nestle against my side.

The teenager narrowed his watery blue eyes. "Hey, why'd it done that? I called it cool."

Connor retorted, "Would you like a stranger poking you? And his name is Larry."

"I didn't poke it," the boy grumbled, and he thumped back down, mumbling, "Such a faggot name. Nothing scary about Larry."

Jefferson said, "I don't think bringing that creature in here is a good idea. We've managed to keep a low profile and keep any of the monstrosities outside from getting in." He glared at Crystal. "If our teenage idiot here hadn't decided he wanted to dig in the trash out back for his useless I-Pod we threw away, you'd never have found us." He glared at the teen. "Right, Ruff?" The boy lowered his head between his shoulders like a turtle tucking into his shell. He studied his plate like it was the most interesting object in the world.

I noticed the useless I-Pod, once a clean shiny blue, but now nothing more than a filthy piece of junk. Ruff grabbed it off the table and stuffed it into his pants pocket.

Crystal cleared her throat. "That's good and all, about hiding out, but we've lost a lot of people. As you can see there's only a handful of us left. We can be useful." She placed a hand down on the counter next to the stove, next to the big man's plate and stared into his eyes. "Even Larry. We will all work hard. I think joining forces would be smart, don't you?"

The man lumbered away from her. He motioned for us to come with him to the front of the building. Pulling out a chair from a banquet-sized table he sat down and clicked on the LED candle on the cracked linoleum top. It barely let out much light. "Take a seat."

We grabbed chairs and seated ourselves. Crystal planted herself to his left. The man rolled his shoulders. "Name's Jefferson Poke."

Crystal stared at him. "Like I said earlier, I'm Crystal." She pointed to me, "Cat." She jerked a thumb at each person, naming them. "And I introduced everyone to your people and you earlier."

Larry had settled on the table opposite Jefferson, who ignored him and opened a dialogue with us. We talked for an hour, answering his questions and asking our own. Jefferson agreed to let us stay. Shadows of night found cracks through the boards over the windows and slipped in like unwelcome visitors. The anemic candle flame couldn't push back the gloom.

Jefferson stood, pushing back his chair. "Let's head back into the kitchen. I can offer you something to eat."

An old woman with straggly, gray hair and wearing big glasses rushed up to him, yelling, "That stupid kid has gone and done it again! He sneaked outside again and left the damn door wide open. Lucky for us, nothing got in. We closed it and locked it, but Ruff's still out there."

Jefferson admonished her and told her to lower her voice. He stomped back to the kitchen and growled. "Stupid brat. I swear I'll wring his scrawny neck when I get my hands on him!"

We all heard a howl, long and loud that startled everyone. Jefferson may not get the pleasure of wringing Ruff's neck. Something else just might do that for Jefferson besides doing other horrors to the kid, too.

Jefferson squeezed through the doorway into the kitchen and headed straight to the back door. He grabbed the knob and looking over his shoulder, he called to Mildred. "Key? Damn it, the key, Mildred."

"Oh, yeah." She dug into the big pocket of the apron she wore over her faded, red checkered dress. Key tight in her grip, she stared at Jefferson with a half frightened, half bewildered look. "You're going to open that door and go searching for that stupid kid? Maybe let in whatever is out there that's making that howling noise?"

"Yes. We can't leave him out there."

Mildred handed over the key. "Maybe the little shit has some smarts and is waiting outside the door." She shrugged. "To be honest, I doubt it."

Jefferson unlocked the door. It swung open with a loud creak. Outside the dark held presence. Malignant, it waited for us to venture outside like a stranger with candy and bad intentions. The chilly night slipped in, and I shivered from its touch. Connor offered to be the first to go outside and search. I caught his arm to stop him, whispering, "No."

Jefferson shook his head. "I can't let you do that alone. The kid's my responsibility."

"No, Jefferson, let me go first." Connor walked out.

I spied some knives hanging along the wall above the sink, and snatching one, I walked outdoors with Larry but waited by the open doorway for Jefferson.

He handed the key to Mildred and said, "Mildred, close the door. But don't lock it."

"Don't lock it?"

"Mildred..."

"Oh, right."

Almost holding his breath, he tiptoed through the doorway. Once he did, she slammed the door.

Jefferson withdrew a long, white candle and a cigarette lighter out of a pocket. He thumbed the lighter once, twice, and a flame flickered, before he touched the tiny fire to the taper's wick to set it alight. The light hardly pierced the gray hell fog that smothered the night. The howling came again to the right of us. The gray crap made everything confusing and frightening. Jefferson took a step forward.

Connor grabbed him by the arm, stopping him. "Let me."

"Why you?"

"Believe me. I'm better equipped for this. You might say... I'm more experienced, if nothing else." Connor faded into the night, no longer in sight.

Larry wanted to go after him. I whispered, "No, Larry, stay with me." He relented and remained at my side.

"How much more experienced than any of us could that guy be?" asked Jefferson.

I didn't look at him. "More than you could imagine."

"I can visualize a lot of things. There's something you're hiding about him. Something about him doesn't add up. Tell me."

I wondered if I should reveal Connor's secret or make something up. If things were normal Jefferson wouldn't believe that Connor wasn't anything more than an ordinary man. Now with the apocalypse, werewolves joined the side of believable these days.

I shoved my hands into my jeans pockets, cleared my throat and opened my mouth. "Connor's a werewolf."

He laughed. Not loud, but a whisper, as if he remembered in time where we were. "Werewolf? Like in those horror movies?"

"Is that so hard to believe after the things I know you've seen? You met Larry. Then there's that vortex."

"But—a werewolf?" I heard him sigh. "Yeah, you're right. I've seen things. I've seen my friends changed by this gray shit and become dead that want to eat you. Why not a werewolf? Did he come from that vortex?"

"Not initially. It appeared over his apartment building six months ago, in California, and vacuumed him up during the full moon. Connor kept his werewolf form until it sucked me up and we, plus Larry, escaped." Larry pressed against me. "Larry's a good demon. Yeah, yeah, I know, are there good demons? But seems Larry is all that, and more."

Howling broke our conversation; seconds later, another howl, obviously from a different creature.

Connor.

"Is that—?"

"Connor? Yes."

From the growling we heard, it let me know that Connor had taken on the other creature. I gripped my butcher knife tightly and took off without a thought. Larry kept pace with me. Jefferson yelled after me to stop, but I paid him no mind. Connor might need help.

Instead, I became lost. In fact, I lost Larry, too. I skidded to a stop. The snarling sounded close by, but I couldn't see in the darkened grayness. Suddenly, a dim, ghostly light surrounded them. I recognized Connor pinned to the ground, as the other one had yellow eyes and it had its jaws clamped down on his throat.

I reacted and darted over, thrusting my knife into back of the other werewolf's head. It let go of Connor and reared up, screaming. Connor rolled over onto his stomach and leaped to his feet, shifting back to human form. He grabbed my hand.

"Come on. Seems that knife must be made of silver. The screaming will bring other things here."

"Silver? The butcher knife? And the werewolf was a guy?" I asked. "What about Ruff?"

"I couldn't find him. The werewolf jumped me. Enough chit chat, company's coming."

His werewolf hearing. Of course. Connor spied his clothing and swiped them off the ground; we fled, and I fought to keep up with him. Out of nowhere appeared Larry, who kept up with us. A tiny beam of light burned away some of the mist and as we drew closer, I saw it came from Jefferson's candle. He had hold of Ruff. The bad boy had come home. We skidded to a halt in front of them. I took the candle from Jefferson and extinguished the flame.

Jefferson said, "Why the hell aren't you dressed, Connor?"

Connor tried the door and found it locked. "No time to talk. The werewolf is dead, but God knows what else is coming. And the damn door is locked!"

"What do you mean, locked? I told Mildred—"

Horrible sounds echoed all around us. Jefferson's eyes widened and he pounded at the door, yelling, "Mildred! Open the damn door! I told you not to lock it."

We heard the clicking of the lock and the door swung open. and we all tumbled inside. Larry hurried past us into the kitchen. He managed to nudge open a cabinet door and ducked inside, the door banging shut behind him. Connor pushed a frightened Mildred to one side, kicked the door shut, and secured it. Something slammed into the door on the outside, followed by an eruption of heavy pummeling. Heart pounding, I prayed that it would hold as exhausted, I slumped to the floor. Jefferson dropped into a chair. Connor put on his clothes when he saw Mildred looking him up and down. The others rushed into the kitchen.

Ruff giggled. It didn't sound normal. We stared at him.

I noticed the unnatural pallor of his face and hands for the first time. He had looked pale earlier, but not as bloodless as he appeared now. His watery blue eyes glowed red and he sneered, revealing jagged teeth. *No, not normal at all.*

"I got your attention. Good." He raked a hand through dirty hair. "I'm hungry."

A young woman not much older than him took a step closer. She hesitated. "Hungry for what, Ruff? What's wrong with you? You don't look too—"

Before anyone could stop him, he seized her and drew her against his scrawny chest. He lowered his head and sniffed at her neck, saliva dripping from his mouth. He whispered, "They thought they kept the monsters outside, but there's one already inside, Zoey. And I'm not talking about the eyeball either. Your blood will do just fine for my first kill."

She wailed and struggled but couldn't fight free. Jefferson and Connor approached, but Ruff hissed at them. He moved away from the wall.

"Keep away. Or I snap her neck. Plus, I'll get to that locked door and let in creatures worse than me inside."

He clutched Zoey tighter to him and crooned to her. "When I was alive, you wouldn't give anything to me, not even the time of day. Now, I'll just take it. Take your blood."

No one moved, as we watched in horror. He levitated to the ceiling out of our reach, the screaming, struggling girl held tight to his chest, and he opened his mouth and jabbed his sharp fangs into her neck. Her screams rose in pitch, as he sucked until he drained her dry. Wiping his mouth on a sleeve, he dropped the husk. Another woman cried out when it almost hit her.

"What happened out there, Ruff?" said Jefferson.

Ruff's eyes glowed. "No one here ever paid the slightest attention to me. Why'd you think I caused all that trouble for you? My parents were the same. Until I trapped them into the room with one of those zombies I lured in. I listened to their screams. No more Mommy and Daddy." He dropped back down to the floor and headed towards the table. He chortled. "This voice talked in my head, telling me to sneak outside. I met this goat-like freak, a real, nasty type. He said if I sold my soul to him, he'd make me into something powerful. I said okay, he slashed my wrists, and I signed my name on a piece of paper with the blood from the cuts. Right afterwards, he jabbed his nails into my neck. My blood bled out and my life with it. I woke up, and well, here I am, a vampire. Isn't that cool? No black cape and funky accent, but hey, still a vampire."

I whispered to Connor. "You never said anything about vampires."

"I always thought them to be nothing more than myths."

"You're a werewolf! Until the apocalypse, I believed shapeshifters were nothing more than a fairytale and you are telling me that you didn't believe in vampires?"

"I saw demons drinking blood when I was stuck in Hell, but they weren't vampires."

I nodded in the direction of the Millennial Dracula. "I would say he's very real."

Ruff said, "Who's next? I'm still hungry." He licked his stained lips.

CHAPTER 15

No one answered. No one approached him to volunteer, either. I didn't blame them, as I had no plans to offer donation of my blood, either.

Ruff lurked nearer, impatient. He growled. "Come on, choose someone, anyone. Or I will."

He leaped at another woman, one that came from our group. Jen screamed and tried to get away but tripped and fell. Her face ashen and her eyes round as saucers, she stared up at Ruff as he loomed over her. Connor snatched one of the wooden chairs nearby, broke off a leg, and pitched it at Ruff's back. The makeshift stake bounced off the vampire's back and splintered when it hit the stove. Wiley Ruff bolted for the door, scattering the rest of us. He cackled like a hag from some badly done B-horror flick and announced, "You missed," as he wrenched the door off its hinges and burst into the night. Useless, the door teetered and whammed to the floor. The grayness remained outside, but scraggly fingers of it wormed along the edges of the doorjamb as if to taunt us.

"Quick, help me get the door back up!" shouted Jefferson, scurrying.

Jim helped him prop it up against the opening. The woman who Ruff had tried to snatch earlier flashed past the husk of the dead girl to the pantry at the other end of the room. She searched inside, tossing things aside.

Her arms jammed full, she hurried back to Jefferson. "Here's a hammer, boxes of nails and screws, and some screwdrivers," she said. "Except for the hammer, I didn't know what size you needed, so I grabbed what I could find."

"Hand it over to Jim," ordered Jefferson.

We all retreated into the dining room while Jim and Jefferson worked. They remounted the hinges and rehung the door as quickly as they could. Once the door had been secured, Jefferson locked it and barricaded us inside. He leaned against the wall, taking a couple of minutes to get his breath while wiping sweat from his brow. Lines furrowed his forehead, and he unlocked the door.

Jefferson said, "I need a couple of guys to take that body outside and toss it in the trash bin out back.

"You can't throw Zoey out like yesterday's garbage," declared Mildred.

"We don't have time to find some ground to bury her. It's not safe to attempt a burial. We all liked the girl, but we can't afford to lose any more people."

Connor nodded. "Jefferson's right and she might rise from the dead if we don't do one more thing before we take Zoey's body out."

He snapped off another leg of the chair and crossed over to her. Kneeling beside her, he jammed it through her chest and the bones beneath, exactly where her heart would be. I flinched at the sound of his werewolf-powered punch sending the wood into her.

Connor bowed his head and said, "I'm sorry, Zoey."

Jefferson unlocked the door. Connor and Jim gathered up her body and carried it outside. Seconds later, they returned, and Jefferson threw all the locks on the door.

Jefferson said, "Everybody, back to the main dining room. We need to figure out the guard duty schedule. I need people for shifts tonight."

I signed up to take watch at two o'clock in the morning with someone from the other group. Jefferson offered food, but after the vampire incident, I'd lost my appetite and wanted only sleep. I said goodnight to Connor and Larry, plus the others, and laid down on the dining room floor, wrapping a blanket around my body and closing my eyes. I hadn't slept long when someone shook my shoulder.

"Hey, it's your watch," mumbled a sleepy male voice. I looked up with one eye and saw it was David from our group. He handed over his weapon and after mouthing, "'Night", I handed him the blanket and watched him totter off to catch some sleep elsewhere.

I got my sorry butt up, rubbed my sleep-dusted eyes, and stumbled into the kitchen. One of the men from Jefferson's group, Carl, sat in his chair tipped back against the wall, and held his rifle like his favorite girl across his lap as he smoked a cigar. The smoke made his face a variation of shadows as it circled around his head like a wreath. I propped my rifle carefully against the wall.

Carl fished the cigar from between his lips and derided, "Looks like someone ain't used to doing this."

I didn't like his smart-ass remark, but didn't answer, just thumped down in a chair across from him. He kept snickering.

"I admit to being human," I said. "Yes, I'm tired, but I can hack being on guard duty, same as you."

The heavy odor of his cigar smoke churned my stomach. A headache pounded in my head like a dozen little men using pickaxes on my brain. I couldn't stop the groan that escaped from my lips, and I clenched my eyes shut as the pain worsened. What I wouldn't give for a couple of aspirins and a glass of water. Or if nothing else, shooting those damn little men mining my brain.

"Hey."

I lifted my head and opened my eyes to find Carl standing over me. He held a glass of water in one hand, and his rifle underneath his armpit. A couple of painkillers nestled in the cupped palm of his other hand. I noticed his cigar bathing in a half-filled glass of water on the sink counter.

Nicking the pills, I chased them down with the water. "Thanks," I said, as I handed him the empty glass.

He set the glass on the counter. "Don't mention it. Besides, I can't have my watch partner out of it."

I leaned forward. "Until my group got here, you never met me before, and here, you're acting like you don't care for me. Why?"

He slid into his chair. "Not care for you? Now why would you think that?" He scratched the scalp under his thinning hair. "Cause you're nothing but trouble. One of the men from your own group, Jim, told me what already happened before you, your group, and your monster buddies came into our lives."

I told him a quick version of what happened to me since the vortex appeared in my neighborhood. To explain to him he was wrong in what he believed. "So, see? We didn't cause that. And stop calling Connor and Larry monsters."

He gave me a dark look. "Well, until you guys came into our lives, we had kept out of the terrors' limelight." He fingered his weapon. "Didn't you just say that damnable vortex thing snatched you before anyone else? Other than that Connor Rojas?"

I didn't like what he insinuated. That maybe because of me, Hell decided to let loose the apocalypse.

Carl's face relaxed as he leaned his chair back against the wall again, his muscles loose. He pulled out another cigar from his shirt pocket and stared at it for a minute, before he jabbed it back. Had he done so because of consideration for me or because he decided he didn't need a smoke?

He looked at me. "Just wanted to let you know how I feel. But no, I don't think you started all this. Although, I'm not ruling out the werewolf or the eyeball."

"They didn't cause this either."

He snorted, withdrew the second cigar from his pocket after all and stuck it in his mouth. Lighting it, he kept silent after that, blowing out rings of smoke and keeping an eye on the back door. Since it appeared that I would be better off keeping watch at the front of the building, I got off the chair and shuffled into the next room. I tiptoed past sleeping bodies on various areas of the floor. Taking a chair, I sat and propped a foot up on another one, laying the rifle across my lap.

Tired, I fought nodding off. But unable to help it, slumber took me.

***

A bright shining light, so brilliant that it hurt to look at it, filled my vision as I stood before the front door of the restaurant.

"Am I dreaming?" I asked out loud.

"This isn't a dream, Cat. Well, it is, but it isn't. Do you understand what I'm trying to say?"

"Not really. Hello, Lisa."

Lisa dimmed her brightness.

"I needed to tell you that George got away. That Heaven called me back. I can't return, either, not yet anyway. What I can tell you is that you're the one who can stop this madness. I learned I was mistaken, as George lied about that bet between Heaven and Hell. A couple of archangels and he are behind this whole fiasco. Disgruntled employees, that sort of thing."

"Let me understand this. I knew that George joined Hell's side because he wasn't happy with Heaven, but there are other angelic beings behind this, too? What was it all about? No pay raises or something?"

"Yes, no, kinda. The two archangels were caught and Archangel Michael sent them to Hell on the express train to it. They're never to return to Heaven because of their transgressions."

"Kinda?" My voice escalated as I became angry. "A couple of birdbrained angels aren't joyful in Heaven so Earth has to be punished for their unhappiness? Where's God in all this?"

Her light became subdued as she cleared her throat.

"Vacation."

"What did you say? Louder, please."

"Vacation." Her voice rocketed a bit more.

"Still can't hear you."

"Vacation!" she screamed, her light flushing orange. "After eons, God decided he needed time off. He went to the other end of the universe."

Well, isn't that swell? The Supreme Being needed a vacation like the boss of a mighty corporation needed a fishing trip? Just left the office to despondent employees? Now isn't that dandy?

I asked, "Well, has anyone sent a message off to God to let Him know what's going on, Lisa?"

"I'm going to try."

"Now tell me how I'm supposed to be the savior of the universe."

"Savior of the universe? No, just of Earth only."

"Spill it. What do I have to do? And why me? I'm nothing special. Why not Connor? He's stronger and faster than me."

"Cat, let's just say, I see something in you. The future has been shown to me in a vision that you will be extra special to this world, but only if we stop Armageddon. I'm sending this archangel down to help you. He's bringing something I borrowed from Harry. Remember the yeti? He had this collection of stuff stored in his attic. A lot of what he had was junk, but there are some things he owned that held the odor of old magic. Magic as old as God Himself. Harry found one object that can blow that vortex to smithereens and send every demon and monster back to Hell. Plus, it can reverse time—back to before this all happened."

She started to twinkle out. "I got to go, Cat. One thing before I do. Be careful with this piece of old magic. It's powerful and if you do it wrong, the Earth is obliterated. There'll be nothing left, not even a speck of dust." She blipped out.

***

I woke up, blinking. Obliterated? That didn't sound good to me. I couldn't understand one thing. Why me? I could see Connor or Larry, Crystal, even Jefferson. Shoot, that jerk, Carl, too. But me? The woman who worked in the Department of Motor Vehicles and the most stressful thing she ever handled, irate customers? But then again, maybe I could be the best man, er, woman for the job, to anyone who survived a week working at the DMV, this would be a piece of cake.

I walked into the kitchen. Carl leaned a hip against the wall, his weapon propped up against the wall beside him. No longer smoking the second cigar, I saw the stub had joined the first one, submerged in the glass of water on the sink counter.

"Get some shut eye out there?" he asked with a yawn.

"I didn't fall asleep."

"Did too."

"Did not."

"Yep, went out there ten minutes ago and saw your chin resting against your chest. Either that or you were meditating. You didn't even wake up when I touched your shoulder."

I slid into a chair and looked up at him with my best defiant expression. "Okay, I nodded off. You can't blame a person when I hadn't gotten much sleep since this all began."

"What's going on?"

Connor stood in the doorway, stretching and yawning. He looked more refreshed than I did. I pondered the unfairness of it all. He'd gotten some good sleep while I learned of my destiny to be savior of the planet.

Carl said, "What are you doing up? You did the first watch, and you should still be sleeping."

Connor sauntered over to the counter and picked up a tea kettle. I hadn't used one of those in years. It seemed pointless, with having a microwave that could heat up water in seconds. Less clutter. Now, I'd rather handle clutter or use a kettle to heat water, if that meant no more end of the world.

"I don't need much sleep." He reached up, opened a cabinet and found a can of instant coffee. After pouring some water into the kettle, he put it on the stove and turned on the gas. At least the gas stove was an old one, and it didn't have an electrical igniter because there was no electricity in Richmond and its environs. *But, you could light the burners with a match too.* I watched as he spooned coffee in several cups on the counter by the stove. He turned with a grin and asked, "Anyone else for coffee?"

"What time is it?" I inquired, bleary-eyed.

"Four o'clock, I think. Hard to tell with no clocks that work." said Carl. "I'll take a cup, werewolf."

Connor helps save our butts and Carl calls him werewolf. I sighed, yawned, and shook my head. "Guess I'm staying up too. I'll take a cup, Connor. Thanks."

It took a little longer for hot water when it was made the old-fashioned way, but when everything was ready, Connor handed each of us steaming cups of coffee. None of my favorite amaretto coffee creamer available, so I had to use the powder stuff I've always hated. To survive in this new world, one had to make changes. Just why did one of those must be my amaretto coffee creamer?

I took a sip and felt the caffeine begin to do its job. Not ready to dance yet, and although it wasn't as strong as coffee house expresso, I went ahead and drained the cup dry.

Holding the cup out, I said, "More, please. It's working."

Connor took my cup, added instant coffee and poured hot water. He handed the cup back to me and I downed it. Carl had a couple more cups of coffee himself, but I had enough caffeine. Besides, I admit, I never cared for the taste of instant coffee. Connor sat down at the table after spreading blackberry jam on some bagels. He had found them in a big pantry. We talked until the first of those waking up wandered into the kitchen like lost souls.

CHAPTER 16

After breakfast, people checked another list that Jefferson wrote up while he ate—this one for chores—pinned to the wall. One by one, they meandered off to perform their assignments. That meant washing and drying dishes, cleaning tables, washing clothes (by hand in big pans), and other assorted jobs. Heck, one man cleaned and checked rifles and guns. For the few not having an errand to do, those grabbed coveted spots and read a book, colored in coloring books or on paper, and one teenage girl, Tina, wrote in a diary. Jefferson told me they got them from Shelf Life Books when they had gone out on a foraging for food and supplies one day after settling in at the restaurant. Connor kept Larry amused by reading to him from a trashy romance novel Larry dug up from the broom closet in the kitchen. I admired Connor for not minding at all that others caught him reading this book, and maybe even questioning his masculinity because of it. Four women brought out a game from that same broom closet and rolled dice to see who would get to go first. A young man settled down at a booth, turned on a battery-operated lamp, and began drawing on some paper. A quick glance revealed him to be quite an artist.

As for me, I chose a spot away from the others at a table in the dining room closest to the front door. I retrieved a notebook and pen from the book bag I'd grabbed before leaving the place downtown. I decided to keep a memoir of sorts when I'd gotten there, writing down all that'd transpired since the first vortex opening. Before now, I hadn't had much time. This would be a golden opportunity to document what had been happening to me since the vortex opened. Maybe if we got out of this with our lives intact and everything back to normal, I could publish it. If Lisa's idea did work, if nothing else, this could be a record for humans to keep if they had to fight Hell again in the future. It wouldn't be published by a normal publishing house—no would remember all this mess once everything was set back—but, I could self-publish it.

I chewed on the end of pen. *Sadly, people will think it a work of fiction, or that I'm crazy to believe that this had ever ensued, except in my head.*

I wrote down the dream I'd had last night. So far, not a single heavenly messenger, whether arch or regular, appeared to me from on high to deliver a message and a so-called magical bomb to save Earth. Maybe deep down inside, I believed I could be savior-of-the-universe material. I wondered if it'd been nothing more than a dream. That the stress of this living nightmare and not eating anything last night, might have been the real reason.

All around me, people done with tasks and curious about each other's group, came together to talk or do other things. Carl dug out a board game and besides a couple of people from Jefferson's group, David and Jen asked if they could play, too. Jim brought out some playing cards he had stuffed in his bookbag, and he got Jefferson, Crystal, Connor, and Lou from Jefferson's group, to play gin rummy. Conversations from everyone else filled the restaurant, but I ignored it all, just fought to remember what I could about the land of the murderous, flesh-eating bunnies and scribbled it all down.

The creak of a door opening lured me away from my writing though, and I paused to look at the front of the restaurant. No longer barricaded, the door hung wide open. I checked to see if anyone else saw it, but everyone kept going about their business.

Okay, that's strange. Have I fallen asleep at the table? Am I dreaming again?

I closed the journal and shoved it and the pen back into the book bag and got up. I inched over to the open doorway, taking care to be ready to run if something like a hungry zombie slipped through. Nothing stumbled in, either by design or accident. Even the damnable grayness didn't allow a tendril to twirl inside.

I stepped outside and was shocked to see brilliant sunlight, something I hadn't seen in a long while now. Its warmth bathed my face, and I fought not to close my eyes and enjoy it. After all, this couldn't be really happening. Right? I glanced over my shoulder through the doorway at the other people. No one hastened to stop me. *That's strange. Why haven't they noticed the opened doorway? Surely, the sunlight must be shining inside, at least a tiny bit?*

When I looked forward again, I found myself not in Carytown, but in a beautiful, serene park. One I didn't remember ever visiting. None of the familiar gray mist was in the air. The sun shined overhead in a pretty, blue sky free of clouds. Birds sang in the trees. Some of them flew out of the branches, and they created a tapestry of reds, browns, blues, and yellows against the sky like splatters of paint on a canvas. It seemed as if Armageddon never happened, at least not here anyway. *That's it, you're asleep, Cat. That's all this is, nothing more than a dream.*

Something startled me; a tall being wearing a shining white robe appeared from out of nowhere. I never saw this person walk up a path or anything, and I never heard footsteps, either. Not one twig had snapped, nor did I hear any leaves being crunched underfoot. And yet, there the figure stood, the glowing rays of the sun sparkling off the robe.

He? She? The slender body made it hard to tell. Peering closely at the figure, I realized the light came from the robe and not the sun.

Okay, not human.

I stumbled over a rock, landing painfully on my rear end. The being stood over me and I stared up, noting the light that fanned around its head, hurting my eyes. I squinted, hoping that would help. Whatever or whoever it could be, it leaned over, and held out a hand of pale radiance.

I shook my head. "I'm not taking your hand, not until you tell me who or what you are."

Is that anyway to talk to an Archangel, my child?

Oh God, it talked in my head! At least, I think I heard words. High pitched, the voice reminded me of dolphin trills.

I wish you would not take the name of Him in vain.

I remembered my dream.

Yes, the Light of Goodness sent me. I am the Archangel Bob.

I sputtered. "The Archangel...Bob?" First the Angel George and now Bob? What about those archangels mentioned in the Bible? The famous ones? I don't remember ever seeing a Bob among them. And why don't you look like George, who looks more human?"

The angel tapped its toe and crossed its arms. *With Armageddon going on and Earth becoming a horror movie, you want to be picky about who comes to you? George is a minor Angel, I am an Archangel. There are more than the initial seven, you know. Besides, do you think that George looks human for real? What he projects is a façade.*

"No, I guess you're right." Bob helped me to my feet. "I assume you brought me something?"

Yes.

"Well, where is it?"

Patience is a virtue, my dear.

"With the possible eradication of humanity and Earth about to become Hell's real estate, you expect me to be patient?"

Point taken.

He withdrew something from within the folds of his robe and held out a box with intricate hieroglyphics etched into the wood. It looked to be quite old. I took it. The texture of the wood felt smooth as a baby's bottom. Not a single sign of a splinter, despite its age. I examined the symbols on it, running a thumb over them. Even though carved, the hieroglyphics felt like metal.

At first, I thought the hieroglyphics to be Egyptian, but I realized my mistake. I swore I'd never seen these before, not in a museum or on the History Channel. I straightened. "What are these?"

Atlantean.

"This came from Atlantis? But that's a myth."

No, it is not. Atlantis was a land where wizards ruled, and white magic, the everyday standard. But the Atlanteans grew arrogant, knowing that being the first true civilization to exist surely made them superior to all, even God. They wanted much stronger magic, so they called forth demons to get it. One of those demons was Lucifer himself. After he contracted their souls, he gave them black magic. However, they learned too late that black magic is not easy to command. The dark magic spiraled out of control and caused the first Armageddon. All of Atlantis sunk beneath the ocean waves, carrying the bad ones down below to drown and sending their souls to their new master. They became the first human-born devils. A few good souls did escape to the lands on the rest of Earth, assisted by God for not listening to the Devil's blandishments. They mingled with the indigenous population and married, and as eons passed, the memory of life in Atlantis faded.

Atlantis! I stared down at the box in my hands. This could possibly be the only thing left from that civilization. I looked up at Bob again, blinking because of his brilliance. "This isn't black magic, right? I assume you wouldn't let me use something like that?"

No, just old, white magic, given to them by God Himself. It was Harry's ancestors who saved it before they fled the mountains of Atlantis and ended up high in the Himalayas. When Harry's many greats grandfather moved down to Niflheim, he took this with him.

"How do I set this off? I'm assuming it's a bomb."

Bob leaned over and tapped lightly on a few of the hieroglyphics carved into the top of the box, pressed beneath it. It whirred and shifted like a living thing in my hands. Frightened, I almost dropped it when Bob snatched it from me. His light grew brighter, and I looked away from the glare.

Never drop it when it is turned on, foolish little one. If you do, the Earth will be nothing but cinders in a second.

He handed the box over to me, and I held it tight against my chest.

Now, you saw where I touched the symbols on the top?

I nodded.

That switched it on. But it is not ready to go off just yet. You need to do what I did, reach underneath the box and press the button that will appear after it gets going. To give you enough time to escape from the aftermath, you need to press it several times. Each press of the button equals a half hour of Earth time. You need to figure how much time you will need. I can tell you that the range of the explosion will be wide, maybe a mile.

I guided my fingers along the bottom of the box and located the button. It didn't feel wooden.

Remember, you need to press the button as many times as you need to give you time to get away from the vortex.

"What? Wait a minute! I have to go to the vortex?"

The Archangel Bob cocked his head to one side. *Yes, I assumed the Light told you in your dream.*

"No, I think I would remember a detail like that."

That is why I told you to estimate how long you need to escape to get far enough away. If you get caught within the wave, you'll die.

I stared down at the box, my gut twisting. "I don't know if I can do all that."

Bob shrugged, reaching for the box. *Well, if you don't think you can do it. . .*

I clasped it against my chest. "No, no. There's no one else that's savior-of-the-world material?"

No, none of your military has survived. None of your police forces or anyone else. There's only you. If the Light of Goodness is right. Bob thrust his face closer, the light dimming low.

I tried to swallow, but my mouth felt dry as dust.

It must be you who sets off the bomb of magic. No one else can do it. It has been foreseen.

Of course, the old you're-the-chosen-one gimmick. I could see that this hero's journey might be short and not so sweet.

I started to say something when Bob vanished. With a sigh, I walked back into the restaurant. The park disappeared as I stepped over the threshold, and the door swung shut and locked tight behind me. The box in my hands proved that it hadn't been a dream.

No one had missed me. I thrust the box inside my bookbag and swung the bag over a shoulder.

You have only twenty-four hours to get to the vortex, otherwise, Hell will win.

"Okay, Bob," I muttered.

I didn't have superpowers, only a box full of magic, and between me and the vortex in downtown Richmond, an assortment of hungry zombies, demons, monsters, and who knows what else roamed the streets. If the pressure didn't kill me, they would.

I dragged my sorry ass into the kitchen and stopped; a delicious odor wafted up my nostrils. I tracked it to the stove, where Jim stood, an apron tied around his waist, stirring a wooden spoon in a big pot. He grinned at me. "We're having vegetable soup for lunch. The veggies are from cans, but it's still good."

My stomach rumbled.

His grin grew wider. "It appears your belly agrees with me."

It looked like one last meal for the condemned. Spying some bowls and a pile of spoons on the counter, I picked up one of each and held the bowl out. "Feed me. Please?"

Shaking his head, he snagged a ladle resting on a spoon rest and scooped soup into my bowl. Others meandered into the kitchen and each took a bowl, lining up behind me. I poured myself a glass of water and headed into the dining room. I sat at the same table I used earlier before the Archangel Bob episode. Connor slid in across from me, while Crystal thumped down on my right and David plopped down next to Connor. Larry hovered by the table, watching us eat.

David growled, "Does that thing have to stare at us eating? Creeps me out."

Connor paused with his spoon in mid-air. "What else can he do? He doesn't eat, and he gets lonely just like you do."

David didn't say anything else, just kept his eyes focused on his soup and ate.

I sighed, scooted my chair a little bit closer to Crystal, and patted the spot on the table next to my bowl. "Come here, Larry."

With a loud whee, he darted over and snuggled next to me. He made sure I had enough room. He chattered away, and though I didn't understand what he said, I said "Aha" and nodded in the appropriate places.

After the meal, everyone carried their bowls and spoons back into the kitchen, where Connor washed them in the sink. Some decided it was time for a nap, others read magazines from a stash someone had snatched from a box in back, or they just talked. I knew this would be the perfect opportunity to slip outdoors. How I would get to the vortex in time by foot I didn't know, but I had less than twenty-four hours to make the effort.

I grabbed my book bag and stuffed a small, loaded pistol and a box of bullets inside, walked into the bathroom, and locked the door. I took a last potty break, then balanced precariously on the toilet and pried away the boards nailed over the small bathroom window. Opening it and ripping away the screen, I threw out the book bag and squeezed through the opening.

My weight had dropped a lot since this all began. Not eating on a regular basis, plus walking and even running—mostly in terror—did what workouts at the gym never could. Still, it was a tight fit. I shimmied and contorted my body like a plump rat trying to work its way through a mouse hole. I panicked when my hips got caught. I wiggled and finally freed myself, and skidded down the outside wall, landing on a pile of odiferous garbage. If those darn zombies wanted to eat something, why couldn't they eat this nasty stuff?

I managed to reach up to close the window, and after swiping the book bag off the ground, I bolted. I prayed under my breath that nothing out here would find the window unlatched and break into the place. Keeping my eyes open for anything that might loom out at me, I kept going. I had only gotten a couple of blocks when I heard movement from behind me. Not daring to look over my shoulder and with my heart in my throat, I scrammed. Breathing hard, I continued praying to higher forces that I wouldn't run smack into the arms of some hell hound or an overly hungry zombie. The vapor had grown thicker and made it hard to see.

I ran into a lamp pole that had the audacity to jump into my path. *Damn, that hurt!* My vision swimming, fighting tears, and glad that I hadn't dropped the book bag or made a sound when I hit the lamp pole. Something bumped into my back.

I guess Lisa and Heaven chose the wrong person. The only kind of hero I would make is a hero sandwich for some terrible creature. Gritting teeth, I twirled around and pulled out the pistol, pointing it. Shocked, I saw Larry. Unfortunately for him, I fired the pistol without thinking. He swerved to the right, and the bullet spun through the grayness. I put the safety back on the gun and shoved it back in the book bag.

"Larry, I almost shot you," I said. "What are you doing out here?"

He beeped.

"You saw me sneak out of the window, didn't you? Decided to follow me, right?"

He beeped twice.

I assumed that meant yes. Although I felt happy to see him, I had to send him back for his own good. "Go back to the restaurant, Larry. I need to go somewhere I don't think you want to go. Do you understand?"

He drew closer and chirped. It looked like he frowned.

I sagged against the lamppost. Time to tell the truth. "I have something in this book bag that will stop Hell and close up the vortex for good." He nosed the bag. "Someone from Heaven came to me in a dream and told me that an Archangel would bring me a special item, a bomb of old magic. This morning the Archangel Bob came and delivered it."

Great, it looked like he didn't believe me. I set the book bag down, reached into it, and took out the box. "This is it. I touch the hieroglyphics on top and it starts up, then you have to press a button underneath several times to set enough time to get away."

I returned the box back into the bookbag. "Please go back to the restaurant."

He shook himself side to side as if saying no, and stood his ground, refusing to budge.

I sighed. "All right, all right. I guess you're coming with me no matter what I say."

"May I join your little expedition?"

I shrieked and reeled around. Connor leaned against the other side of the pole. He straightened and pressed his hand against my open mouth, his other hand pushing my jaw up to close it. "Shhhhh. Haven't you learned yet that noise might attract a horde of fiends?"

I was rewarded with his exotic scent, a combination of man with a husky hint of canine. Disappointment filled me when he withdrew his hand.

"Connor, you too?" I looked around, trying to find others from the restaurant. "Anyone else with you? Am I really that inept in escaping that everyone knows that I left?"

"No, just me and, apparently, Larry. Larry, why didn't you tell me she left instead of just following her?"

Larry whined and looked down toward the ground.

Connor patted him. "It's all right, Larry. Lucky for me, I discovered the unlatched bathroom window, fastened it, and fixed the boards. Jefferson let me out by the back door." He crossed his arms. "I can tell you they all think I'm crazy for going after you, Cat. I tracked you here. Even in human form, it didn't take long for a werewolf to catch up with you." He glared and shook a finger at us. "The both of you are lucky something else hasn't caught wind of you yet. Now, let's head back to the restaurant."

I took a breath and said, "No."

His eyes widened. "What did you say?"

"I said no. There's something I have to do. Something important. Honest, like save-the-world kind of important."

"Now what can be im—" He frowned as I shifted the book bag from one shoulder to the other.

He pinched it before I could stop him.

"Hey!"

"What's in here, Cat?"

I tried to snatch it back. "Nothing that should concern you. Take Larry and the both of you go back."

Ignoring me, he explored inside. With a hiss of surprise, he hauled the bomb out. Stupid me, I made a grab for it, but he held it away from me. "Cat, what is this?"

I shrugged and lied. "Nothing. Just some box I found when we stayed in the hotel, that's all."

"No, I'm sure I would have seen this. Besides, I can sense the lie you're telling. Cough up the truth." He sniffed the box and sneezed a couple of times, and his eyes widened as he looked at me. "It has the odor of powerful magic! Tell me where you got it."

How dare the nosy werewolf and his damn keen nose ruin my mission. Most people, in my experience, were easy to fool long as you kept a poker face. But then again, most humans can't get the impression if you're lying or telling the truth by your scent either.

I gave up. "Okay, I had this dream last night."

"And?"

"My friend, Lisa, the Light of Goodness, came to me and told me I'm this hero of the moment. That an Archangel from Heaven would come to deliver this box to me. This morning, the Archangel Bob arrived and handed over this bomb that I'm to set off around the vortex. It's supposed to close it up, send all the bad guys back to Hell, and reverse time and set everything right. But I have to do it within twenty-four hours or Hell wins."

"You're telling me that this little wooden box is a bomb?"

I glared at him. "Can't you sniff out that I'm telling the truth? You said the box reeked of old magic, right?"

"Oh, you're telling the truth, at least as you believe it. And yes, this thing is loaded with old magic. Not sure if it's white or black. I'm just not sure it's the full truth by your heavenly buddies, or if it's George pulling some strings."

He brought the box right to his nose and took another whiff. His nose wrinkled and he looked at me. "It is definitely made of old magic. The strongest old magic I've ever come across. Trouble is, I can't tell if it's good or bad news for you, for all of us."

Great. I remembered my dream. Lisa had come to me, and I had met an Archangel. I didn't know Bob all that well, but I felt sure that Lisa wouldn't give me a bum rap.

Sometimes you just had to take a leap of faith. I took the box back.

"If I'd wanted to keep hold of it, you wouldn't have gotten it," he said with a smirk.

I stuffed it back in the book bag. "Yeah, I know."

"I'm going with you." He nodded at Larry. "She needs both of us." He started walking but stopped as if he'd realized we hadn't moved. "Well, what are you two waiting for? Cat, how long do we have?"

"Maybe eighteen hours, tops." I curled my hands on my hips. "Hold on there, mister, you're not going to try and convince me to stop this nonsense, or throw me over your shoulder and carry me back to the restaurant?"

"No. If you believe this box will stop Armageddon, I'm with you." He muttered under his breath as he marched away, "I just hope I'm wrong about who really gave this box to you."

"I heard that, Rojas," I said as I trotted after him, Larry right beside me.

Five hours later and I figured it must be almost nightfall; we still hadn't come close to the area where the vortex was located. Connor decided we should stop for the night in a small building that once housed a burger joint. Settling down for the night when we only had about thirteen hours left didn't seem wise to me.

Before we could enter the place, Connor checked it out. After he deemed it safe, he motioned to us to come on in. Feeling somewhat hungry, I came across what one might call "science projects" inside the fridge. A search of some shelves and I discovered hamburger buns and a couple of tomatoes still good, so we had tomato sandwiches sprinkled with a few spices I also found. Afterward, I slid in a booth while Connor checked the building to make sure we were safe. We'd been lucky so far today. Exhausted, I laid down my head, using some kitchen towels as a makeshift pillow. A few minutes couldn't hurt, could it? I nodded off.

"Wake up," said a voice breaking into the start of a good dream. "You've got to keep going. You now have only eleven hours left to do your job."

I murmured, "Leave me alone."

"Wake up."

I grumbled but lifted my head. I massaged a crick in my neck and searched for the owner of the voice.

"Here."

A tiny television sat on a counter in one corner. A dazzling light radiated from the screen. *WTF!*

"It's me. Lisa."

"Lisa?" I asked in a stupid manner.

"That's what I just told you, didn't I?"

I sat up straighter. "Snippy, aren't we?"

"Whatever. If you stay here overnight, you won't get to the vortex."

I stumbled to my feet. "It's dark out there. Besides, Connor said we should stay here until morning. If I go alone, I know I couldn't find my way."

The light dimmed. "I have confidence in you."

"Sorry. But dang it, even if I kept walking straight through all night, there's not a chance I'd get there in time. Help me out here. Otherwise, you take the stupid bomb to the vortex yourself. I can only do so much."

"Yes, I know. I'm sorry, Cat."

She said nothing else for a couple of minutes, before she spoke again. "I'm not supposed to do this. I mean, I already did more than I should have by sending the Archangel Bob to you."

I leaned my hip against the counter. "Right. I thought you said Heaven isn't behind some bet. And yet, you act like this is all hush-hush to Heaven, as much as Hell."

"God doesn't know about this. He is still on that vacation. I never said that some Archangels and demons don't want the end of the world to happen. But on a technicality, I can only give you so much help."

I grabbed each side of the TV. "Lisa, you're talking about people's lives here. Living, breathing lives. This isn't some board game."

"You're right. Here's what I am going to do." She drifted out of the set, just as Connor and Larry awoke.

Partially shifting, Connor became defensive. "What's going on, Cat?"

"It's Lisa. Remember the light being who took on George?"

He crossed the room to stand next to me. Larry peered over his shoulder. Lisa's light dimmed a bit. Did Connor intimidate her? I tried to stop him as he got up close and personal with her.

"What's Heaven going to do about this mess?" demanded Connor.

She dulled. "Nothing." She brightened again. "But I am going to even the playing field here. I will open a small portal, one that Cat can step through and be right at the vortex within a few seconds."

Connor laid a hand on my shoulder. "Right now, at night? Can't you do this a few hours from now when it's morning? Yes, that Hell vapor doesn't make daytime sunshiny, but add the pitch darkness of night to it, and she won't be able see her hands in front of her face, much less anything else." He added with a growl, "If this is truly a bomb. It smells of old magic. I'm not sure whose side you or any of the others are really on."

"What I will send her through is a time and space portal. She'll arrive in the morning and not at night. I know better than that, werewolf. Though it being dawn, it will only give her an hour to set the device." A wisp of light came through the TV screen and gently touched my face. "Cat is my friend, and I would never harm her."

Connor snarled, "But you can send her right into the clutches of all those terrors that will be waiting for her. You'll let her do Heaven's dirty work. She won't have much time to get away after setting your damned thing up. Is this how you treat your friends?"

Tired of the bickering and knowing I'd made my choice, I broke in. "Hey, it's my choice." I stared at Lisa. "Get me that portal ASAP."

A strange sound filled the place and a human-sized vortex, dark as night, opened in the middle of the kitchen. I snatched the book bag from the table and stepped toward the whirling mass.

Connor called out. "Cat, wait."

I paused at the portal's doorstep. Larry floated over, hovering on the other side of me while Connor took my hand. "You're not doing this alone."

Sadness filled me. "I can't ask you to sacrifice your own life, nor Larry's, either."

Larry bumped against me and chirped. I looked back at Connor, and he tucked an errant strand of hair behind my ear. He pressed his forehead to mine, whispering, "Hopefully, when this is over...I'd like to see if that night in the hotel meant something more to you. It did for me."

I glanced over my shoulder. "Lisa, we're go—" She had vanished.

Growls erupted from outside. I saw the faces of drooling zombies plastered against the big, glass door. Hand in hand, Connor and I entered the portal, Larry close behind. The zombies crashed through glass and ran for us, their hands clawing the air.

The portal closed. The vortex spun us like some mad ride through time and space. I closed my eyes and prayed, hoping I didn't throw up on myself.

CHAPTER 17

We shot out of the portal. I landed on the concrete and Connor on top of me. His heavy weight knocked the air out of my lungs. Larry shot out last but managed to stay in the air above us. Connor climbed off me, jumping to his feet as I lay there for a minute, hurting. Damn.

Rolling over, I checked the book bag to inspect the bomb. Phew, it didn't look like it'd been turned on. Examining it close, I saw no parts had come loose. Even as ancient as it was, I'm sure being made of magic didn't make it unbreakable.

I climbed to my feet and stared at the mayhem surrounding us. We had been dropped off just a few yards from the vortex. Like a factory, it churned out demon after demon. Boxed in from all sides, I saw the zombies with dead eyes lurch toward us.

Connor stripped his clothes off and shouted over the vortex's noise. "Come on, Larry, we got to keep them away from Cat and give her enough time to get to the foot of the vortex."

He became the wolf.

Gnashing his fangs, he tackled one muscular demon that had thrown itself at me, and both he and it fell to the left. Rolling, punching, and biting, it was almost hard to tell who was who. Seizing my chance, I dumped the bag and dashed for the vortex, the box tucked beneath my arm like a football. Connor and Larry kept most of the evil away. I dodged others like a football player trying to make a touchdown. Incredible sheer luck—or maybe heavenly intervention—kept me out of harm's way, and I made it to the howling gyre.

The swirling mass had stopped spitting out the unholy for now.

Not knowing how long I had before it started up again, I dropped to my knees close as to it as I dared. Just as I was ready to turn on the bomb, something hooked my shoulder. A foul odor jammed up my nostrils.

"Sorry, but I can't let you do it."

I looked up.

Azazel loomed over me. He tightened his grip, his claws digging into my skin and he dragged me to my feet. He planted his ugly mug, nose to nose with me. My eyes watered as his disgusting smell overpowered my sinuses, but I couldn't turn away. Suddenly, Azazel restrained me; luckily it wasn't a choke hold. The others backed away, letting their lord have me. Ruff, the juvenile delinquent vampire, was with them, grinning like a big idiot.

"Cool," the vampire chuckled. "I get to watch Lord Azazel tear you to pieces. He said I get to lick your blood off the ground afterwards."

Why didn't the dawn just fry the little bastard?

Azazel snarled, "I should have known Heaven couldn't keep its snotty nose out of our business." His grip tightened and I began to choke.

He slapped my face hard and reached for the box. With tears blinding me and the side of my face smarting, coughing, I fought to keep him from getting it. I might as well have handed it over because he plucked it from my fingers with a snicker. He handed it to an imp who ran away like a spider monkey to settle down and watch.

Azazel taunted me. "Heaven must be in desperate straits if they have to scrape the bottom of the barrel by using humans to do their dirty work."

I spit out, "You should know all about dirty work, Azzie."

He glowered. "Don't call me Azzie."

"Why? Afraid all the demons here might think less of you?"

He bellowed and shook me. My teeth hurt from banging against each other.

"No. I am a demon lord, bitch, so call me Lord Azazel."

I wrinkled my nose and swept my eyes over him. "You smell like a goat and look like one, too. So, why would I call you lord of anything...Azzie?"

Azazel slapped me again, then ignored me and stared at the vortex. He laughed at something he saw. One clawed hand on my head, he forced it around. "Look."

"No," I said, gasping.

Two big demons used Larry like a basketball. They bounced him in rapid succession against the concrete street, and then tossed him back and forth between them. As for Connor, he was hedged into a corner by a group of the undead. He snapped at fingers grasping for him.

The whole situation was dire.

Azazel forced my head around to look at him again. A shit-eating grin split across his face, almost hiding his piggish eyes.

"It doesn't matter, Azazel. Connor and Larry knew what would be in store for them helping me. Even if this doesn't work, and Hell does take over Earth, there will always be pockets of rebels everywhere. They'll fight you tooth and nail until the end. That's the thing about us humans, we don't go down without a fight."

Azazel dropped my arm and with a roar, punched me. I dropped to the ground. The bastard towered over me, no longer smiling. Forget help from Heaven. There had to be something I could do. Scared and hurting, I couldn't think of one darn idea.

Azazel said, "What I am going to do to you will be monstrous and it makes me feel all warm and fuzzy inside. You'll be nothing left but a tattered soul. And, like I promised the bloodsucker here, he gets to lick up all the blood that will be splattered." He flashed a fetid grin. "If there's any left, that is."

I closed my eyes and waited. I shot them open again, when a familiar voice came to my ears.

"Hey, can I join in the fun?"

I saw George float down, hovering in the air above Azazel, his wings flapping from behind his coat. He smiled, and as the vortex's wind caught the ends of his black leather coat, he looked like a crow in flight.

The demon lord cut his eyes at George. "What do you want, pansy? Can't you see I'm about to tear this mortal apart?"

The grin dropped from George's face. He stared at me. His eyes turned black. "I just wanted to see these three losers get what they deserve."

At that moment, I stamped on Azazel's hoof and somehow got free of the bastard's grip. I darted away in a blind panic and crashed right into something. I screamed, kicking a foot out like some demented ninja. No terrible fiend would stop me from what must be done. I stopped my foot within inches of his baby blue iris. "Larry? Oh, Larry!" I threw my arms around him, hugged him, and released him. "Where's Connor?"

He pivoted his whole self to the left, and I saw Connor being forced down by Ruff. The vampire giggled and lowered his head to try and bite Connor's neck. Larry flew over to Connor's side. Azazel had a couple of his fiends catch me and bring me to him. After having one of his boys immobilize me, Azazel joined the others to fence in Connor and Larry. George ambled over.

Connor roared, snapping his jaws at the vampire's face, but Ruff dodged. Connor saw George and snarled, "What are you doing here, you angelic turncoat?" With a maniacal grin, Ruff punched him. Connor's head smacked back.

George shrugged. "I couldn't let Azazel get all the souls, especially yours and Cat's. I'm at the bottom of Hell's corporation you know, and I needed some bargaining chips to climb my way up the ladder. I heard Azazel here might be trying to stage a coup to take over Hell from Lucifer. I figured I might just see how well he does. Big L hadn't given me that great of a deal to defect from Heaven's graces."

I screeched, struggling in Azazel's hench-demon's hold. "So, you're not going back over to the side of light at all? I should have figured you're nothing more than a creep."

Azazel approached George. "I'm tired of Big L this and Big L that. It is time for another to take over Hell. I can do a way better job than Lucifer has done since the Fall. And you know what? I don't like you, George. If you'll stick it to Lucifer, who's to say you won't do the same to me in the long run? I'm going to solve this little problem I have with you right now." A sword appeared in his hand.

His face like stone and his eyes obsidian, George fanned out his wings, creating a wind. The wind became so powerful that many of Azazel's henchmen and zombies were blown away, one by one. He had a terrible beauty about him. and I scooted away from him and Azazel when my captor gawked and let me loose. Something bad was about to go down.

His sword materializing in his hand, too, George said, "I'm just going to separate your head from your shoulders, goat face."

But Azazel had his own magic. "*Rat Tos Montos!*" The sword flew out of George's hand, hitting the ground with a clang.

Connor power punched Ruff in the face, which flung the vampire toward the vortex. Then, he dove for the sword and snatched it before Azazel could, and whirled around to slice through the demon lord's neck. But Azazel seemed to know what was coming and ducked, dissipating with a nasty laugh. Another entity that looked like a horse with iron legs galloped at Connor, and he swung the blade and severed its head from it neck. The head dropped to the ground, crushed to a pulp beneath its hooves. Not waiting to see if it was dead or not, Connor began hacking at demons and zombies right and left, howling as he did so. George snapped his fingers and another sword popped out of the air into his hands. He joined the fray, slitting and slashing at bodies. The imp that had the bomb, placed it on the ground and merged into the fray.

Connor yelled, "Duck, Cat!" His sword passed over me and sliced through the thing that appeared behind me.

I barreled away to a spot where I would be kept out of the bloodshed, nicking the box off the ground before I did. Larry joined me. "I don't know what George's game is, Larry, but here's my chance. Guard my back. Okay?"

Not waiting to see if he agreed or not, I scrambled over to the foot of the vortex and dropped to my knees. I fingered the hieroglyphics on top of it, just like the Archangel Bob showed me, and the box whirred and moved. Sweating, I bent my thumb underneath, located the button, and held it there as I tried to determine how much time we would need for escape. I pushed the button several times. My heart pounded against my chest each time I did.

One time. Two times. Okay, that's an hour, right? Shit, why didn't I determine all this back at the restaurant? I pressed a couple of more times. A couple of hours had to be enough. I hoped I did the timing right. I propped it against the bottom lip of the vortex, stood and was ready to bolt when arms wrapped around me.

"Oh, no, you don't," whispered a voice into my ear.

Oh no. Ruff.

Why hadn't the vortex sucked him up? I struggled, but I couldn't free myself. Low laughter, cold as ice, rumbled by my neck, followed by something wet on the skin there.

"Tasty. I smell your blood. It's so rich, salty, and full of iron. Let's have a taste. One little sharp nip, the—"

Something slammed into my tormenter, knocking me free of him. Ruff punched Larry. I saw a piece of wood from some sign the vortex must have broken but never sucked up, and I snatched it off the ground. As graceful as a ballerina, I twirled around and thrust the sharp end of the wood into Ruff's skinny chest, working it in deep. I leaped back and watched him drop to the ground, twisting violently. One last earth-shattering scream and he exploded into dust particles. The wind from the vortex carried them into its mouth. *Had I really staked a vampire? Wow!*

There was no time to fist pump the air about what I'd done. "Come on, Larry. The vortex is starting up again. We need to get away before it draws us in. Now!"

Larry and I bolted to a nearby building and got inside. We stood at the locked glass door and watched as more zombies and demons emerged from the vortex. Others surged from other areas of Richmond, too. These joined the demonic hordes Connor still fought. Shocked, I saw that the traitorous George stood back-to-back with him and that they both fought together. When did the fallen angel become an ally?

I unlocked the door and stepped out, yelling over the shrieks from the fiends and the vortex's roar, "Connor, we have to leave! We only have an hour or two before the bomb goes off!"

His ears swiveled in my direction. Thank goodness for werewolf hearing.

He howled.

Larry left the building and began to shove me away from the vortex. I dug my feet in. I couldn't understand what he was doing. "No, we've got to get Connor to come, too."

He stopped nudging, bumped me off my feet, and he settled under me, lifting me into the air. We accelerated, evading flying creatures that dove at us. I struggled enough that I toppled off Larry and hit the ground, the air knocked out of me.

Frightened and hurting, I sprang to my feet and ran, pursued by Hell's minions. I tried to get back to Connor, but they headed me off, and I sprinted away from them. Not looking back over my shoulder to see if they still chased me, I swore I could still feel their spit stinging the back of my neck as I thundered down one street and took a right.

Could things get worse? When had anything these days turn out for the better? I glanced over my shoulder and saw the yellow, bloodshot gaze of a malignant spirit, full of hunger and anger. It looked close enough to reach out and touch me.

Just as I took another right turn, something captured me from behind and knocked me in the back of the head. Excruciating pain slammed into my head, and I crumpled to the pavement, darkness washing over me.

***

Groggy, I scrabbled to my feet and tried to walk but found myself held fast to something. I tried to move my hands and my feet, but they were bound like the rest of me. I was tied securely to what seemed to be a tall stake in the middle of a giant effigy constructed of twigs, leaves, and brush. A large, evil creature loomed in front of me, holding a long stick that appeared to be a torch, thankfully, unlit for now. A shit-eating grin played upon its ugly puss.

"Ah, the bitch has awoken." Azazel came into view. He wore a long black robe with a hood and leaned over to poke around the hair on the back of my head. I cried out when he touched the bump there. He whipped his head around with a snarl to the other being.

"Did you have to hit her that hard, Bumbles? The sacrifice must be perfect. That means no gashes, bumps, bruises, nothing."

Bumbles? There's a creepy-looking thing named Bumbles?

Azazel slapped the other demon's face and wrenched the torch out of its paws. "Get out of here. Back to Hell with you. And don't you breathe a word of my rebellion to Lucifer."

Bumbles sniffled and walked away, swaying side to side with its bulk. He stepped through a watery shimmering. It shrunk until it vanished with him. Azazel flashed a dark grin at me.

Acid gurgled in the pit of my stomach. I flinched. *Why does he have me trussed up to this stake? He said something about a sacrifice. The torch...oh no!*

"I am so glad you made it easy for me to grab you," he said, patting the side of my face like a benevolent father. "But mortals are so dumb. That's why we have possessed your bodies so easily for centuries."

"Come on, Goat Lips, get to the important stuff."

Holding up the stick, he said, "Do you know what this is for?"

Does he think I'm an idiot? Of course, I knew. The acid in my stomach sputtered like a small eruption from a volcano.

His eyes shone like orange fires. "I am going to light it and set fire to this effigy holding you. Once you're sacrificed, all the suffering you and your kind have gone through will have been for nothing." He seemed to savor that for a second, before continuing, "My legion will take over this stinking planet. Afterwards, we'll head down into Hell to defeat Lucifer and take it over."

"How can burning me stop everything?"

"Because I say so!" he spat, globs of spit from his mouth hitting my face.

Maybe the sour grapes of being Lucifer's go-to boy had made him try one last attempt to even the score. Either that, or like any villain in a story, he thought he was the ultimate demagogue.

I saw Larry floating next to me, also tied to the stake. Below him on the rushes, laid something that looked like a filthy light bulb. *Now why does it look familiar? That can't be. . .*

Azazel clapped his hands and laughed as he saw I knew who was with me and Larry. "Yes, I lured that stinking Light of Goodness here. That's what the trollop looks like after an injection of hell spawn. As for that stupid eye demon, he has been nothing but a burr in my backside from day one. I must say, this will be a great sacrifice, three for the price of one." He laughed until tears of blood pooled in his eyes.

"Let Larry and Lisa go. You have me."

He set his jaw like stone; his eyes, gleaming deadlights; and the hollow edges of his cheek sucked in. "No. Larry is nothing but a traitor to his kind. He should be here with the rest of Hell wanting to cook you, but is he? Since eons ago, he's been a thorn in our sides." He punched Larry and knocked him out. "With his and the Heaven's bitch's death added to yours, that will just sweeten the deal. And when I finally have Lucifer all trussed up and chained to one of his nasty torture devices in Hell, my victory will be complete." He frowned. "No, wait, I also need to get that double-crossing turncoat, George, and your mangy cur. Eventually, Heaven has to be greenlighted to be destroyed, too. Details, details, I hate details."

A bright, scarlet flame flickered at the tip of the torch. He brought it closer, its heat searing my skin. I refused to give him the satisfaction of me crying out, as I bit my lip.

"A bonfire will keep the bad spirits away." Azazel cackled. "Oh wait, a bad spirit is lighting it, so I guess that's a lost cause." His cackling grew more demented as he thrust the fire at the effigy's feet, and it caught. Tossing the burning torch right into the rising fire, he vanished.

I huffed and puffed, blowing at the flames. Like that would put them out. The heat worsened as the fire ate up the kindling closer to my feet. I tested the bindings on my legs, hands, and body, but still couldn't get the tight binding to loosen or tear apart from the stake. I thought about screaming for help, but I figured no one would be in the area, and besides, it might attract the wrong kind of help. I could reach Lisa with the toe of my tennis shoes, and I tried to wake her, but she didn't budge. Larry wasn't much help, as he was out for the count, too.

Out of nowhere, a freezing wind whipped up and instead of fanning the flames, it froze them. Feeling relief for a second, I wondered what games the demon lord played now. Instead of Azazel, Connor popped in with George, dressed in a pair of black jeans, a blue T-shirt, and boots.

"Free her," said George. "The bomb is about to go off, and Azazel might come back. Hurry."

Connor untied me and did the same to the unconscious Lisa next. He handed her over to a disgusted George. "Take her."

"You've got to be joking."

Connor untied Larry. The eye demon had regained consciousness, and he floated out of the effigy. "Take care of Larry, too," warned Connor, "otherwise, I can't be responsible for anything he does to you."

With a sigh, George carried Lisa and led Larry away. Connor went to work on my bindings, cutting with a switchblade, and had me free in minutes. We bolted out of the effigy, following George. We walked on a dirt path in the woods. A glimmer of light showed ahead, and I pushed aside some thick brush. We stepped out into sunlight, just above the James River. I recognized the area.

Belle Isle. A small island that's also a city park in the James River, where you had to cross a swaying, suspension footbridge to get to. I doubted that Azazel brought us here that way though. Many old and ruined Civil War era buildings were scattered about the island. It had been the site of a Civil War prison camp for close to 10,000 Northern soldiers. Many of them had died here, and because of that, ghostly sounds and sights had been reported at Belle Isle.

Catching up to the others, I could understand why Azazel might think of burning Larry, Lisa, and me in a Wicker Man fashion here. I didn't understand why George kept helping us, and I had big reservations about him.

George halted, "We're on—"

I broke in, "Belle Isle. Yes, I know. I used to come here for walks. I know the history and the ghost stories behind this place, too. Is that why Azazel tried to sacrifice us here?"

"Enough of the chit chat." He ignored my question and clapped his hands.

A small vortex appeared and George jumped through a whirling column of colors with us on his coattails. It opened in a clearing among trees near my neighborhood. My house was a couple of blocks away, but taking a shortcut through the woods would halve the distance. I stepped on a small, almost hidden path and I darted ahead, grabbing hold of branches I almost ran into and letting them loose. I heard the others behind me block them, though at one point I heard a muffled oath. It sounded like George.

I smiled.

"Sorry," I said, not actually feeling sorry at all.

"Connor," I asked in a low whisper, "how did both of you get away from the vortex, and why are you letting that creep help us?"

"George agreed to help me save you. He's had a change of heart. He wanted to get back into Lucifer's good graces and volunteered when the Devil asked him to stop Azazel."

I turned my head to look at him. "You didn't agree to anything, did you?"

"No. I didn't."

Somehow, that didn't reassure me. I suspected a lie, but until I had the time to dig the truth out of Connor, it would have to wait.

Larry twittered. He left George when we stepped out of the woods and onto my street. Uttering a long whee, he zoomed over to me. I hugged him. "Looks like we're almost home, buddy."

Impatient, George said, "Come on, the clock's ticking and we don't have much time. It's only minutes before that damnable bomb goes off. And when Azazel finds out that you're gone, he's not going to be happy. Save the hugging for when we're out of this mess. Lucifer wants this rebellion ended. He's going to be livid that one of his demon lords is behind it. There's a special spot for traitors like Azazel. Believe me, when I say that no one with any smarts wants to end up in that place. It's Hell within Hell."

His wings unfurled and he flew off, dropping Lisa into my arms. Connor outpaced me and, breathing hard, I struggled to keep up with him.

Everything was quiet and nothing moved, not even a breeze scattering leaves. I didn't see any of the Hell fog. After seeing it for days and days, the lack of it bothered me. You think I would be happy to see it gone, instead, it intensified my fear. So many empty homes and motionless cars in driveways and along the street.

We almost made it to my house: Azazel and at least fifty of his allies stood between it and us. We halted at my mailbox.

"Hello, Azzie," said George, sounding unsurprised as he lazily descended.

"Don't call me that, you two-face bastard," replied Azazel with a growl. "I am Lord Azazel to you from now on. To be frank, just Prince of High Darkness will do. You may have stopped the effigy from burning and sacrificing the twit and her friends, but I had a backup sacrifice that did succeed. I put a stop to that miserable magical bomb. It won't be long before I'm in charge. You're going to wish you'd joined me when it happens." He whipped out a long sword with a blade that glowed with a crimson sheen of fire.

Looking bored, George snapped his fingers and his obsidian sword appeared in his hand. It flashed with black fire erupting from its tip.

No one moved. Azazel turned his head to stare at me. Hatred and lust scorched in his eyes.

"Wait until this is all over, girlie," he said with a promise of retaliation, "and when I have won and both Hell and Earth are mine to do with what I wish, I will play with you. Over and over."

I almost shuddered, but I decided not to give him that satisfaction. Instead, I stuck out my chin and didn't look away.

"I don't think so, Goat Boy." Connor put his arm around me.

A black look slithered over Azazel's face. Guess the "Goat Boy" had been a bit too much.

With a bellow and his sword flashing flames, he charged George. George laughed and met the demon's sword with his own, the clash ear shattering. Red and black fire shot through the sky, and the melee began. The rest of the demons hustled toward us.

Oh, God! We had nothing to defend ourselves with. Connor grabbed my hand and tugged. "Run! Into your house."

"But they're in front of us."

He took off, dragging me. "We'll try to slip around them. Larry, keep them busy."

The eye demon hightailed it and as he got to the horde, he back tracked. They chased him like the dimwitted idiots they were, and gave us time to reach my house. Lucky for us, I had left the door unlocked and Connor and I sprinted inside. Larry streaked over the leaping demons that tried to catch him and right over the threshold. Connor slammed the door shut behind him and locked it. I wondered how long the door would hold when they began to ram it.

"Cat."

I frowned. "What?"

"Cat. Look."

Connor stared out of the living room window. I joined him and peeked. The cavalry had arrived. Angels and demons together. Brilliant with light, the angels carried Heaven-made swords and fighting staffs. As for the demons, they radiated a terrifying beauty and were held aloft by coal black wings. These had to be the original fallen angels that had been cast down to Hell.

One of the most handsome men I had ever seen led the fallen ones. But, as I stared at him, I saw dim shadows in his eyes, his purple skin, and how grim his features really were. This had to be Lucifer himself.

I watched all of them force back the rebellious devils until a large hole appeared right next to the old maple tree in my front yard. Black smoke, burning ash, and unearthly shrieks erupted from it. The hole spiraled into the air, revolving around and around like child's toy top as it became a vortex.

We ran outside and cheered. Except for Larry, he trumpeted like a small elephant. One by one, the evil ones got sucked in the vortex, cries of agony melding with the nauseating odor of brimstone. Only one was left when the hell hole snapped shut.

Azazel.

He still crossed swords with George, oblivious to the beautiful devil I knew must be Lucifer behind him. Azazel whirled around and his eyes widened with terror, and he dropped to his knees, sobbing. Lucifer reached down and grabbed Azazel by the throat, shook him; then he laughed and vanished with the bawling pretender to the throne.

The angels and demons that previously fought together, parted. Mistrust glittered in each of their gazes, but with the strife done, things had returned to normal for Heaven and Hell. But the angels saluted their demonic counterparts in an act of solidarity that most likely would never occur again and rocketed out of sight. The fallen ones leapt through the vortex with unearthly screams. The hell hole vanished like a zipper being pulled closed.

George wiped demonic blood off his sword onto the browning grass of my yard.

"Hey, does this mean that the Earth is back to the way it was before the vortex opened up? No more Armageddon?" I asked with hope.

"At least for this time around. Big L agreed to Archangel Michael's deal that if Heaven would help him retrieve Azazel, all bets would be off." He walked past us and headed for the house. When we didn't immediately follow, George hollered, "Waiting for a formal invitation, are we?" Once inside, he stood over Lisa and waved a hand over her. Her light returned and it brightened as if she smiled, before she dissipated. George continued, "Anyway, that's it. Lucifer and the demons are back in Hell, and it'll be eons before another bet is wagered with Heaven. Earth is back to normal. Look through your window and you'll see your neighborhood is back."

I did as he suggested and saw cars traveling down the street, my neighbor next door mowing his lawn, and a family going for a walk. I even saw a sparrow flutter onto my lawn to peck at the dirt. I turned around and watched with distaste as George wiped what blood was left on his sword on the coattails of his leather duster. To my surprise it didn't leave a stain. He tossed the sword into the air, and it dissolved until nothing of it remained.

"Ready?" he asked Connor.

I grew apprehensive. "Ready for what?"

George grinned. "He died back there at the vortex. Didn't you notice since we came to you on Belle's Island until now, that he never once shifted? His curse ended when he died. He did it for you, begging me to save your life and find a way to save Earth. Pity he did it for such a silly reason like love and not for any gain. Oh well, a soul is a soul."

I turned to Connor.

He nodded. "It's true."

I faced George. "Oh no, you're not taking Connor."

George's visage transformed and I saw his true self for the first time. He said, "A bargain's a bargain. He died saving someone else, and he offered his soul to me to save yours. That's that."

My blood boiled. "I bet you set up what all those angels and demons did here earlier."

"Now would I do something like that just to gain Hell one crummy soul? You're giving me more power than I have."

I looked into Connor's eyes. "You don't have to go. You know this was manipulated by that the son of a bitch somehow. We can find a way out."

Connor looked sad. "I have to. He's right. I died today. I gave him my word to let him take my soul to save you. I'm sorry, Cat." He took my face between his hands and kissed me tenderly.

I began to cry; He wiped my tears away.

"I don't want to leave you or Larry. . ." Tears gleamed in his eyes.

"Guess I got to do something about this," said George from behind me.

I felt something pass through my head and I dropped. As if from a great distance, I could hear Connor yelling, "You didn't have to do that to her." A great roaring filled my ears.

I cried out, "Connor. Larry." I blacked out.

***

I woke up, gasping for breath. I wasn't lying in my front yard. Instead, I found myself on something soft, like a pillow and mattress, a blanket covering me. Shards of pain wrenched through me. I saw an IV drip inserted in my arm. The white walls like you find in a hospital surrounded me. *How'd I get in here? Where's Connor and Larry? Where's that creep, George?*

I turned my head to the opposite side of my bed and saw a shadowy figure sitting in a chair. This figure got up to pull a string at a lone window and raise the blinds, letting in a stream of bright sunlight. The light illuminated the stranger, and I saw it was Connor.

He wore a pair of black jeans and a blue T-shirt with a running wolf on the front. Turning, his eyes widened, surprised to see me sitting up. With a concerned look on his face, he ran to the door and threw it open. He yelled, "Nurse! Nurse! She's awake!"

A woman dressed in a sky-blue top and matching pants, a name tag pinned to the blouse, rushed into the room. Connor pointed at me and whispered something to her. She came over to my bedside.

"Awake finally," said the woman, smiling down at me. "How are you feeling?"

"I've have a headache, otherwise..." I frowned at her. "How did I get here? " I looked at Connor. "Where's Larry, Connor?"

The nurse left the room and brought back a tall, African American man in a white coat, a stethoscope hanging around his neck.

My doctor?

He looked down at me with a kind smile. "I'm Dr. Trask. I see you've finally awakened. We were worried about you."

I asked, confused, "What do you mean—?"

"You were in a coma, Mrs. Viggolone," said the doctor. "For about four weeks."

I sputtered, "A coma!"

"But you're awake now, and we'll need to run some tests to determine that there are no lasting effects." He turned to the nurse. "Nurse Shelby, please schedule all the procedures I listed in her chart."

"Yes, Dr. Trask. Right away." She bustled out of the room.

Dr. Trask patted my shoulder. "I'm going to leave you for a few minutes, but I think Mr. Rojas here can give you some answers to those questions I know you have. He hasn't left your side since the accident. In fact, he's the one who brought you in." The doctor moved away and left the room, leaving me alone with Connor.

Connor pulled the chair closer to my bedside and sat down. Using the hand not attached with the IV, I felt the bandages that covered the back and top of my head. Horrified, I looked at Connor. "They performed surgery?"

He took hold of my hand and held it gently. "Yes, they did. I'm sorry. But the wound had cut deep and kept bleeding."

"What happened?"

"You ran through the intersection, and my truck blindsided your car. I'm sorry."

"That was you." I asked, feeling numb. I sat up abruptly, jarring my head and increasing the pain. "Oh, my God, I remember it all. I left work at the DMV that Friday afternoon and I stopped at the supermarket for a few groceries. I don't know why, but I tried to beat the red light. This big red truck slammed into my car. Did that really happen?"

When he didn't answer, I added, "I see myself lying on the street and feeling nothing, just pain, loads of it. Something wet is streaming down from the top of my head and pooling beneath my head. My blood. I blacked out." I gave him a fixed look. "But I must know you. I was dreaming about you. But I never saw you before I blacked out. Right?"

Connor said, "I guess you must have seen me getting out of my truck and running over to you, otherwise how would you know me? We never met before the accident. I'd just moved to Virginia from California."

"Your name is...Connor, Connor Rojas. Now how would I know that?"

"Well, the doctor just called me Mr. Rojas," he said, "and as for my first name, I've been talking to you while you were in your coma. I told you my first name, introducing myself. I had always heard coma victims could hear people talking to them and that this kept their brain active. See, even my name can be explained away." He smiled.

My breath caught over his beautiful, soul-catching smile.

"I guess that does explain things—" Still groggy, I closed my eyes and drifted off.

I always had later to get more answers.

***

I awoke and thought I heard Connor speaking to someone else. I didn't see him or the other person in my room, though. Maybe I imagined the conversation. He would return. I smiled and snuggled against the pillow.

Something materialized on the chair by my bed. Large and round, it looked like one big eye. It chirped. I screamed and fell out of bed. My drip tore out of my arm, and I stared at the creature from my position on the cold floor.

WTF! It must be some drugs in that IV.

Grabbing hold of the bed, I pulled myself up and began to hobble away from the thing. I headed for the door when something floated in front of me. It was the creature. I nearly slipped, but I managed to stay on my feet and skidded toward the window. Though why I went that way, as I wasn't planning to open the window and climb out to escape.

I don't understand. I've been in a bad vehicle accident and I can walk? My head didn't hurt, no aches or pains, anything. Something felt wrong here.

I stopped at the window and moved around until I faced the eyeball coming at me. I cried out, "Go away, please, go away, you—"

Larry. His name is Larry.

I remembered everything. Not a dream, but something that really happened. No car accident. No surgery. Not sure about the surgery part, I touched the bandages on my head and yanked them off. There were no stiches, no soreness, no shaved head. Just my head and all my hair like normal. I jerked around to the window. Numb, I stared through the glass. Larry drifted over to hover at my side.

I looked at him. He stared back, unblinking.

"You're Larry. Okay, why is Connor here and not in Hell, and why is he trying to make me believe I had some terrible accident? That we never met?"

Larry bleated, then did something I thought he couldn't do. The television in my room came on. Only it wasn't a TV show. I saw Connor and some strange man standing in a hospital corridor. The stranger looked familiar, but I couldn't figure out who he was. I looked at that man on the screen, but my head began to ache. Either, my mind refused to remember him, or someone put a...

...*mind block*? Now, why would I think that?

I turned to Larry. "What's going on?"

CHAPTER 18

One minute I stood at the window in the hospital room, the next minute I found myself popping into a broom closet with Larry. The tiny place smelled rancid from old bleach and moldy water in a plastic mop bucket. One foot stuck in it and the other slid on a still wet, mop head.

I managed to get off the mop without any mishaps but the stuck foot was jammed tightly into the pail. I dragged the stupid container over to a cracked plastic chair in a corner. Wearing a hospital gown that bared my rear end, the scratchiness of the chair's seat hurt. It took me a couple of minutes to liberate my foot. I got off the chair and opened the closet door a crack. Larry hovered next to me.

"Larry, what's going on?" I lowered my voice to a whisper. "Do you see something?"

He turned and looked at me, neighed like a horse, then circled around me to push me toward the opening. I placed a hand flat against the wall next to the door.

Wondering what he wanted me to see, I squinted through the tiny space. To my surprise, I saw Connor standing next to the good-looking man from the TV. I noticed the man wore a black leather duster and withdrew a cigarette from a packet and placed it between his lips and lit it. He still seemed familiar, but my head still hurt, making it hard to figure out where I knew him from. Easing his left hip against the wall, he took a puff. I watched the smoke from its burning end rise into the air shaped like miniature horned devils. *How did he do that?*

The blond man removed the cigarette from his lips and stepped away from the wall. "Well, are you ready to go to Hell?"

Connor thumped down into a chair right beside him. "No, George, but I'll never feel ready, will I?"

I remembered who the other was. Not a man at all, but a former angel turned bad-boy devil. Anger burned in me.

He's not taking Connor to Hell, not if I have anything to do with it!

Just as I was about to open the door all the way, Larry bumped against me, stopping me. I glared at him, saying in a harsh whisper. "Let me go. He's not taking Connor anywhere with him."

George's voice drifted into the broom closet. "Remember, Connor Rojas, you gave me your word if I helped you save Cat and stop Azazel, you would forfeit your soul to me."

Barely breathing, I jerked my head around to the crack again.

George stepped up to Connor and dropped a hand on his shoulder. "There's no saving you from any dire circumstances or like that game mortals play, no getting out of jail or passing go."

He flicked the burning butt to the floor and crushed it beneath the heel of his boot. But he didn't release his grip on Connor's shoulder. "Damn, I'm going to miss cigarettes, beer, chocolate, and sex," George said with a sigh. "Being immortal can be a bitch sometimes. As an angel, you can't indulge in guilty pleasures and as a demon, you can, but not down in Big L's territory. Only he and a few of his handpicked fallen brethren can." He snorted. "I thought being on the low rung of the angelic ladder in Heaven bad, but it looks like Hell won't be any better. Oh well, let's go, it's time to catch the express train to Hell."

His grip on Connor's shoulder slid down to the upper arm and he squeezed. Connor dug in his heels and made it hard for George to drag him away. With a face full of tight lines and his eyes a soulless black, the demon planted it closer to Connor's. With a voice deep and dark, he said, "You're a dead man. You died back there at the vortex. Did you think you and Cat can have a happy life together? You a corpse and she a living woman?" He smiled as Connor looked away. "I thought not. Time to take your medicine. Lucifer is waiting for you. I heard he's got just the place for you to stay, too."

Connor said, "Promise me you'll ensure she'll never remember me."

George didn't answer.

Connor's voice escalated, demanding. "Promise me!"

George loosened his grip. "Okay, I promise. I thought you'd like her to retain memories of you."

Connor shook his head. "You had her recollecting me as the man who hit her in some car accident. I rather that she wouldn't remember me at all, especially not that one." He stood tall. "I'll reminisce for both of us. Her sweet face and our one time together will help me through whatever Hell throws at me. I'm ready, now, get your hand off me!"

George withdrew his hand and Connor stood. The fallen angel snapped his fingers and a deck of cards appeared on his palm.

"Do you know how to play poker?" he asked.

"I used to play, long ago. It's been a while."

George took out a few cards as they both walked down the corridor. "Well, I played it a couple of times. It's another vice I became attached to while on Earth. This might be a good time to get together and have a few games. I'm sure we can find a few more lost souls to join in."

I slipped out of the closet and tiptoed after them, Larry close behind. They left the hospital, and through a window, I saw a vortex appear in the middle of the hospital parking lot and something long came thundering out of it. The thing rolled over some parked and moving vehicles and drew to a stop in the hospital parking lot. It looked like a nasty, blind worm with fangs. *It's the express train to Hell.* I shivered.

A door swung open in its side and a demon in a conductor's uniform stepped down some small steps. In his claws, he clutched a lamp glowing with eerie, green hellfire.

"All aboard," he called out. "Last chance to get to Hell. All lost, damned souls, come and join us."

Spirits walked, flitted, crawled, and flew from within the hospital. Not one of them looked happy. Not even using the steps, they passed through the flesh of the worm. Those gone, George climbed the steps, Connor right behind. After they'd boarded, the conductor trudged up the steps, and one by one the steps folded up, disappearing. The door faded and with a melancholy wail, the train headed up to the sky and came back down to speed through the vortex. The rip snapped shut after the tail end slipped through. The vehicles it apparently destroyed appeared if nothing ever happened to them.

Not caring that it was cold or that my naked ass and back were on display, I ran barefooted out of the building, yelling. "Connor!" Too late, I stared at where the vortex had been, oblivious to honking horns from a couple of cars. I dropped to my knees. My heart felt as if it had been ripped out of me. I began to bawl. It was the first time I heard Larry cry. The sounds of our misery joined the blaring noise into a concert of pain.

CHAPTER 19

Two nurses burst through the emergency room entrance. Larry dissipated. I babbled about Larry leaving me, and while one of them crooned softly to me, both helped me off the ground. One stayed with me, while the other ran back into the hospital and got a wheelchair. After I was settled into it, they pushed me indoors. The door closed behind us and they wheeled me down the hospital corridor to my room.

Everything became a blur after that. One of the nurses stayed to help me into the shower and turned on both hot and cold water. She divested me of my dirty hospital gown and handed it to the other nurse to take away. I shivered as the water sluiced over me. Grabbing a washcloth and bar of soap, one of the nurses took care as she washed all the dirty areas on my body, especially my knees, hands, and the bottoms of my feet. The last part I had to try to stand on one foot, leaning back against the tiled wall. The other nurse helped me so I wouldn't slip and fall. Then the first nurse returned to pour shampoo over the top of my hair and worked the growing bubbles into the strands of my hair. My hair rinsed of soap and looking shiny clean, it was dried with a big, fluffy towel before Nurse number one drew a fresh hospital gown over my head. That done, she left the room while Nurse number two led me to bed, but I fought being tucked in.

"Let me go," I cried. "I need to find Connor."

"Now, now, Ms. Viggolone," said the nurse. "You had a bad accident, and Nurse Johnson and I didn't see anyone else out there. Just climb into bed. I don't understand how you managed to get outside, as you just came out of a coma."

I grabbed her arm and twisted it. "Look, Nurse"—I peered at her nametag and saw Aaron on it—"Aaron, I need to find Connor. The longer you hold me here, the easier George will get him all the way down to Hell."

She blinked tears. I'd been rougher on her than I had realized. She asked, "Who's this George?"

"A former angel who decided he'd rather be a demon." I dropped Nurse Aaron's arm when Nurse Johnson returned.

They looked at each other. Before I knew what was happening, Nurse Johnson hooked her arms around me and her knee poked me in the back as she forced me onto the bed. The gown slid off my naked rear end and I mooned the room. I struggled, trying to kick back at her. During the altercation, Nurse Aaron ran out of the room, returning a couple of minutes later with a needle. She pricked it into one of my butt cheeks. Whatever it contained, the stuff roller-coastered through my veins and within minutes, I quit moving as my body grew heavy. I managed to roll over onto my back and my last words I slurred at them were not printable.

Nightmares chased me through my sleep. Frightening ones full of demons and zombies and amidst it all, Connor being dragged by George toward a hole where a scarlet light spun, rocketing toward the black night sky. I ran after them, wanting to save the one man who I really cared about. I stumbled as if I struggled through heavy sludge, my feet clumsy. I tripped and fell to my knees. Something wiggled against my legs and I looked down and saw what seemed like a zillion tiny maggots swarming all around me and up my legs. Someone's shrill screams echoed in my ears, hurting my eardrums, and I realized they belonged to me. Demons and zombies came out of the grayness and surrounded me and out of the corner of my eye, I saw George stuffing Connor into that hole. I screamed again as another demon collided and bashed me back down to the ground and the mass of maggots surged over me, crawling into my mouth. The screaming turned into a gagging, choking reflex, and I swallowed a lot of the nasty, squirmy things.

I woke up with a start, in the hospital room, my gown soaked from sweat. The room pitch dark, I glanced at the window. The drapes had been drawn back. *It's night.*

A full moon shone its face as it stared through the window, its moonbeams lighting up a portion of the room.

Dragging my eyes back to the room, I swore the shadows in the corners moved. Unnerved, I groped for the lamp on the nightstand, next to the bed and wiggled my fingers over the on/off button. I pushed it and light from the lamp flooded from my side of the room. Shadows banished like exorcised ghosts and I lay back on my pillow, slowing down my breathing and from there, my erratic heart. *Calm down*, I thought.

Frustrated, I wondered why I hadn't done something more to stop George, to keep Connor here. If I had done that earlier, I wouldn't have had that terrible nightmare. Instead, I whined like a baby and did nothing.

Connor's dead. He's nothing more than fodder for the worms. No, that's impossible. I don't believe he's gone for good.

With the apocalypse ended, Connor and I could have explored our connection further. Other couples had met under weird circumstances before. Okay, most people didn't have an apocalypse to start a relationship.

I sat up, my hands twisting the sheets. There had to be something I could do. But I had to agree with those nurses, I needed to get well enough to check myself out of this hospital first. Dragged down, out of it, I didn't feel ready to take on another cause. Not yet anyway. When I could though, I would find someone, maybe a medium or a detective, and track down Connor, or even that bastard George. *Georgie Porgie, you better beware, because when I catch up to you, you're going to find out how much I will kick your ass.*

Leaving the light on, I lay back down and closed my eyes, waiting for sleep to overcome me. I drifted off, this time without any nightmares.

Seemed I didn't get much slumber when someone stopped by my side of the bed and called out in a cheerful tone, "Good morning."

I ignored the salutation, by rolling over onto my stomach and burrowing deeper under the covers. It must have encouraged that same person to shake my shoulder. My voice raspy with sleep, I flicked my shoulder and grumbled, "Go away. Let me sleep a little longer."

"Rise and shine. Breakfast is here."

I flipped onto my back and blinked the sands of sleep out of my eyes. A woman I never saw before stood over me. She wore a cheerful tunic with kittens and puppies playing across it and blue pants. In her hands, she held a tray of covered dishes and flashed me a big smile. She looked like one of those cheerful morning people, the kind I used to work with at the DMV who fluttered into the place and made the rest of us feel more depressed than we already were. Unlike those of us who needed caffeine to survive the workday, especially at the beginning of the day, morning people seemed to exist on nothing more than happiness, making everyone else consider murder. There had to be a place reserved for their kind in Hell. I bet before the Earth had been put back to rights they didn't get made into zombies. No, I bet they became demons and sat at the right and left hand of Lucifer himself. I despise morning people.

I sat up. The nurse set the tray down on a small table attached to the bed and swung it around and over my lap. She reached behind me to plump up my pillows and make me more comfortable. I didn't say a thing, just watched her with a wary eye.

Her grin grew wider if that could be possible. "Where is our lovely smile, this morning? I brought you a good breakfast. Eggs and bacon, toast buttered with real butter and a couple of pancakes with some low-fat syrup.

As for coffee, we have decaf. We've got to watch our caffeine intake."

Okay, I really hate the bitch. Decaf coffee? What did she think I was? A martyr?

I stared down at light-as-air, fluffy scrambled eggs, crisp bacon, toast light brown and buttered, and downy pancakes. It looked good except I didn't eat breakfast too often. I existed on yogurt or half a bagel with fat-free cream cheese. If I kept eating like this during my stay here, I might need to be rolled out after I got discharged.

"I want yogurt—with strawberries or blueberries in it, and coffee jam-packed full of caffeine." I crossed my arms and stuck my bottom lip out. "I don't drink that watered-down excuse decaf coffee, ever."

She laughed and picked up a fork and stuck it in the eggs. "Now, now, you need to eat enough to heal faster. You do want to go home as soon as you can, right?"

I scratched an itch alongside my nose and thought about what she'd said. Okay, I'm not a breakfast eater and I'm not a morning person, but I wanted out as soon as I could. If that meant I had to force a big hearty breakfast down my throat to gain that, I could handle a few extra pounds. The sooner I got myself discharged from this hospital, the sooner I'd be able to get Connor back.

Taking up the fork, I speared some of the eggs, shoved them into my mouth and chewed, swallowing. I did the same for everything on the plate. The breakfast tasted super and even the decaf coffee seemed okay, but the nurse stood there, arms folded, and watched me like some demented blue bird of happiness. Feeling an itch to see what would happen if I poured my coffee over her head, instead I kept eating. But I really wanted to dump it all over her instead.

Everything down my throat and in my belly, she whipped away my tray and set the table back to where it belonged. "Where's your brush? I'll brush your hair out."

"I don't have a brush."

She stared at me. "No brush? I know that Nurse Gottering said you came here with nothing, but I thought she was mistaken."

"Well, she's right and you're wrong. I ate your breakfast, now get out." I lay back down. "Let me have a few winks of sleep."

She bustled up. "Oh no. Time to get cleaned up."

I rose back into a sitting position and glared at her. "Look, what part of get out did you not even begin to understand? I'm not a morning person, I lost someone close to me, and your bright and cheerful attitude sucks. Leave me to my misery and go bug some other patient."

Her grin evaporated and her eyes darkened. She stomped over. Placing both hands flat on the mattress, she leaned over me like a hungry vulture.

"Archangel Michael told me to take this job and watch over you, but you can bring out the devil in even a being full of goodness, Cat."

Shocked, I stared at her as I realized what she had just said. A being full of goodness. She called me Cat, too. Only one being of—"Lisa? Is that you?"

Her smile shone like a warm sun. No wonder she symbolized happiness personified.

With a snap of her pearl pink fingernails, the door closed, and she folded her arms. The nurse's uniform disappeared and a glowing being stood beside me, her radiance illuminating the room. I thought her smile shone bright before. Now, the brilliance of her presence seared my eyes, and I closed them.

"Open thy eyes, Cat." Cheerful as ever and yet, still demanding. She would have made a superb drill sergeant in the Army or Marines. I stole a look by cracking my eyelids a bit, my lashes shading my pupils.

"Your light," I mumbled. "It hurts."

Lisa toned down her brightness. Not as much as I would have liked, but not super nova killer, thank goodness. The light still not a comfortable level, but I could handle it.

"Why are you here?" I said, dubiously.

"Because God sent me as He knows you well. He figured you might try and get out of here, like yesterday, and go after Connor. Right now, Heaven can't have that."

I threw back the covers and got out of bed, angry. "Why? Connor gave his life for me and you're telling me that God is going to let his soul be damned?"

She sighed and unfolded her arms. "No. All is not what it seems. Stay here and get better. Wait and give it time. You will see him again. That's all Heaven is asking. Have faith."

I snorted, pacing the floor and waving my hands around. "Have faith? Look, maybe in the movies someone goes to Hell and gets out. But that's make believe, not reality."

Her voice became more pleading. "Please, just give it some time. Heal and get your life back together. All is not what it seems." Her voice gentled and grew tender. "Sleep."

I grew drowsy and fought it, not wanting to give into the urge to get back in bed and lay down. Damn it, Lisa had done something to me. Like someone hypnotized, I crawled back in bed, and she drew the covers up to my chin. Just before my eyelids dropped, I heard her singing a psalm.

"Lisa," I said, yawning. "Are you telling the truth about Connor?"

"Yes, you will see Connor again."

I closed my eyes and drifted off.

CHAPTER 20

I remained in the hospital for a few more days. They released me on Thursday. They didn't know why I had nothing wrong suddenly, calling it a miracle. I hadn't been visited by Lisa again, or any of the angels or devils. Never saw Larry, either. If I didn't know better, it looked like I'd imagined everything. That it was a coma dream. Though even the coma appeared never to have happened.

I rode home in a cab, staring out the window on my right, not noticing anything until my home came in sight. I sat up, one thought spinning in my mind. That it didn't look like anything had been touched. That the vortex had never appeared that long-ago Friday afternoon. A niggling voice of doubt crept in, saying again that maybe it had been nothing more than a fantasy. I narrowed my eyes, thinking back to Larry popping into my room and then taking me to listen to Connor and George. I clutched the small tote bag to my chest that held a few articles of clothing and toiletries a nurse had gone to my house to get for me when I said I had no one to bring them to me.

Pulling the door handle of the cab, I got out at my front door after paying the cabbie. The cab rattled away, and I ran up to my front door, unlocked it and entered, the door slamming shut behind me. Not breaking stride and tossing the bag onto my couch, I headed straight for the extra bedroom that held my laptop. I stood over it, powered it up and watched as the icons appeared onscreen. I frowned as I glanced at the time and date on my computer. How long had it been since that fateful day?

Unless nothing ever happened.

I sat down and picked up my cell phone lying next to the laptop. No doubt, I'd left it and never even took it to work with me that Friday. After all, if it had been with me when I left work that afternoon, it wouldn't be here now, would it? Not after an accident. I keyed in my work's phone number. It rang three times before someone answered. I found out they knew that I'd been in an accident and had been in the hospital for seven weeks. They made no mention of a vortex or monsters.

I told my supervisor, Betty, that I was fine and home from the hospital. "I can go back to work Monday. I'll bring the doctor's note with me."

Betty replied in a monotone voice. "See you then, Cathleen." She clicked off.

Yeah, they missed me. They really missed me. *Not.* I needed a vehicle until I could get a new car; I made a call to a car rental agency and after arrangements were made, they promised to have a rental car driven over to my address right away. Connor Rojas' vehicle insurance would pay for it. He'd left the card of his company. According to the discharge nurse at the hospital, he already called them to set things up.

I tried getting into a movie on TV that afternoon after my rental car came, but instead, it bored me. After what felt like a lifetime of battling demons, zombies, and Armageddon, even if it was a nightmare, a movie on SyFy just didn't grab me. A real demon would have made lunchmeat in five seconds of the special effects creation terrorizing the city. With a click of the remote, the TV shut off and I got off the couch. Spying my purse and the car rental key on the coffee table, I snatched them and strolled out the door.

I climbed into the car and drove down I-95 to downtown Richmond. No sight of the vortex or the gray fog, just the same old city scene. A homeless man smoked and supported his body against a mailbox on one corner. Two drunken men stumbled out of a seedy bar, laughing and punching each other. People wandering by ignored them. Vehicles motored down the streets. I parallel-parked across the street from the library, and dodging a truck and a SUV as I ran across the street, I made my way up the steps and into the Richmond Public Library. Not too many patrons inside. I couldn't even find the librarian we had talked to, much less a trace of a ravenous monster.

I stepped back outside and sat on one of the steps, feeling empty. No, I didn't want Richmond to be the way it had been during those terrifying times, glad it had gone back to normal. *If it wasn't a dream.* I never felt so fucked up.

But I was close to being driven out of my mind from an boring, humdrum life. Now if I had Connor with me, and Larry, too, it wouldn't be so bad. Except Connor said he'd hit my car with his truck and there's no such thing as a demon that looked like an eyeball.

I couldn't stay here though. I rose and dusted off the back of my jeans. Two women gave me a peculiar look as I walked down the steps, crossing the street to my car.

Thanks to there not being too much traffic on the road, I arrived home in twenty minutes. Inside my house, I tossed the car keys and my purse onto the coffee table, but they missed, falling to the rug. Not caring, I continued to my bedroom. Kicking off my shoes, still dressed and miserable, I took a sleeping pill that had been prescribed for me and scrambled under the covers, huddling and staring at the wall. Tears welled up in my eyes and they bubbled over.

Life's a bitch and then the one man who meant something dies. Except he never died. It had all been nothing but a fucked-up coma. I didn't even have Larry here to make all sorts of sounds at me, trying to comfort me in his strange but endearing way.

I wrapped my arms around one of my pillows and laid on my stomach. At last, the pill worked, and I fell into a deep, dreamless sleep.

***

I awoke, befuddled at first before I understood I was home and not at the hospital. Shadows had lengthened in the bedroom, and I realized it must be either late afternoon or early evening. If it had been night, the bedroom would be so black I couldn't see without light. I threw off the covers and climbed out of bed.

My clothes wrinkled from sleeping in them, I padded on stocking feet to the kitchen and heated a can of soup. Sipping from a glass of tap water, I poured the soup into a bowl and carried both over to the table, thumping down in the chair. One spoonful of the soup and I threw down the spoon. Nothing tasted right. The tears returned. I pushed away the bowl and laid my head down and sobbed.

What's that? My cheeks tearstained, I shot up. Nothing. That's when I heard it again. A tiny sound, it grew louder by the second.

Had someone broken into my house? I got up and went over to the drawer that held all my kitchen knives. I opened it, taking care to do it as quietly as I could, withdrew a sharp butcher knife and crept toward the doorway. My hand pressed against the wall beside it, I peeked around the corner and saw nothing but the darkened room.

That's when I saw it. Something shaped like a big ball, it seemed a part of the darkness until it shifted like a detaching shadow and rose over the shape that was the couch. I gripped the knife close to me, and I bent my knees, waiting. It came closer and closer. I caught my breath, as it floated halfway past me into the kitchen. I leaped and thrust my knife at it, stopping myself in time before I impaled the top of Larry's eye.

"Larry!" I said, dropping the knife as I realized how close I came to doing harm to my dear friend. *My God, he's real. Real. I could have killed him.*

Okay, he has no eyebrows and yet, I swore he lifted one at me, as if he heard my thoughts. "Kill me? I'm a demon, dummy."

Shaken, I retrieved the knife and lay it onto an end table. "Why didn't you come to the kitchen first and not the living room? You scared the crap out of me."

He whimpered. I opened my arms. With a squeal, he raced into them, and I closed them around him tight, hugging him. "Oh God, Larry," I said, crying tears of joy, "you're real, so that means Connor's real. That means it did happen. I'm so glad you came back to me, dear friend." I drew back, still holding him. "Connor's gone to me, but I still have you."

He chirped.

I laughed. "You can stay with me, always. Of course, I guess we'll have to be careful and not let anyone see you. Can't have you become some government experiment."

I swore I heard him laugh as I hugged him again. It sounded soft and short, so I couldn't say for sure though.

That night I made him his own place in the bedroom I used for my office, leaving him to stare wide-eyed at the Internet as I went to bed. For the first time in three weeks, I fell asleep without a heavy heart. Although, I still dreamed of Connor.

The weekend sped by fast and I had to go back to work Monday, hard for me at first. I'd become used to fantastic adventures now, and the DMV was boring and mundane. But I had to support myself and now Larry, and at least this was a job. I suffered in silence and worked, getting through the day.

The week inched along, slow as a turtle, taking its time to get to five o'clock on Friday and finally the weekend. None of my co-workers noticed or cared—to them, life went on as usual. Of course, no one ever observed how tedious life had been before the vortex, either. Friday arrived without fanfare and when the DMV closed, I raced out of the parking lot like a mad thing, aiming for home. I stopped at the rental box outside Kroger to rent the movie I promised Larry we would watch. I also planned for us to watch one of the movies from the *Star Wars* trilogy I owned on DVD. I told him that everyone should see the *Star Wars* Saga at least once in their lives.

Pulling up to my driveway, I frowned; a shiny black truck was already in it. I parked behind it and shut off the engine. Checking out the rest of the neighborhood, I looked for a salesman, or even a couple of religious types selling their church to an unsuspecting population. I didn't see anyone. With purse, keys, and the DVD rental in hand, I climbed out of the car.

Worried about who owned the truck, I walked up to my front door and found it wide open. *Oh, oh. Not a good sign.*

I sneaked into the house and eased the front door shut with a soft click. I heard laughter coming from the extra bedroom/office. My purse, the DVD, and keys now on the couch, I seized a lamp, deciding it might be better at braining if I needed to do that. I slipped off my high heels and tiptoed in stocking feet, grateful for the rug that covered the hallway and muffled my footfalls. *Oh please, let Larry be all right.*

I paused at the bedroom door and opened it a crack. The laughter boomed louder. It sounded like men. At that moment, Larry screamed like a horse in agony, and I threw open the door and rushed in, brandishing the lamp high above my head.

"Get your filthy paws—" I stopped, shocked. It couldn't be. "Connor?"

The lamp slipped from my hand and hit the floor. Larry rose above the computer as Connor stood. Connor had longer hair and he needed to shave, but he looked good.

It was the other man who stood next to him who had me swoop down, retrieving my lamp weapon again. "You," I hissed. "Why are you here?"

George sighed and rubbed the back of his neck underneath a lot of long blond hair. "Put the lamp down, Cat. I can explain."

I didn't put down the lamp but held onto it as I moved to stand next to Connor. He hugged me, and he felt as solid as any living person and not a ghost. He kissed me on the mouth.

I stood back, giving George the eye. "Okay, spill the beans."

George frowned. "The beans? How can I spill any beans if we don't have any to spill?"

Connor said, "Shut up, George. She expects you to tell her how we got back to the Earth." He looked at me. "Actually, let me tell it instead."

He sat back down in front of the computer and I grabbed a seat nearby. I put the lamp down—close by just in case—and waited. What he said next almost had me falling out of my chair.

"I'm no longer dead."

"What?"

He grinned. "I have been given a second chance, thanks to George here."

George muttered, "Really, no thanks is necessary."

I swung my gaze to nail George, suspicious. "What did George do?"

"To get back in Heaven's graces, Lisa had him aiding them so I could be set free. We had a little game of poker with Lucifer himself and George won. Well, he cheated, sort of. But he is a fallen angel and who else could cheat better. It couldn't be me, or I would never be alive again, so that meant George."

I leaned forward. "Is that what I overheard at the hospital about a poker game?"

Connor looked startled. "You were there?"

"Larry teleported me to there and we watched you. When you both vanished, I thought I'd lost you for good."

He closed his eyes for a minute, hiding the pain I glimpsed in them. "I'm sorry, Cat." He reopened them.

"What about the werewolf stuff?"

"I'm no longer a werewolf, a human same as you. Isn't that great? Death has a way of breaking the curse."

George shrugged and muttered again. "Yeah, great. Mortality. What everyone needs."

"What is up with you, George?" I asked in exasperation.

Connor smirked. "George is now a mortal, too."

"What?" I jumped up out of the chair. "First, he was an angel, then a devil. So how can he be mortal now? I never heard of such a thing, outside of the movies."

Bitter, George spat out, "Because Heaven doesn't want me back and Hell never wants to see me ever again, even when I die."

I walked over to him. "Are you saying you've been kicked out of paradise and the pit of evil, too? You screwed up so bad that no one wants you?" I snickered. "Oh, this is rich." I sobered up. "That means Earth has the bastard now. Not so good."

George thumped down in the chair Connor had vacated. "It's not funny to me. After eons of immortality, how can one get used to this lump of flesh? All right, I like smoking, the sex will be cool, too, and eating is great, but to make me mortal? How could God and Big L do this to me?"

"Hush!" hissed Connor as he stood up and turned to me. "Best news, I got a backer to open up a paranormal investigation business. You know, help supernatural beings in trouble, mortals, too, when they are being plagued by something of an extraordinary nature. Even investigate haunted places and rid people of pesky ghosts. George will be my partner. This way I can keep tabs on him."

"Who's the backer?"

Me, Cat. Well, God essentially. He agreed with me that mortals need some good souls to protect them. I am hoping you will join them in the business. After all, you saved your world from Armageddon.

Lisa? I looked up at the ceiling where the voice in my head came from.

Goodbye, Cat. It has been good being friends with you. Maybe we will see each other again one day. Her voice drifted away. I felt a momentary sadness, then squealed and leaped into Connor's arms.

"Oh, angel's wings!" said George, as I kissed Connor. "Get a room you two."

As for Larry, he settled down in front of the computer and brought up the game of solitaire onscreen and began to play, using his magic.

I quit my job at the DMV the next day. Two weeks later, I joined Connor, Larry, and George at Vortex Paranormal Research and Investigation. I felt excited about a whole new way of life for me at VPRI.

And the best thing about my new job?

George is my assistant.

Revenge is sweet.

About the Author

Pamela K. Kinney gave up ignoring the voices in her head a long time ago, and has written horror, fantasy, and science fiction. Her horror short story, "Bottled Spirits," was runner-up for the 2013 WSFA Small Press Award and her poem, "Dementia," was in the *HWA Poetry Showcase Vol VII*, and got her a mention in Best Horror of the Years, Vol 13. She has a story and a poem in *The Haunted Zone,* a horror anthology with stories and poetry written by women military veterans, released in 2024. Her YA dark fantasy novel, first in the *Moon Ridge, Virginia* trilogy, *Demon Memories*, was released October 15, 2024; she is working on the second book in the *Moon Ridge, Virginia* trilogy.

Pamela and her husband live with one crazy black cat in Virginia. Along with writing, Pamela has acted on stage and film. She is a member of Horror Writers Association, Virginia Writers Club, and James River Writers.

Other Books by Pamela K. Kinney published by DreamPunk Press

Nowhere Land
Demon Memories – first in a YA horror trilogy
Maverick Heart – a novella

These titles are available from your favorite bookseller, or from www.dreampunkpress.com.

Pamela has short stories published in fiction anthologies and magazines/ezines, plus an article in a nonfiction anthology, *Ghost on Every Corner*. Find out about these at her website: www.PamelaKKinney.com.

www.ingramcontent.com/pod-product-compliance
Lightning Source LLC
Chambersburg PA
CBHW072104300726
48975CB00003B/698